1 Last Betrayal

1 Last Betrayal, the explosive third installment in the Angeline Porter Series, brings the heat, intrigue, and grit that we've come to love from Valerie J. Brooks, the queen of the femmes-noir thriller. Steeped in suspense, chilling encounters, and shocking twists, Brooks drops us into the dark underbelly of organized crime, and we love her for it.

~ Heather Gudenkauf ~ NYT bestselling author of *The Weight of Silence* and *The Overnight Guest*

Like the first two books featuring the disbarred Oregon attorney Angeline Porter, *1 Last Betrayal* is meticulously crafted by a writer who never seems to take a false step: every clue, every revelation, every betrayal dovetails into the next one. The secondary characters – a conflicted detective, a cold-blooded mobster – are expertly drawn, and the narrative's sexual aura, like its portrayal of grief, is refreshingly realistic. But in the end, Angeline – analytical, morally grounded, deeply courageous – remains the book's anchor, a principled woman who refuses to give in even as the walls close around her in what, for my money, is Valerie Brooks' finest novel to date.

~ Tim Applegate, *Flamingo Lane* and *Fever Tree*

The third book in the Angeline Porter femme noir trilogy begins with a bang when our heroine races to Florida only to find her half-sister is missing. Hot on the trail, Angeline is thrown into a life-or-death fight with the Boston mob. A twisty plot, great locations, and a gutsy protagonist you'll root for all the way. A fabulous finale to a sophisticated series that can also be enjoyed as a stand-alone title.

~ Kaira Rouda, USA Today and Amazon Charts best-selling author

With 1 Last Betrayal, author, Valerie J. Brooks, has delivered a seductive, intricately twisted suspense-thriller that's nearly impossible to put down. When onetime defense attorney, the tough-yet-vulnerable Angeline Porter, investigates the disappearance of her half-sister, she's plunged into a sinister underworld of double-dealing, corruption, kidnapping, and murder. Nothing is what it seems, and no one can be trusted. As you start 1 Last Betrayal, get ready for a wild ride with plenty of suspense, action, and shocking surprises.

~ Kevin O'Brien, *New York Times* Bestselling Author of *The Night She Disappeared*

The Angeline Porter trilogy comes to a gripping climax in 1 Last Betrayal. This atmospheric thriller can be enjoyed on its own, as all the plotlines and dark secrets of the two previous novels are recapped to converge in this final installment. Readers will fall in love with Angeline, a whip-smart former criminal lawyer who's on a mission to rescue her half-sister Bibi from the Boston mob. Unsure who to trust—the under-cover FBI agent, the brother she didn't know she had, or the possibly corrupt cop who all say they are helping her—Angeline falls back on her own wits and courage to reach the final twisty conclusion.

~ Lis Angus, author of *Not Your Child*

~

Tainted Times 2

In Valerie Brooks' scintillating new suspense novel *Tainted Times 2*, Angeline Porter, the tough but vulnerable Oregon attorney who first appeared in the author's remarkable debut *Revenge In 3 Parts*, continues to unravel the sinister narrative threads woven around her sister's tragic death. And once again Brooks keeps the pages turning by constructing an intricate and engaging story. From the first paragraph to the last, *Tainted Times 2* unfolds at a breakneck pace, each startling new revelation about Angeline's troubled family adding to the book's genuine emotional depth. A muscular, laser-focused, compelling new entry in this one-of-a-kind trilogy.

–Tim Applegate, *Flamingo Lane* and *Fever Tree*

With *Tainted Times 2*, Valerie J. Brooks has delivered an intriguing thriller that crackles with tension. Amid the cast of fascinating characters Brooks has created, disbarred attorney, Angeline "Ang" Porter emerges as a gutsy, likable heroine. You'll find yourself caring about her and rooting for her. Filled with clever plot twists, *Tainted Times 2* is a real nail-biter from the first page to the last.

—Kevin O'Brien, *New York Times* Bestselling Author

~

Revenge in 3 Parts

"...a striking and complicated protagonist."
"...genuinely surprising plot turns."

"...a whirlwind of deceit, theft, blackmail, and worse."
—Kirkus Review

"Beware of disguises and those who wear them. Val Brooks has crafted a cunning tale of revenge, grief and unwanted desire that lets you walk the streets of Paris, Portland, and Kauai as bereft sister, confident attorney, vengeful murderer, and confused lover. By the time you're done, you and your anxious narrator are left wondering which of those identities you'll need to go on living with yourself."

—Paul Skenazy, former thriller reviewer *Washington Post*, and author of *James M. Cain*

"*Revenge in Three Parts* is a swift, seductive, menacing tale of extortion and murder. Like the great James M. Cain, Brooks strips her story down to the bare essentials, effortlessly blending classic noir (urban settings, unexpected narrative detours, a suspicious money trail) with uniquely modern components, including a professional computer hacker, Snapchat, and the Ashley Madison dating site. With its breakneck pace, intriguing cast of characters, and unabashed eroticism, *Revenge in 3 Parts* is a wild, wicked, and utterly delightful ride."

—Tim Applegate, *Fever Tree*

"The author treats you to a strong intelligent, gutsy woman who writes her own rules and throws herself into a dangerous situation of her own creation. As has been said, 'well-behaved women seldom make history'—or good novels."

—Wendy Kendall, "Kendall and Cooper Talk Mysteries" podcast

"Revenge is a dish best served hot, at least in Valerie Brooks' *Revenge in 3 Parts,* a sexy fast-paced tale of family, love, and murder. Brooks' settings are characters too: two-faced lovers who charm as they kill. Can't wait for Brooks' next noir!"

—Cindy Brown, Agatha-nominated author of the Ivy Meadows mystery series

"Jan Myrdal famously said, 'Traveling is like falling in love; the world is made new.' In *Revenge in 3 Parts*, Valerie J. Brooks offers up a darker, if no less enthralling view of globetrotting. With *Revenge*, we follow jaded criminal lawyer Angela Porter as she seeks to avenge her sister's tragic death. With a whip-crack voice and delicious twists, *Revenge* is a thoroughly engrossing page-turner."

—Bill Cameron, author of the award-winning Skin Kadash mysteries

"Button up your trench coat! Valerie J Brooks' *Revenge in 3 Parts* puts an original twist on the classic elements of noir. *Revenge* successfully and poignantly balances travel destinations with the darkest compulsions of the human heart. Brooks' future travel destinations promise more creatively chilling mysteries!"

—Chris Scofield, author of *The Shark Curtain*

"*Revenge in 3 Parts* in twist after twist keeps our senses reeling as Angeline, an ex-attorney who believes in ultimate justice, comes closer and closer to the truth of why her sister committed suicide. Follow Angeline to the edge. Does she ever find what she seeks? Is she willing to go for the ultimate revenge, one that might tear her own life apart or even take her life? Find out in this tense noir mystery set in Paris, Portland, Oregon, and Kauai."

—Patsy Hand, *Lost Dogs of Rome*

1 LAST BETRAYAL

THIRD BOOK IN THE ANGELINE PORTER
TRILOGY

VALERIE J. BROOKS

This is a work of fiction. All characters, organizations, and events in this book are either products of the author's imagination or are used fictitiously. Any similarity to real persons, living or dead, is coincidental and not intended by the author.

BLACK LEATHER JACKET PRESS

ISBN 978-1-7323732-4-2 (paperback)
ISBN 978-1-7323732-5-9 (e-book)
Library of Congress Control Number: 2022910742

For Alexx, Maddi & Iree
The Stars in My Earthly Heaven

"Never attempt to win by force what can be won by deception." — Machiavelli

"The intellectual tradition is one of servility to power, and if I didn't betray it I'd be ashamed of myself." — Noam Chomsky

1 LAST BETRAYAL

1

I f I ever get out of this alive, I'm going to have a tattoo needled on my arm like others of my generation. Of what I don't know. But if I'm alive, I'll be able to make a decision then. I'm throwing off the conservative persona I once had as a criminal defense lawyer. My sister Sophie would be saying, "It's about time."

From Portland, Oregon, I'd hopped a red-eye and was on my way to Hollywood, Florida. I was back in the game and in the right headspace, ready to bring down the Boston mob once and for all while protecting Bibi, my sister Sophie's twin. Bibi needed me. She was tough, but this mob had a new and younger crime boss. Talia "Shawn" Diamandis. She didn't play by the old-fashioned rules of mobsters.

Like the rest of the world, there was no honor anymore among thieves, whether they be members of gangs, political parties, or religious sects. There was no "one for all and all for one." That only happened in the movies. So to energize my fighting spirit, I put on my headphones, pulled up "Rebel Yell," one of Sophie's old favorites, and put it on repeat. We used to jump up and down to that song in her living room—but that was before the mob.

Yes, I was back in the game, but I wasn't happy that I had to leave my dog Tempest again. How I'd ever come to love a dog that much, I'll never know. Maybe I relate to her being a rescue. More probable is how much we've been through together.

The plane dropped and bumped, almost spilling my coffee. The pilot announced that we were hitting some turbulence and to keep our seatbelts fastened. I shook my head. What did he know about turbulence?

Then the plane bucked and dropped hard, causing a few people to swear and the flight attendant to grab onto a seat. A child cried. I took a deep breath. The plane continued to buck and weave back and forth. Finally, it leveled out and a collective sigh went up from the passengers. My phone was clutched in my hand. It remained silent.

I closed my eyes and leaned my head back. Why hadn't Bibi texted me? Maybe, hopefully, she'd fallen asleep. Bibi and I had been talking and texting for the past twenty-four hours about Shawn and what to do about her. But what did you do with a mob boss telling you that you were part of her "organization" whether you liked it or not? As my sweet, dead husband Hank would have said, Bibi was in "deep shit." I knew what that deep shit was like. I'd been in it for a few years.

Shawn sure had cojones. She'd already broken into Bibi's apartment—and in broad daylight. What I found frightening was how thoroughly Shawn had prepared. She knew about Otto, Bibi's dog, a dog that should have scared the daylights out of her. But Shawn had fed him a treat while telling Bibi that there would be a meeting of the three partners, and Bibi was expected to join them. Join them, as in becoming one of the partners.

My main question was "Why?" Why would Shawn take such a risk as to get into Bibi's apartment just to tell her that she was expected to make this meeting? She could have met her in the lobby. I had a hunch: Shawn needed to know the layout of the apartment and get friendly with the dog. She planned on breaking into the place again. Again, the question was *Why*?

Bibi reported the "break-in" to management, a report was filed, and the police notified. Security camera footage was watched. But nothing seemed amiss. Shawn never showed her face and seemed to enter the apartment no problem, so she could have had a duplicate keycard. Nothing suspicious. Bibi was pissed because the police said she must have given Shawn a card. As I said to Bibi, a large wad of cash would have bought a duplicate from someone in the hotel or was there some type of master keycard?

My phone dinged, and I jumped. It dinged with two more messages. It was Bibi.

I'm in danger. I'm not paranoid! Otto keeps growling. There are footsteps outside my door and muffled voices.

I didn't tell you this before, but I found incriminating evidence against the mob in Betty's stuff. I created a safe place for it. You'll figure it out.

If something happens to me, promise you'll take care of Otto. You know what he's like. He's sweet and needs his ugly striped afghan. He also knows a lot.

I reread the texts. Fuck! It was 4:02 a.m., and we wouldn't land for another two hours. I texted back.

Don't answer the door, Bibi. Don't let anyone in. Call the police.

I tried to stay calm. Footsteps and voices didn't necessarily mean anything. Maybe it was nothing more than late-night revelers or an assignation. Yet my heart raced. Shawn had been there once. Why not again? I texted another message and tried to convince myself that she would text back and say it was nothing. Had Otto barked at the noise? He wasn't much of a barker, more of a growler. He was a big gentle brute the size of a Shetland pony, but there's only so much a dog could do against greedy criminals who were willing to kill people, never mind dogs. But Shawn had already made friends with him. OK, what else? Bibi carried a gun. Good. But you had to be willing to shoot to kill. I knew very few good people capable of that, even in a life-or-death situation.

I sent another text.

Do you still have your gun? Load and keep it handy.

A text came in. I almost dropped my phone.

It was my lawyer. I ignored him.

I squirmed in my seat. Why hadn't Bibi told me about the incriminating evidence before? What had she planned on doing with it? I chewed a cuticle. Maybe she didn't really trust me.

Being trapped on a plane made it impossible to do anything. I had to keep my wits about me though. Did Shawn know about the incriminating evidence? I doubted it. My bet was on Shawn targeting Bibi's inheritances—two huge estates and all the assets. What a rat's nest of relationships! Bibi's godmother, Betty Snayer, had been the crime boss of this mob until she died trying to kill me in Kauai. But before that, Betty had taken in a young, homeless, talented black girl, my half-sister Bibi, and given her a life in the arts. Then Betty had fallen for Shawn, at the time a streetwise, ragged, coke snorter who had addicted Betty to sex and white powder. That left Bibi adrift as to Betty's affections. So, there I was with a new half-sister who didn't know I'd killed her sainted godmother. What a mess.

The first-class flight attendant leaned over the empty seat next to me. "Anything I can get you, Ms. Porter?" She smiled with her bright red lips, her eyes sparkling behind her cat-eye glasses.

"Scotch, please. A double."

I wiped my sweaty palms on my jeans. After sending another message to Bibi, I waited. Again, nothing. Finally, resigned, I set the cell on the empty seat next to me, and when my drink came, I tried not to knock it back, but that was impossible.

Maybe Bibi *had* called the cops, but I doubted it. I knew she didn't trust the FBI. Being African American, she probably didn't trust the cops either, especially after they did nothing to follow up on Shawn. I rubbed my chest, drew in some air, and let it go. Sophie often scolded me, saying I held my breath when stressed. Taking advice from my dead sister? Better late than never.

I pushed up the window cover. The bright light made me wince. Below, the ocean bordered the serpentine edge of land. Lakes littered the middle of the state. The pilot announced we were flying over Orlando and Disney World. People oohed and aahed.

On the seat next to me, I found my notebook and pen under the *New York Times,* and as I flipped open the notebook, my hand trembled. I'd always been pretty good at compartmentalizing, something I found necessary as a lawyer, but it was getting more difficult. I needed to keep my mind busy until I was off the plane and could make calls. I wondered where Gerard was. I figured from our conversations that he was back undercover with the mob. When I told him I was heading to Florida to help Bibi, he told me not to and was upset when I wouldn't back down. When he realized I wouldn't change my mind, he said he'd meet me there. Fine.

I made a fist, squeezed, then shook out my hand, needing to write something down, maybe work through what I knew and come up with a plan of sorts. Since my law school days, I'd written to-do lists, observations, even lists of conjectures and theories about people and cases. It kept me focused. It also helped me solve dilemmas, and even, at times, find something that wasn't immediately apparent. Clients were told to keep a journal of every move they made, with dates and times, plus anything that could help their case. People were unaware of the evidentiary heft a written journal provided when entered into court records. I'd won several cases on the written word alone when the opposition had what I called a wormy case.

But what to write?

The scotch had warmed its way down to my body, and I could feel my nerves relaxing, my brain focusing. I tapped the pen against my lower teeth. Going back to the beginning with Shawn, I wondered why Betty had been interested in her? Bibi said it was cocaine-fueled sex. I believed that. Betty was older and not a looker, so it could have been the excitement and ego boost. I believed Bibi when she said Betty took Bibi in because she saw her talent and wanted to support her. Being a cynic at heart, I figured Betty had done that to make herself feel good. I'm sure it made her look good to her wealthy patron friends. Bibi was beautiful too—a dark version of Sophie—dizygotic twins from different fathers. So that would give Betty even more cred for being inclusive. A great way to get grants for her non-profit art ventures.

There I go again—the cynic.

The flight attendant swooped in and removed my cold coffee. I ordered another scotch, a single this time, thinking about Gerard, my FBI special agent pain-in-the-ass contact. In the beginning, he'd suspected Bibi was another one of Betty's lovers. Men. They always think sex is involved. Sometimes it was. I could attest to that.

So how had Shawn become the crime boss of Betty's mob? Maybe Betty had put her in charge when she went to Kauai. I know that Betty was using heavily by the time she came to the island. She was in Kauai, doing a godmotherly thing—setting up a hit on Bibi's brother who hated Bibi. Bibi was adopted and the parents favored her over their flaky son. Her brother lived communally on Kauai and dressed as the grim reaper to get peoples' attention about climate change. So, he didn't fit his parents' mold. Bibi, however, was the golden child, always thankful for everything they did for her. But they died before the will was changed, and the brother inherited the bulk. Hating Bibi, he gave her nothing. Betty figured she'd get rid of the brother so Bibi would inherit. At least Betty felt she was protecting Bibi. I wonder if Shawn had put that idea into Betty's head, thinking Bibi would eventually bring in even more assets to the "organization."

When I met Betty in Kauai, I didn't know I had a sister named Bibi. I didn't know a lot of things. I was hiding out from the mob. They wanted the millions my sister Sophie stole. But Betty knew who I was. I was the one who had killed one of her partners—in self-defense. But that didn't matter to her. She must have been overjoyed to think she could take care of two marks on the same trip.

I had to assume that Shawn took over the crime boss position when Betty and her bodyguard never made it back to Boston. Gerard and I thought Shawn was a minor character, one of those people who target the wealthy to live luxuriously for a while, snort coke all day, then when things go dumpster, they disappear. She fooled us.

Plus, I had to remember she was a good actor. Shawn had gone from messed-up street urchin to high couture. What really bothered me was her telling Bibi that she laundered the money for the mob. True? Or was that a way to entrap Bibi? If Bibi knew that, she'd be vulnerable if she didn't join the mob. Shawn was smart, no matter her motive.

I sipped my second scotch. If I kept in lawyer mode, I could keep my shit together. So, who was Shawn? Did she have a police record? What was her M.O.? I'd lost the connection with Snoop, my hacker, just as she was going to tell me what she found on Shawn. I haven't heard from her since, and that's not good.

Shawn might be a psychopath, but she had to be a strategist, someone with patience, someone who had planned her ascent with the crime group. This was conjecture, but her actions pointed to it.

This felt good, building a case, listing all the possibilities, hopefully tracing them to their logical conclusion either with evidence or what I'd discovered in the process.

I listed questions about "Shawn the Strategist":

- Getting Betty hooked on cocaine: loosens the tongue, makes her vulnerable
- Reason for admitting money laundering: trap Bibi into the gang; something else?
- Need background check on her: laundering takes guts, know-how, and connections
- Has Shawn already taken Bibi somewhere? Under guise of meeting?
- How much does Bibi know about Betty?
- Maybe Shawn knows more about Bibi than I do

I SUSPECTED that Bibi couldn't live in Betty's house all that time and not notice any illegal activities. But Bibi seemed to have no idea, and as she said, she'd been fully engaged in school, her art, and her friends.

The plane's engine noise changed. We were approaching Fort Lauderdale. I slipped on my shoes and buttoned my military-style jacket, readying myself for landing. I'd dressed with a casual elegance so people would take me seriously but not authoritatively as with a suit. Instead of perfume or aftershave, the cabin smelled like a locker room, and I hoped I didn't smell that way. I thought of how Gerard

would smell when I met him. As if reading my mind, Gerard
sent me a message.

I'll get to The Circ before you. Meet you in the residency
lobby.

BETWEEN MY TEETH, I HISSED, "ASSHOLE." He'd insisted on
meeting me in Florida, but I told him to do *nothing* until I
got there. That was like pissing in the wind with him.

I finished the scotch. I couldn't get off the plane fast
enough.

The pilot came on the intercom and gave the usual
instructions, telling everyone to take their seats, buckle up,
seats upright, tray in position. The flight attendant quickly
gathered up all the bottles and glasses. I snapped my tray
into place, gathered up everything on the empty seat, and
threw them in my satchel, something I'd bought because it
was more like a briefcase but not a briefcase. The flight
attendant had just buckled herself in when the plane
dropped like a trap door had opened. Someone squealed. A
kid cried. Then the plane leveled off.

With my heart in my throat, I forced my mind back to
Bibi and Betty. From everything I knew, Betty wanted Bibi to
devote herself to being an artist. What if Betty had recognized Shawn's killer instinct and started grooming her to
take over the business?

I checked my cell one more time. Nothing from Bibi.

The plane headed toward the landing strip. I held the
notebook against my chest. As a defense attorney, I'd met
many criminals and could usually sniff out the liars. Bibi's

panicky text from Florida was not something easy to fake. But I had no body language to go with this to assure me she was being straight with me.

Far too many unknowns.

I sat back, closed my eyes, and prepared for landing.

s the plane taxied to our gate, everyone's phones lit up, rang, and pinged. I had one message from Gerard.

I'm at The Circ. Where are you?

I MESSAGED BACK:

Do nothing until I get there. Comprends?

I THOUGHT MAYBE USING his native French might get his attention. But he always did what he wanted. I wished I could trust Gerard, but right from the beginning, he'd made mistakes, caused by his mission and his obsession with finding a rogue FBI agent. The rogue agent was suspected of joining this mob and working at the highest level, but in all the time I'd known Gerard, he hadn't uncovered one name, one lead, not even a shadow. He met my sister Sophie, Bibi's twin, while working with this Boston mob and involved her with this family of extortionists. They'd tragically fallen in love.

As I strode over to the luggage carousel, I tried to shake the past that Gerard represented. I understood the power of love, but Gerard had not understood my sister. When Sophie fell in love, she became obsessed and did things ordinary people wouldn't. For the love of Gerard, she had seduced my husband and stole his business money, all to supposedly save Gerard from being killed. She'd been manipulated. Betty's partner had told Sophie that Gerard had used her to get the money. She'd never had enough confidence in herself when it came to men. Why? I don't know. She could have passed for Marilyn Monroe. She was that beautiful. But beauty wasn't always a gift.

As the plane opened for us to disembark, I stayed seated. I wiped my eyes, remembering Sophie hanging from her living room overhead light fixture, wearing that blue dress. That is one image I'll never be able to wipe from my memory.

Now I had Bibi to worry about with this same organization.

I swallowed hard and looked at my cell. I tried Bibi again. Had I hopped a red-eye to Florida for nothing? The Glock 19 I'd packed in my suitcase would do me little good if something had already happened to Bibi. Unless someone was waiting for me, too.

My phone dinged. Yes!

Oh, damn. It was my "new" brother.

Please let me know if I can do anything. I have you
arriving this morning? Do you need a ride from the
airport? This is Ian. Ian McKnight. In case you don't
recognize the number.

NOT RECOGNIZE? I should have been beat, emotionally and
physically, but I thrived on stress. Most lawyers do. What
exhausted me were the lies, betrayals, and uncertainties. Ian
had shown up in Oregon under an alias to test me, to see
what I was like before he confessed to being my brother. I
was bone-tired of not having anyone to trust or believe in.
Now I'd been reminded that there was a new member of the
family, my half-brother, Ian, another product of one of my
mother's affairs. The mom who keeps on giving me siblings
long after she was dead. Ian lived in Naples on the West side
of Florida. So, what was he doing on the East Coast? And
why did he always show up wherever I was? He felt like a
stalker, not a brother.

While fellow travelers popped up from their seats like
Whack-a-moles, grabbing at their luggage in the overhead
bins, I stayed seated and tried calling Bibi. No luck.

I brushed my hair back and applied lip balm as people
waited for the door to open.

Maybe I was too suspicious. Ian explained that he was
excited to have a sister as he didn't have one, and now he
did. OK. Maybe it was that simple. Could Ian possibly turn
out to be a trusted ally? Maybe *that's* why I'd intuitively told
him I was going to Florida to help a half-sister. I didn't tell
him details, but he'd offered to help in any way he could,

said he could be there in a couple of hours, just call. The trouble was he was just so excitable. And it couldn't have come at a worse time.

I stood, trying to stay patient as passengers juggled their carry-ons. I slipped between two people. Were they ever going to open the plane's door?

If only I could get back in touch with Snoop. I trusted her. Come to think of it, she was the only one I trusted. Gerard needed to tell me if she was all right. When I was on the phone with Snoop when we were cut off, she not only was going to give me intel on Shawn, but was also going to tell me something about Ian. I wonder if the Feds nabbed her? Gerard had warned me not to stay in contact with her. Could that be it? Gerard knew she was going to get busted? He and I had lots to talk about.

Another call to Bibi. It went to voicemail.

Amidst all this craziness, I'd given hardly any thought to what should have been my biggest surprise—I had a father. I had a living father. Someone who might tell me more than I ever knew about my mother. Someone who might love me as a daughter. Someone who was sane, thoughtful, and would be there for me. Hopefully, after Bibi was safe and we took care of the mob, I could meet him, and we'd form some kind of relationship. I'd been an orphan for years since my parents died in the car "accident." After Sophie's suicide, I remained the last of my family. Now, with DNA, I'd gained two siblings and a father. Were there other siblings out there?

I swallowed hard, the faint taste of scotch in my mouth. The plane's door opened. I grabbed my satchel, filed out, and raced toward the baggage area.

3

The crowd thickened inside the airport, and I raced to baggage. As I dodged people, I asked Siri to call The Circ residency apartments. I needed to talk to the manager so I could have access to Bibi's apartment, but I was put through to a desk clerk who told me visitors had to check in before being allowed to access the building, and the resident had to grant entry. Any door into the residency section could only be opened with a card key. I told the desk clerk my name, my relation to Bibi, and the situation.

"Did my sister Bibi leave any directions for you in case I showed up when she wasn't home?"

"Just a moment." Nails tapped on a keyboard. "No, she left no instructions. I'm sorry."

"That means something *has* happened to her. She would have left instructions if she'd had to leave because she knew I was coming today."

"I understand, but we have strict rules. Unless she left your information and instructions to let you in, I can't do anything." She then explained that she could try calling the apartment and, if there was no answer, could send someone up to Bibi's to knock.

"If she doesn't answer, we need to go inside. As I told you, someone gained access to her apartment without her permission."

"We can knock but can't enter. Maybe she's walking her dog? Or has gone off to shop or meet someone and forgot to leave instructions?"

I lowered my voice and spoke slowly. "No matter where she is, she'd answer her cell. All these factors—unable to reach her, no cell contact, no instructions for me—point to a dangerous situation for her."

"Perhaps she lost her cell," the young woman added. She paused. "Perhaps you should call the police?"

"Please get your manager on the line."

I waited. A few seconds later, she returned to tell me the manager would call me as soon as possible.

Why didn't I call the police? Because as a lawyer, I knew I didn't have enough evidence for them to gain access to her apartment. Plus, I wanted to be the first one through the door. The police would never give me access to her place once they were in there.

I wiped sweat from my upper lip and waited near my flight's carousel. I turned my phone's volume up too high so I wouldn't miss a call or message. Someone smelling of laundry soap pushed past me as the bags came through.

When my cell rang, it almost jumped from my hand.

"Hello, Ms. Porter, this is Carla Santiago, The Circ's residency manager. There was no answer at your sister's apartment. Are you close by?"

I told her I'd be there in about thirty minutes if traffic allowed and agreed to meet her in the lobby. She told me where to park and what to say to the concierge—I was a special guest of hers.

My suitcase arrived. I grabbed it and headed to pick up the SUV rental I arranged on the plane. Just from the limited amount of rushing around, I was already sweating, and outside it was eighty-seven degrees. Inside the SUV, I programmed the GPS for The Circ, connected my cell to its charger, turned on the air, and fumbled in my satchel for my sunglasses. The SUV had a faint hint of cigarette smoke combined with a throat-tightening air "freshener." I already missed the cool, moist air of the Northwest.

The traffic was as I remembered—license plates from all over the country, many from Massachusetts and Ohio, some from Canada, fast drivers and elderly dawdlers mixed with the crazies. I had to whip in and out and give a finger to one driver who got on my ass and honked. My hands hurt from clutching the wheel. Thankfully, GPS kept me focused. I needed coffee. I needed to pee. Before I drove up to The Circ's residency building, I pulled into a parking space along the street, a large, impressive traffic circle with shops, a large city park, a Publix. I opened the hatch and glanced around. I pulled out my gun case from my suitcase, unlocked it, loaded my Glock, and slipped it into my satchel. A loaded, accessible gun was against the law in Florida, but this was about my sister. Gerard would no doubt be in the lobby, and together we'd figure out how to get into Bibi's apartment.

As I closed the hatch, a naked man riding a bicycle on the sidewalk headed my way. His only article of clothing seemed to be a fedora wrapped in purple fairy lights. I'd expect to see that in Oregon, but not here. He slowed, tipped his hat, and said, "Careful of that thing," and pointed at my shoulder bag.

4

The naked guy threw me. I hopped into the car and sat there for a minute. Had he seen the gun? My heart thrummed. No, he couldn't have. I'd been careful. Even if he had, so what? He was a crazy, naked guy on a bike.

Still, something about it reminded me of Paris and the homeless man dressed in a dirty Santa suit. He saw me just after I'd poisoned—or thought I'd poisoned—Gerard. I'd left Gerard lying on the ground across from the Eiffel Tower among thousands of people celebrating New Year's. I ran and almost made it back to the Paris apartment, but just before I got there, the homeless Santa Claus popped up and pointed a finger at me as if accusing me of killing Gerard. It still causes goosebumps up my arms.

I smacked the steering wheel. "Snap out of it." I exhaled like blowing out a candle. I'd give my left ovary for a cigarette.

I had to get to Bibi. I knew she thought Otto would protect her, but big bruisers were typically suckers for a poisoned treat. At the same time, the ankle biters barked themselves to exhaustion.

The hotel was a short distance. I pulled up to the entrance. The Circ—a grand, white, multistoried Art Deco hotel, studded with glass—glowed even in the morning light. Palms and oleanders textured the ground level. Across from The Circ, the sizable park showed a healthy green. Had Bibi taken Otto there for his morning constitutional?

As I handed the key fob and a tip to the parking attendant, I asked about Bibi. He remembered her and said he hadn't seen her that morning.

His name tag said, "Tony." I took a good look at the young man and filed his face to memory. I'd question him later if necessary.

I rushed inside. You could have landed a small plane in the lobby.

And there was Gerard, walking toward me. At first, I wasn't sure it was him.

He looked different. He looked good. He looked rested, his dark hair thick and neatly trimmed, his brown eyes clear. No facial hair now. His fashionable jeans slung low on his hips. His amber-colored, short-sleeve shirt moved like silk. Someone had done a makeover on him. He looked very Floridian, even down to a tan. Or was it just a disguise? This look of his, this fake local, turned me off. I guess I'd outgrown the love of a "well-dressed man." Something had changed in me, but I had no time to figure it out.

He kissed me on each cheek then swept his lips across mine. Son-of-a-bitch. I felt the blood rush to my face. What was the deal? I felt his breath on my face and smelled something new, like a citrusy aftershave. Even his nails were neatly trimmed. And was that a Movado gold watch on his wrist? No, probably a knockoff.

I stepped back, almost a jump. My pulse raced, but not with pleasure. I blurted out, "Bibi hasn't returned any of my messages. Something *has* happened to her." I started to explain that the residency manager wouldn't let us into her room when Gerard stopped me.

"We will get into the apartment, Angeline." His French accent was thick, and not for the first time, I questioned whether he was French or only posing. Who the hell was he?

A woman and young man entered the lobby. The young man took the concierge's desk chair.

The woman asked Gerard, "Agent Duvernet, is this Ms. Porter?" She held out her hand, and I shook it. "We spoke on the phone. I'm Carla Santiago, the residency manager. Agent Duvernet has explained the situation. Follow me."

Damn him. This is why I hadn't wanted him here. What exactly had he explained? I told him to let me handle it first. But I had no choice now except to follow them, teeth grinding.

On the elevator to the eighth floor, I watched Gerard charm the woman. Just how long had he been here in Florida? Maybe I should be asking if he was an FBI agent. But I'd witnessed other FBI agents react to his name and recognize his credentials. For the first time, I realized I'd never seen him work directly with anyone. Did I know for sure that he was undercover? Or that there was a rogue FBI agent? When the elevator door opened, I stood to the side, letting him and the manager go first. He gave me a quizzical look and motioned for me to join him.

"Are you all right, Angeline?"

A stupid question. No, I wasn't all right. I hurried ahead. All I cared about was getting into Bibi's apartment.

At Bibi's door, I knocked several times before banging on

the door. "Bibi! It's Angeline." Nothing. Visions of Sophie hanging by a noose blinded me.

Then I heard a sound so insignificant I could easily have missed it. On the floor on my knees, I put my ear to the door. "Otto?" I thought I heard something. "Otto!" A faint scratching.

"Otto! Hello, boy. Hold on. We're coming. Just a minute."

Otto whined.

5

I jumped to my feet. "It's Bibi's dog. He'd bark if he were OK. He must be hurt. That means Bibi is—"

"Excuse me," Gerard said to the manager, cutting me off. He brandished his FBI credentials again and said, "Legally, I can have you open this door. I believe a person's life or health is at risk."

Gerard's French accent had all but disappeared. The manager didn't react, perhaps considering what to do next.

"I assure you that under the legal search exception of ensuring the safety of others, you can legally unlock this door for me. You should also call the police."

She called the police while unlocking the door. I tried to open the door, but Otto blocked it. Gerard helped me push him aside. Otto was panting hard, froth at his mouth, but he was alive. He seemed to recognize me. "Hang in there, Otto. We'll get you help." Thankfully, when I adopted my dog Tempest in Kauai, I learned about canine health real fast. I had to. The mob had taken her and was going to kill her if I didn't hand over the money that Sophie had stolen. They knew my weak spot.

Otto let me check his gums and under his eyelids, but both were white instead of pink. Not good.

"Ms. Santiago," I said. "The dog has been poisoned. We need a vet *now*."

The manager shouted into the phone, "Get the veterinary hospital to send someone. A large dog has been poisoned. It's a police situation."

I walked over to Gerard, who stood near the couch. I gasped. The room had been turned inside out. He put out an arm to hold me back. He was taking photos with his cell. I looked over to where he pointed. The glass coffee table was smeared with what looked like blood. One of Bibi's sandals was under the table.

My hand flew to my mouth.

I felt sick. Gerard put his hand on my shoulder. "Don't," he said. I had no idea what he meant. Don't throw up? Don't cry? Don't scream? Don't lose your shit?

But I knew better. I flicked his hand from my shoulder and walked around the apartment, not touching anything, just visually searching. The laptop was gone and so was any visible external hard drive. It wasn't hard to guess why this apartment had been ransacked. Or who did it or had it done. But what had they done with Bibi?

The manager stood in the doorway, glancing back and forth between the apartment and the hall, holding her cell phone to her ear, mouth moving rapidly.

Gerard caught her attention during a short pause in her phone activity. "I'm suggesting you call security and have all camera footage secured. The police will want it."

The manager kept talking on the cell while Gerard took more photos.

Before the cops came and kicked us out, I hurried into Bibi's bedroom and took photos too. The bed had been pulled apart, mattress upended, bedding balled on the floor. Drawers were emptied, beautiful underthings scattered across the floor, clothing in the closet ransacked. Even boxes of Bibi's art supplies had been dumped. The exposed intimacy of the scene was frightening. Not that I believed in Him or Her, but I begged God to keep Bibi safe.

Back at Bibi's desk, I noted everything I could remember from her work area in New Hampshire when I first met her. I figured Shawn had taken anything that could hold incriminating evidence about the gang, like Bibi's cell, laptop, papers, files. All her framed computer graphic art had been ripped from the walls and the backs removed. The art was strewn across the table and floor.

Two were face up. In New Hampshire, when Bibi and I first met, she had four pieces framed and hung on the wall. Black faces and bodies, an angry crowd holding baseball bats and signs, naked people dancing, and a stack of dead black bodies piled like logged trees. I shuddered.

But one of the pieces on the floor was new ... and odd ... unlike her other work. A smaller piece too. A digital painting of a black man. He wore a suit with a bowtie, had a perfect oval head with a receding hairline, close-set eyes, and a thin mustache.

With my back to Gerard and the manager, I slipped the small art piece under my blouse. Call it a gut move, but I had to have it. All the investigation team would do is dust for fingerprints.

I looked over the room. By the looks of the upheaval, Shawn had to have had help. How could one person contain a dog and a woman while ransacking the apartment? Unless, of course, she had knocked Bibi unconscious. But Bibi needed to be conscious to walk out. No one was going to carry her. That would raise an alarm to see a grown black woman carried from the premises. The security footage would identify her and whoever forced her from the building.

My mind buzzed, and I tried not to think about what they'd do to Bibi. The statistics weren't good. After twenty-four hours, the chances of a kidnapping turning fatal shot up to eighty percent. We needed to find her soon. I knew why they'd taken her. Tearing up the apartment and the blood on the coffee table meant Bibi hadn't talked, hadn't told them anything—*if* she knew anything.

But Bibi had information. Her text had said she'd hidden it, so I looked more closely at her desk, hoping for a clue of where it could be, something that—

"I'm sorry, Miss, but you need to vacate the premises."

A policeman stood next to me and motioned me toward the door. The room filled with men in blue. Already, a detective was talking to the manager. Ms. Santiago called me over. I looked for Gerard. He was gone.

The detective held out his hand and smiled. "I'm Detective Arturo Prosper." His hand was warm, dry, firm, and confident, not pushy. He was unusual too. Most detectives didn't wear a uniform or suit. They were usually rough around the edges, sometimes unkempt, even potbellied. If you saw one on your property, you'd call the police. That's because they spent most of their time in the office at a desk, never on the dangerous front line like cops.

"Ms. Porter?"

I pulled my hand away. "Yes?"

"Ms. Santiago says this is your sister's apartment? I'm sorry and hope nothing has happened to her. What do you know about the situation?"

"I'm pretty sure she's been forcibly taken."

He nodded. "Excuse me just a moment." One of his officers leaned in and said something into his ear. Detective Prosper listened, brows furrowed.

When he turned back to me, I wondered what was going on inside his head. He asked, "Did you touch anything in the room?"

"No, of course not." I said flatly. I wasn't offended. It was a professional question.

"That's good. Thank you." He smiled. "So, Ms. Porter, where did your FBI friend go?"

OK, this guy was good. One of those who could act pleasant and appreciative of your help then catch you off guard with a pointed question. A good strategy if the other person hadn't dealt with it much.

"I have no idea."

To Ms. Santiago, he said, "Did you see Mr. Duvernet leave?" She nodded and indicated the stairwell. He sent two men to check that out. I noticed he hadn't called Gerard "Agent Duvernet," so that implied he wouldn't until he had confirmation from an FBI badge or ID via the local FBI.

"You just arrived?" he said to me. I nodded. "From where?" I told him. "A long flight," he said.

A veterinarian team exited the elevator, causing a commotion with the police. The Detective motioned to the cops to let them pass.

I could feel Detective Prosper's eyes on me as I hurried over to Otto and knelt. Otto's panting had slowed, and he didn't look good. I rubbed under his chin. "You'll be OK, boy. Hang in there."

After the vet tech gave him a precursory exam, they loaded the dog onto a carrier.

"Was he poisoned? Will he live?"

She gave me a wary look. "It looks like a poisoning. He's

alive now, but whatever he was given could have irreparably damaged his stomach and liver."

I knew what that meant.

We swapped information, and I watched them as they took poor Otto away.

6

In the hallway, I sank onto my haunches with my head back against the wall. Two-way radios clicked and transmitted info from the scene. The investigative team scoured the apartment, photographed everything, and bagged evidence. Two of the house cleaning employees spoke with Ms. Santiago. When no one was looking, I pulled the art piece from under my blouse and slipped it into my satchel.

Detective Prosper walked over, looked down at me, and said, "Are you all right?"

I looked up. "Yes. Just afraid for my sister." I sucked back a sob. It was getting to me.

"I understand." He paused. "Do you know why your FBI friend left in such a hurry?"

"He's FBI. He doesn't tell me much." I didn't try to hide the frustration in my voice. I didn't like this position of Prosper looking down on me. Pressing against the wall, I pushed up to standing.

"What do you know about what's going on here?"

To establish I was no grunt but to get on his good side, I

said, "I'm a former prosecuting attorney from Oregon." I lied because law enforcement didn't like defense attorneys. "I flew here on a red-eye because yesterday a woman who had no access to Bibi's apartment was sitting on her couch when she came home. This person threatened her."

"Yes, I read the report on that. We didn't have anything to go on and nothing was stolen. Plus, it looked like the woman entered legally with a swipe card."

I charged ahead. "That means someone affiliated with The Circ gave her the swipe card or had a second one made for that person. The employee might be connected with this case, but more probable they were paid a tidy sum for a duplicate key." I gave him Shawn's full name. If Gerard wanted to have any official cooperation from the locals, he should have stuck around.

"Thank you," he said as he wrote more in his notebook.

I told him I'd keep him informed of anything that developed. This man gave off the air of being trustworthy. But again, I don't bat one hundred in my people assessment skills. "How long have you been on the force?"

"Fourteen years here in Florida. Excuse me a minute." One of his men had waved him over.

I thought I discerned a slight accent, possibly Canadian. Many Canadians lived in Florida after retirement at least half the year. Maybe he had family here.

A hotel employee came over with a bucket of bottled waters on ice and handed me one. I downed half of it. This was a robbery and missing person case for the time being. The critical evidence was the blood on the table. It still needed to be determined as human. Never assume anything. If human, did it match my sister's?

If so, that would make this a significant case that needed to be solved quickly if Bibi were to be found alive. I needed access to everything. Most of all, I needed the trust and cooperation of Detective Arturo Prosper.

When he returned, I said, "I'm worried sick about my sister. I know what this outfit can do." My throat caught. "I'd appreciate it if you'd keep me in the loop."

"I'll do what I can. And may I request you do the same? She'll try to reach out to you as soon as she's able. I hope it's soon."

"Deal."

"Can you give me your FBI friend's number?"

"He's working a big case. He only contacts me." That wasn't a lie. He never answered my calls. The detective waited for more, but I just shrugged.

"So, did your sister just move here?"

"Yes."

"Can you tell me why?"

"She wanted to leave Boston and get a new start after losing her godmother, her benefactor. Bibi's an artist, and maybe she heard this place was friendly to artists. Maybe due to her ... being biracial? I don't know. Oh, she did say she had a friend here, so she had a connection, but I have no idea who that is."

"You flew out here to help her, yet you don't seem to know much about why she moved here." He didn't say this accusingly. His voice was mildly husky, even comforting.

"I just met her. I didn't know she existed." I waited for a reaction, but none came. He had a good poker face. I didn't explain about the twins, my mother, and what I'd learned in New Hampshire. I needed to talk with Gerard before the cops knew everything. Why the hell *did* he leave?

One of the detective's men asked him a question which he answered, then turned back to me. "It sounds like you have quite a story to tell. Can we talk down at the station?"

"I need coffee."

He smiled. "We have some of that at the station."

"Anything to eat there?"

"I'll get you a sandwich." He didn't ask what kind. "Just one question right now. If your sister was taken, do you know why?"

"Bibi has incriminating evidence about her deceased godmother who was the head of a group of Boston extortionists. That's who Agent Duvernet is after."

One eyebrow rose, but that poker face remained. He jotted something in his notebook, turned to a nearby officer, said something that I couldn't hear, and waved a young female officer over. As he spoke with her, I finally checked him out. Up until now, it had been too chaotic, but now I needed to know who oversaw my sister's case, whom I was dealing with, what kind of man he was. I needed to make him an ally.

Physically, he bore healthy, rugged masculinity, unlike the bald neo-extremist look so many cops adopted, *and* he had cheekbones women would swap for their firstborn. His thick, wavy hair was gray at the temples. Detective Prosper also didn't wear a wedding ring.

His demeanor impressed me most. He'd been polite, sympathetic, and direct so far with no dismissive retorts because I was a woman. Too good to be true? We'd see how he did when I went to the station for interviewing.

"Ms. Porter, this is Officer Walsh," he said. "She'll be taking you down to the station and bring you back to the hotel if that's all right with you." He pulled out a card and wrote something on it. "Call me anytime. I've written my cell number on the back."

I nodded.

"We'll do everything possible to find her."

I appreciated his kindness, but I was beyond trusting anyone.

The hotel manager offered me a room, and I thanked her. "Does Agent Duvernet have a room in the hotel?"

He didn't. I was perplexed and pissed. I took one last look at Bibi's room and the team working it, then left with Officer Walsh for the station.

7

A t the station, officer Walsh waited while I went through security to use the ladies' room. I needed coffee, pronto, as jet lag was catching up with me, never mind the stress. The dominoes kept falling, and I had no idea how to stop them.

What would I do if I lost Bibi?

When Officer Walsh held open the door to the interview room, she told me to take a seat. I turned to her and said, "This is the interview room?"

She nodded. "Everyone reacts like that when they see it for the first time. Can I get you some coffee?"

"Please," I said as I gawked at the room and took a seat on a dark navy-blue sofa that faced a coffee table and two beige armchairs.

Usually, the standard non-secure police interview room would be painted industrial white or gray with a table and three or four desk chairs. This room was painted a sunny white tinted with tangerine, just enough color to remind me I was in Florida, the state of excess. Two framed posters of Hollywood, Florida hung on the opposite wall advertising a "Crime Tour" of the city.

When Officer Walsh returned with the coffee, I said, "Whose bright idea was this?" gesturing to the room.

I hadn't meant to be snarky. I desperately needed that coffee.

"You can blame Detective Prosper." She handed me the paper cup. Her smile said she admired the detective.

I sipped the thick, hot sludge. Cuban coffee, something I'd tried when Hank and I visited the Keys. Still not a fan.

The officer handed me a napkin, and I thanked her.

Detective Prosper walked in, thanked Officer Walsh, set down a recording device, a file, his coffee, then handed me a sandwich. I opened the wrapper. A Cubano. I took a bite.

The recording device seemed unnecessary. I'd already noted two high-definition IP cameras in the corners and, to the right of me, a two-way mirror.

He settled in a chair and crossed his legs. "What do you think? Of the room?"

"Interesting. Colorful. I can't wait to see your interrogation rooms."

"Similar, only the sofa isn't so comfy."

So, he had a sense of humor. Good, but I wanted information. I wanted to know if they'd found something hidden, something she'd said that could throw this criminal group into the nearest croc-infested swamp. Then I thought about how she'd asked me to take care of Otto if something happened to her. I shivered and cupped the coffee in my hands as if I were freezing.

Detective Prosper said, "Are you cold? We can turn down the AC."

"No, fine. Just a little jetlagged and worried." I sipped the coffee.

Prosper opened his file, and I watched him, trying to stay quiet. I was determined not to rush him. "Thanks for this," I said, holding up the sandwich. "I think better with something in my stomach."

"That works best for me too."

"Anything on my sister?"

Someone knocked on the door and stuck his head in. "Hey, Art, here's the blood analysis you wanted."

I leaned forward and set down my coffee. Prosper took the papers. My heart raced, and I tried to see the papers. After a glance, he looked up. I couldn't read him or the papers.

"What is it?" I asked.

"The blood on the table doesn't match your sister's."

"How do you know?"

"Your sister is O+. The blood on the table is A+."

"How do you know my sister's blood type?"

"She was arrested a few times when she was homeless in Boston. Squatting, B&E. Not surprising for someone on the street." He wasn't looking at me. He continued leafing through the papers and drinking his coffee.

"Oh," I whispered. "At least we know it's not her blood on the table. That's good."

He held up a piece of paper. "Something else. We searched for Tamara Shawn Diamandis's name and found only one person who fit the age group. She died from an overdose in Boston."

"So 'Shawn' is ghosting."

"Looks that way."

"Anything else?" Relieved at least about the blood, I tried a bigger bite of the Cubano, but my mouth was so dry I couldn't swallow. I washed it down with the coffee.

Prosper continued reading the file. I waited, not wanting

to be pushy. I pegged him as being thorough and thoughtful.

Finally, he said, "At the apartment, we found several fingerprints that belong to your sister, and The Circ employees, cleaning staff, etc. Thanks for not touching anything when you were in there."

The look he gave me now set me upright and rigid. "What?"

"We found something odd, however." He paused and studied me.

Was he playing me for a reaction? I held his gaze. "What was it?"

"We found prints belonging to your friend Gerard Duvernet."

I'd already told him we hadn't touched anything. So, Gerard was making me look like a liar. "Where?"

"In the living room area and kitchen."

I was relieved to hear they weren't in the bedroom. If he'd even touched my sister, I'd have—

"We also found a dirty wine glass pushed deep into a cupboard. Using the county crime lab's Rapid DNA machine, we identified the DNA as belonging to Duvernet. When we contacted the FBI, they said they couldn't give us any information on him."

"Couldn't or wouldn't?"

"Same thing."

I tried to keep a neutral expression even though I snapped up *that* detail like an alligator snapping up a yappy Shih Tzu. His fingerprints? His DNA on a wine glass? So, he'd been in Bibi's apartment before I'd arrived. But why had Bibi saved his dirty wine glass? Was she suspicious of him and had kept it for this exact purpose? To expose him for some reason?

Then it hit me. Who had interviewed Bibi in Boston? Gerard or someone else? When was he put in charge of her protection? Or was he? Had he used Bibi as bait to draw out the new crime group's head of operation? Or did it have to do with—

"Did you know anything about this? About Duvernet being at your sister's?"

"No." I said in almost a whisper. "No, I did not." If the detective could read me, he'd note that I was pissed.

"Does any of this make sense then?"

I decided to keep it simple with the detective. "None of it makes any sense."

What I was thinking was, "WTF, Gerard?" Then I remembered how I felt when I first saw him in the lobby, his tan, how he looked like he'd been in Florida for a while. But the tan could be fake. That didn't matter. He had gone full-tilt Floridian for a reason. Mentally, I ran through some possibilities, one of them being Bibi had never met him and had struck up a friendship with him, not knowing he was FBI. But when I first arrived, he went with me to Bibi's apartment, so he must have known she wasn't there. Hell, he probably knew the place had been ransacked but wanted to act like he and I were seeing it for the first time. But the wine glass? He'd been at Bibi's drinking wine which meant they had been in casual conversation, maybe had even been attracted to each other. Maybe they had started at the bar and then gone up to the apartment. I was so hot with anger that I could feel the blood pounding in my neck.

I pulled at my blouse and flapped it a bit, needing air. Needing a cigarette.

"Are you doing OK, Ms. Porter? Or should I call you Mrs. Porter?"

"No, I'm not." I stood. "And would you please call me

Angeline? All this formality is like something out of 'Downton Abbey.'"

Detective Prosper smiled. "How about a cigarette break?"

"Great idea. Do you have extra?"

He stood, pulled out a pack, and motioned toward the door. I grabbed my Cubano. We avoided the busy front offices by heading down a hall and going through a small eating area and kitchenette. He opened the heavy metal door for me, and I stepped outside.

8

I followed him to a picnic table under a big tree and sat atop the table. The detective flipped back the top of a Marlboro Light pack, drew out a cigarette, handed it to me, and lit it. I took a deep drag and felt the comforting smoke at the back of my throat and the calming expansion of my lungs. The long luxurious exhale. The next drag. When I opened my eyes, the detective was watching me.

"Any possibility of you giving me Agent Duvernet's cell number?"

"I've been calling him on a burner, but he hasn't been answering. Now it's not working." I took it from my satchel and handed it to him.

He tried. "It's dead." He gave it back to me.

"You're not smoking," I said.

"I don't smoke."

"You're kidding."

He shook his head.

I snorted. This guy was beyond different.

"So, what happens next? Did you find her car? Did you

find anything? I want to help. It's my sister and I feel responsible."

"Let's find a way for you to help with the investigation. I know it's not easy waiting on others. I'm not good at it either." He put his hands in his jean pockets and didn't speak at first. I waited. Then he said, "I want to make sure we still have a deal. You said you'd keep me informed if I'd agree to do the same."

"I know, but being a former lawyer, I know you can't promise me anything of the kind. You'll only tell me what you can. And you won't tell me anything if I somehow come under suspicion, right?"

"If that happens, you'll know because I'll engage with you in an entirely different way. You'll recognize it. I can be a bastard when I need to be." He smiled. I didn't doubt that.

"What about Bibi's car?"

"It was parked in its assigned parking space and locked. We took fingerprints from the door handles, but nothing, just hers and the parking attendant's."

My Cubano, forgotten on the picnic table, attracted two noisy gulls that swept in. I jumped off the table as the gulls fought over the sandwich and other gulls noisily joined them. Prosper and I moved away.

I thought about Otto and wondered if he was eating, hoping he was getting better. Maybe I could stop to check on him on the way back to The Circ.

Prosper and I ended up near the door, not needing a shady spot this time. The clouds rolled in, heavy and dark.

Prosper said, "We found something in the apartment that I'd like you to identify if possible."

We were so close to each other now that I could detect a scent I couldn't place, something that didn't smell like cologne or aftershave. He also had a three-inch scar on his neck under his ear.

"What is it?" I asked.

"An acrylic nail."

The cigarette hung forgotten from my fingers. I took a drag, crushed it on the concrete pad, and threw the butt into the trashcan by the door. "A fake nail. No. Not my sister's." I crossed my arms over my chest, trying to visualize Bibi, trying to remember. "At least I don't think she wore fake nails. I bet it's Shawn's. Bibi told me Shawn's nails were long and manicured."

The gulls made so much noise fighting over the sand-wich that I wished I'd grabbed it and thrown it away. I clasped my hands together and squeezed. It helped me focus.

Prosper said, "What do *you* think happened to your sister?"

Hadn't he asked me that before? I was too tired to remember. "Sorry, I don't know," I said. "I was sure Shawn and her gang had taken her. Bibi had evidence about the mob."

But another scenario popped into my head. I considered it before speaking, then looked away from Prosper. "OK, what about this possibility? This time, Shawn visited Bibi with one of her goons and said Bibi needed to go with them. They were holding a meeting with some business partners, and it was time for Bibi to get involved. I don't know why they'd want her but bear with me." I turned to Prosper. "Bibi didn't want to go, but Shawn insisted. Plus, she told Bibi that it wouldn't be more than an hour or two, so leave the dog. Bibi went reluctantly, wanting to know what it was all about. But what if they needed her for some other reason? What if something's going on that none of us have a clue about?"

The stench of dead fish wafted by. Even though the sky was overcast, I could already feel the back of my neck getting burned.

"OK," Prosper said. "But what about the ransacking?" He opened the door, and, thankfully, we stepped inside the air-conditioned lunch area. Two officers were drinking coffee and talking but stopped when we came in. We walked into the hall to speak privately.

I thought about the possibilities, my lawyer brain happily engaged even though this was my sister we were talking about. "There could have been a second guy who stayed behind, poisoned Otto, and searched the room."

Prosper scratched his chin. "True, but that would mean three people had been allowed unauthorized access to the residency section of the hotel."

"That could be anything from delivery people to fake IDs." I waited for him to say something, but he didn't. "An acrylic nail should provide DNA to ascertain Shawn's identity, right?"

"Possibly. We'll find out. I ordered DNA analysis on it." Deep grooves appeared on his forehead, his eyes squinted, and his mouth hardened. "Is there anything else you can tell me that might be helpful?"

I didn't know why, but I hated that word *helpful*. For some reason, it felt patronizing. But I was tired. And I did have something else. "Bibi's godmother was the head of the Boston gang. Now that she's dead, we might be dealing with leadership infighting like in law firms. The head of the firm dies, and the partners fight over the territory. Sometimes the nastiest, hungriest, least moral one drives out the others." My personal experience could attest to that, but I wasn't about to tell Prosper any of my stories. "In this case with the extortion group, I don't know all the players, but I can tell you the ones I do know."

I told him about Rena, Betty's cousin, and Ralph, a relative of Betty's former cohort Sam who was dead. I didn't tell him I'd killed Sam in self-defense.

"Do you have last names?"

"Sorry, no. But Ralph and Rena worked the business end of things—financials, taxes, legal, that stuff. I'm sure the FBI knows."

"Thanks for your help, Angeline. I'll have Officer Walsh take you back to the hotel. I'll call you."

As he escorted me to the front of the station, he said, "Tomorrow's meeting about your sister's case will go from about eight o'clock to nine. Why don't we meet after that? I'll fill you in."

"Right. I'll need coffee at least."

"There's a cafe a few blocks from your hotel. I'll call you when my meeting ends."

"And whenever you hear anything before that, you'll call me, right?"

He gave me the name of the cafe. I watched closely as he spoke with Officer Walsh and was relieved to see no male power trip, only courtesy.

We shook hands, and I thanked him. As he pulled away, I sensed a sadness in his expression. Did he know something I didn't? Was he bullshitting me about sharing knowledge? I watched him walk away, and then I left with Officer Walsh.

9

On the way to Officer Walsh's cruiser, I thought about poor Otto, what the veterinarian could tell me about his condition.

"Officer Walsh, would you mind taking me to the Veterinary Hospital?"

There, the vet confirmed he'd been poisoned. Otto was stable, but they didn't know the extent of the damage yet and would let me know after the test results were back.

"So, this person intended to kill the dog, right?" Walsh asked the vet.

The vet looked tired. "Yes. Whoever did this had the option of sedating Otto, but they didn't. There are many ways to knock out a dog without killing it. The person gave the dog enough to kill Otto but not quite enough for the dog's size. They could have underestimated the amount, or the dog put up a good fight and didn't get the full dose."

Otto was resting, so I couldn't see him. I gave the front desk clerk a credit card and my contact information. Otto had to live for Bibi's sake. I'd promised to take care of him in case anything happened to her. In case she—

Tired, I turned away and rubbed my eyes, wondering if Bibi was dead. I shivered. The vet tech handed me a tissue. I asked to use the bathroom. I needed to call home to the two ladies caring for Tempest to see how *my* dog was doing. It was hard to believe that I'd only been in Florida for one day —a very long day.

On the short drive to The Circ, I dried my eyes and asked Officer Walsh what she thought of Detective Prosper.

"I admire him. Everyone does."

"How is his success rate at solving his cases?"

She looked genuinely surprised. "He's one of the best."

"Tell me about him." I wanted to know the guy I was dealing with. Was he trustworthy? Would he work with me? I also needed a distraction. "I thought I detected a slight Canadian accent."

"Good catch. He grew up in Canada. He trained and worked there before marrying an American. Then he came here."

"What's the deal with the interview room?"

"A Canadian thing. Make a person comfortable so you can observe normal behavior. Later, if there's an interrogation, we can compare that behavior with his more relaxed behavior. It's amazing how it helps identify if the person's lying."

The hotel came into view. My focus faded.

When we pulled up to The Circ Hotel, she asked, "Do you know who the best liars are?"

My brain kicked out an automatic response. "Gamblers and Secret Service."

"You knew that? You're not a private investigator, are you?"

I guess no one told her I was and always would be an attorney, whether I was licensed or not. I side-stepped the question with something that had been bugging me. "Detective Prosper seems sad."

"You picked up on that, too? Yes, he tries to hide it, but he lost his wife to cancer about a year and a half ago. He adored her."

"That's rough."

We sat in silence for a moment. Ironic that the detective and I both lost our spouses around the same time.

"You're lucky to have him on your case."

I thanked Officer Walsh for the lift and stepped out. The sun bled into a bank of dark clouds over the city. I was ready to lie down. I had a headache from either the heat and thick muggy air or hunger. The gulls had eaten most of my sandwich.

In my hotel room, the bed had been turned down, and a dinner mint was left on the pillow along with a lavender-scented eye mask. Ms. Santiago had given me a suite with a view. I called her office, left a message thanking her, and asked her to call me in the morning. I wanted the names of a few employees, such as the housekeeper on my sister's floor and the car park attendants so I could "talk" with them. I was also going to hit up the bartender in the Olivia. I knew that Bibi drank. When I first met her in New Hampshire, we'd knocked back a few tumblers of scotch.

After ordering dinner from the Olivia Restaurant downstairs, I asked, "Is there any way I can get a bottle of scotch delivered to my room?" Of course. So, I ordered the best, not caring how much it cost me.

I hung up my few clothes and put my laptop on the desk. When I looked for a drinking glass in the kitchenette, I spotted Andy Warhol's painting of Marilyn Monroe, reminding me of Sophie who had looked so much like her. I raised my empty glass to the image and said, "Well, Sophie, if you have any power wherever you are, how about doing something to save your twin?" I drew a ragged breath as a jagged knife of grief ripped through me. I could not lose this sister too.

I had no way to call Gerard now, but it didn't matter. It was a one-way street with him. He'd made the right decision about leaving, however. He and the detective would have been at odds right away. Besides, being FBI didn't do him any good when it was a local case, especially with him being undercover.

Admittedly, my faith in him was now in single digits, quickly headed to the negative range. How could he allow this situation with Bibi to happen? Why hadn't the FBI protected her? She'd given them her full cooperation as far as I knew, and what had they done for her? Nada. Zip. A major fuck you.

But what threw me off was the blood found on her coffee table. It wasn't hers. What did that mean? Had Bibi struck a blow to her perp, maybe Shawn? I should have been relieved, but I was too confused. None of it made sense. There had to have been a struggle if there was blood.

My gut went back to that transcript of her FBI interview in Boston. I wanted a copy. I needed to know what they'd asked of her and how she'd answered their questions. I needed Gerard to get a copy for me.

Out on the balcony, lights popped up across downtown Hollywood. The air was so thick with moisture it was hard to breathe. Yet live Cuban music played in the distance. The locals were used to the humidity. Horns sounded as traffic navigated the circle below. Palm trees drooped. In Kauai, the palms would be swaying in a gentle breeze. I clutched my stomach. I didn't want to know, could not imagine, what had happened or would happen to Bibi. The only reason they'd take her was to torture the truth out of her. I shuddered.

As I leaned on the railing, I tried to distract myself from visions of Bibi's torment by going to the analytical lawyer brain and questioning what I knew. It was one of the best tools an attorney had—flip what you know, question everything you'd been told, try to see your blind spots. Use the "what if" starter.

I hadn't done that so far. Personal stakes could blind a person to the reality of a situation. So, where to start? One question would get me started.

What if I were wrong?

About all of it.

What if Bibi had been involved with the mob from the start? What if she and Shawn had cooked up this scheme to bring me here and take me out, for good. But why? For shoving Betty, Bibi's godmother, off a cliff in Kauai?

But they *didn't* know I'd killed Betty. No one knew. There were no witnesses. It took months to discover the bodies. Besides, it was self-defense. She'd tried to kill me, we struggled, and she went over. No one saw it, so who was there to tell them what happened?

Gerard. Gerard could give me up.

But he only knew what I'd told him. He hadn't witnessed it. At least not to my knowledge. Besides, it was best for him and the FBI to leave it as is. And why would he tell—

A knock at the door. I froze, then grabbed my gun from my satchel.

"Room service."

My dinner. Of course. I stuck the Glock in the back of my jeans just in case.

The waiter rolled in the food tray, set out the dinner on my table, and handed me the bottle of scotch plus a snifter. I signed for it. After the waiter left, I poured a finger of scotch, threw it back, and sat down at the table. Fork in hand, I hoped I could handle the ravioli stuffed with fresh Florida lobster. Small careful bite after small careful bite, I finally felt myself again. Even my stomach calmed down.

Out on the balcony, I checked the weather. A breeze had come up and blown away the heavy air, softening the evening. Back inside, I poured a half snifter of scotch and took my notebook to the balcony. Below, leaning over the hood of a car, a young couple were making out. The way they were going at it, I sighed, envious of their youth, of a world centered on their lips and hands.

I sat in the rattan chair, turned on Spotify for a little music of my own, and it went to Roxy Music's "More Than This." I thought, *No shit.*

This is what I have, a world centered on posing questions to myself.

- Gerard.
- What about him? Is he lying about being undercover?
- He was scruffy, exhausted, stinky in NH. Was that for real?
- Now he's all Don Johnson of Miami Vice?
- A quick-change artist or what?
- *Who the hell is he?*

I underlined the last sentence. Gerard was getting in the way, becoming more a detriment than an ally. I needed to mine the truth, cut through his bullshit. But how?

Out toward the ocean, the sky held dark clouds, but sun managed to break through for now. One thing I knew about

Florida—the state was accommodating to criminals. Major thought:

- What if the gang had moved to Florida?
- Gerard could be using Bibi to get inside the mob.
- Is that why Bibi moved to Florida?
- Had Gerard struck up a deal with Bibi in Boston?

I DRANK the rest of my scotch. Gerard had been adamant about me staying in Oregon for my safety and Bibi's, but I hadn't listened. I wrote furiously.

- Had Gerard insisted I not come because he was afraid I'd interfere with his plan?
- Had my appearance jeopardized Bibi's life in some way?
- Why *again* hadn't he protected Bibi?

Damn. That seemed most logical. He hadn't wanted me to come because he used Bibi as a lure to net the mob. He'd used her. Just like he'd done with Sophie.

- Sophie had died because of him. She stole millions for him; then he abandoned her. Why didn't he bring the gangsters to justice then?
- Bibi's apartment was ransacked. Blood was on the coffee table. Now she was missing. Why had he let that happen?
- Gerard wasn't protecting *anyone*. He wasn't after the mob.
- His goal was to catch the rogue FBI agent. Period.

My cell rang.

"Ms. Porter ... I mean Angeline ... this is Detective Prosper."

"Who?" I underlined the last line I wrote. Fuck. Bibi was in grave danger.

"Detective Prosper."

"Oh, yes. Any news?" I looked at the time. Nine-thirty in the evening? I stood up, and my legs went wonky.

"We've done a quick view of the security camera from both the residency building and hotel. Have you had any word from your sister?"

"No. I would have called you right away if I had."

That, of course, was a lie. If I did hear from Bibi, I might call him—or I might not, depending on the circumstances. I couldn't trust anyone now.

"The security footage shows your sister leaving her apartment with two other people. The first one, we'll call 'Shawn' for now. They looked like they knew each other, and it appeared she walked away willingly. But we'll need to examine it closer."

"Who was the second person?"

"A man. He followed your sister and Shawn but never let the camera see his face."

Speechless, I walked the perimeter of the room, trying to think of something to say, something that made sense. Even the sense of relief I should have felt—that my sister had walked out on her own steam—wasn't there. I tried to think back on anything she'd told me that would make sense out of this, but I couldn't.

"Porter, are you still there? I mean Angeline?"

"Yes, I heard you."

"I've put in a request to run the clearest images through

the MPD's facial recognition software." He paused. "We won't get anything on the male figure, though."

"If Bibi walked out of there, talking with Shawn, then someone else ransacked the room after they left. She wouldn't have left willingly if they'd poisoned Otto. Did you identify whose blood was on the coffee table?"

"Not yet."

"No matter how it looks, those people tricked her, and she's in danger. I'm certain of it." I pinched the bridge of my nose. What was I missing? Why wouldn't the pieces come together?

A police operator on the radio announced a 10-66. So he was in his car, still on the job.

"Look, Porter, I mean Ange—"

"Oh, for God's sake, call me Porter. I like it better anyway." I liked it because only the men were usually called by their last name.

"OK." He sounded relieved. "What I was going to say is if your FBI agent friend contacts you, tell him to contact me."

He knew that Gerard was around somewhere. Maybe he suspected something personal between us.

After we hung up, I stepped out onto my balcony. Moonlight sent shards of light across the ocean. Somewhere someone was barbecuing. Below, in the Arts Park, a dog pissed on a concrete bench. Sirens sounded in the distance. An arguing couple stepped out onto their balcony next to mine, so I hustled inside. Hank and I never argued. What would he advise in this situation? I had no one by my side and no one to trust. But I had to remind myself that even he'd betrayed me.

Enough self-pity. I called Tempest's dog sitters. It was seven o'clock there. Yes, she was doing great. They'd just walked her. Could they give her special dog treats? Sure. Why not?

I laughed at myself, grabbed the remote, and settled onto the sea-green couch. The women on "The Housewives of Miami" were arguing. Why the hell was everyone arguing? And who was that freak of an older woman on the show? Had she deliberately done that to her face? I fumbled the remote, clicked off, and stretched out on the couch.

Just as I was nodding off, there was another knock at my door. This time I knew it wasn't room service.

10

I jumped off the couch and grabbed my semi-automatic again, nerves finally shredded. A second knock, this time louder. I slugged back the remains of my scotch. "Liquid courage," my mom used to call it when my father drank and accused her of not loving him.

Through the door's peephole, I saw no one. Then bang, another knock, and now I was ready to shoot whoever was there. I opened the door and pointed the gun.

"Gerard!" I didn't let him pass. "You asshole!"

He wavered, listed to the left.

"Are you drunk?"

He lunged.

Luckily, I jumped back and slid the gun into my waistband.

"Do you *want* to get shot?"

He grabbed the doorframe to steady himself.

I tried to see his eyes, but he pushed past me and went to the sink where he drank a full glass of water.

I tried to slam the self-closing door, but I had to shove it closed, making me ready to slam Gerard to the ground instead.

"What the fuck, Gerard! Just what the fuck!" I walked over to him and grabbed his arm.

He set the glass down, pulled me to him, and kissed me. Hard. When I tried to pull away, he put his hands behind my head and held me there. I tried to wriggle free, but his lips were full and hungry, causing a hot thread to run from my mouth to my pelvis. He wouldn't let go, my arms dropped, and he pulled me to his chest, holding me firmly with one hand at my head and one on my back. I buckled. How pathetic. Am I honestly making out with a drunk? He *was* drunk, wasn't he? He tasted like a mint and something salty, but he was such a good kisser. My arms reached up to his shoulders, his neck, his face. I'd regret this, I knew I would, but it had been so long, so long without...

He backed me to the bedroom, our thighs pressed together. Our lips never separated. My mind kept screaming "Stop!" while my body couldn't get close enough to his. I wrapped myself around him like a second layer of skin. When we reached the bed, he slid my gun from my waistband and laid it on the bedside table as if he'd done this a million times. Then he gripped my buttocks, hoisted me up, and laid me down. While holding my arms over my head, he kissed my neck. God, I wanted him. He straddled me and looked down with narrowed, lustful eyes. Oh, those eyes. Had he looked that way at Sophie? Had he swept her up like this? Straddled her?

I shoved him hard. What the hell was I doing? I shoved him again. "Get off me," I spit. "Get off, or I'll scream."

He slid back, stood over me for a moment, then lurched away and out of the bedroom. I sighed, not knowing if it was with regret, relief, or both. Then my hotel door closed.

I stayed there for a moment, confused as to what had just happened. When I managed to pull myself together, I sat up and groaned. Standing, I stepped on something. A phone. I picked it up. Gerard had dropped a burner.

11

I quickly brought the burner to life. It hadn't locked.

Grabbing my Glock from the bedside table, I headed to the kitchen, where I slipped the gun into a drawer. After taking a minute to clear my head and calm down, I scrolled through the phone. Only one number had been repeatedly used for that burner, both incoming and outgoing. Did I dare call it? Maybe I should call the number from my cell. But then the other person would recognize my incoming ID.

If I did call, would it blow something of Gerard's that was in the works? Gerard's hunt for the rogue FBI agent? Maybe my sister's case? Something important? Or maybe this had nothing to do with either her or me. I kept tapping the phone to keep it alive so it wouldn't lock, but I couldn't keep that up indefinitely, so I memorized the called number.

At 10:30, I went out on my balcony. The couple next door was gone, probably making love in a champagne euphoria. I swiped a hand across my mouth.

I couldn't make up my mind about the phone, so I made a deal with myself. If Gerard didn't return for it in half an hour, I'd call the number. But what if he'd gone someplace and passed out? What if he didn't know he'd lost the burner? And why was he drunk tonight? What had triggered that? Something had kicked him over the edge.

Wait. What was I thinking? Inside, I stood over the sink, picked up his glass, and smelled it. No telltale liquor smell. He hadn't even tasted of booze when he kissed me, just mint and salt. So, was he drunk or acting? Was the whole sexual gambit a way to disarm me and stop me from thinking so he could plant the phone? Was I being paranoid? Of course.

Gerard was not careless. I found it hard to believe he'd accidentally drop a burner.If he left it on purpose, he wanted me to call the number. Was that why he didn't lock it? One possibility.

The other possibility? If he were drunk and *had* accidentally dropped it, something was messed up, or he'd screwed up something and wanted ... what? Me? As a distraction?

My lips felt sore. I licked them. I could taste him.

I'd been attracted to Gerard from the beginning, even when I'd gone to Paris to poison him.

Our bodies so often betray us. How little it took to fire up the old dormant urges. How did anyone keep a coherent thought in their head when pheromones and hormones and body parts came alive like dropping coins into a pinball machine?

No.

This is precisely what I shouldn't do—be physically and emotionally thrown off guard. Gerard didn't make mistakes. Plus, he didn't have the hots for me. Dropping the burner wasn't an accident.

I stared at the phone, waiting for eleven o'clock.

When I heard the knock on my door, I smiled despite myself. I didn't need to make a choice. He'd sobered up enough to realize his burner was missing. I pushed it under the chair's pillow so I could play him a little. *What burner? I didn't find any burner.* Smiling, I headed to the door. He knocked again.

Wait, that didn't sound like him—three sharp knocks, then a pause, repeat. Gerard's raps were close together. I grabbed my gun from the kitchen drawer. My muscles tensed. My mouth went dry.

I held the Glock steady with both hands, but could I use it on a person? I saw someone through the peephole, but they had their back to me. I waited for another knock.

"Who is it?" I yelled.

"Detective Prosper. Can we talk?"

What? At ten-forty-five at night? Had he found Bibi? Was she dead? I felt sick. My chest tightened. I shoved the gun into the drawer again, trying to keep my legs under me. Damn him. I checked the peephole and opened the door.

"Sorry about the time, Angeline." He waited. The cop with him waited outside by the door.

"Is something wrong? Did you find Bibi? Is she—"

"We haven't found her yet, but..." He looked at my face. "What's wrong? What happened?"

"Why are you here so late? What do you want?" I was shaking. Bibi? Gerard?

"What happened?" Prosper kept a neutral tone and expression. "Duvernet was here. What did he do?"

Did he know? My fists clenched. So much for trusting the guy. I lowered my voice. "So, you have someone watching me."

"What did he want?" Still that neutral tone.

I let out a long-held breath. "Come in. I'm not talking about this standing in the doorway." I sat down at the kitchen table and motioned him to sit down, but he didn't. Fine. Fuck him, too.

"Gerard turned up drunk. After I gave him a glass of water, he grabbed me." I locked eyes with the detective. He didn't blink or react. "Agent Duvernet was once in love with my sister Sophie. I believe he's damaged from the job that involved my sister's death. He should feel guilt. He made a mess of it." I was still shaking, but I sounded professional. "I'm no psychologist, but I think because he was drunk tonight, he projected the love he had for Sophie onto me." I acted like it was no big deal and shifted in my chair.

"Why tonight? Has he done this before?"

I wanted to say, "None of your business," but I shook my head and said, "No."

"Did he rape you?"

"Oh, God, no." I snorted. "No. I think the poor guy must see something of Sophie in me, but I have no idea what that is. She looked like that." I pointed to the Warhol Marilyn Monroe behind him next to the door.

So, he's here about Gerard, not Bibi? When did I give up my anonymity? My privacy?

He looked over at the Marilyn print, then back at me, cleared his throat, and said, "I think you underestimate yourself, Ms. Porter."

What was with the formality? Why was I back to Ms. Porter? I let the silence hang between us.

Prosper pulled out a chair and sat opposite me. "Duvernet had to have some purpose. Did he say anything to you? Let you know why he was drunk? Anything at all?"

"He wasn't here to chitchat, Detective. He was drunk. End of story."

"Yes, but if he didn't expect to get away with the sex, then he came for something else."

"How do I know he didn't expect to get away with sex? Let me repeat what I said. He was drunk, and I turned him out, OK? No harm done."

"Do you have feelings for him?"

"That's none of your damn business. Besides, what does it have to do with my sister's case?" I gave him what Dad used to call my stink eye. He didn't answer. I was tired and pissed. Will this day ever end? "You've had someone watching me. Either I'm under suspicion, or he is. Which is it?"

"Neither." Prosper leaned forward on the table and studied me. The scar on his neck stood out redder and more noticeable. "I'm trying to understand the people who are involved in this investigation so I can do my job. Personal feelings get in the way, and I need to know if his feelings for you will interfere with finding your sister Bibi."

He'd used Bibi's name to make this personal, to draw me in, to show that he cared. Did he?

Fucking men. I leaned across the table and enunciated clearly. "Look, let's get this straight. I threw his ass out. Just as I would *anyone* who made a drunken sexual advance." I paused. "And it's none of your business whom I screw." He flinched. "And just for the record," I was on a roll now, "I don't like having a cop stationed outside my door unless I'm told about it first. Now tell me something about Bibi or get the hell out of here. I haven't slept for forty-eight hours."

Outside, a dog barked. And barked. Then yelped as if someone hit it. I flinched and thought of Tempest, my pooch back home. I bristled and said, "I hate that."

Prosper muttered, "I'll check on it when I leave."

An awkward silence fell between us.

Prosper stared at his open hands. Finally, he said, "Look, Porter, I'm sorry for the late visit. I should have notified you about stationing someone outside your door. As an attorney, I'm sure you've dealt with detectives who *can* be destructive to a case, even act illegally. But I would never—"

"I get it. You're on the up-and-up. Good for you. What else do you have?" I was too tired for this bullshit.

"I don't have you under surveillance. The officer is there for your protection."

I snorted with laughter. "*Protect me?* Where have I heard *that* before?" I popped up from the chair. "I need people to quit saying they're protecting me when they're using me." I looked down at him. "The short story, Detective, is I had a husband who betrayed me, a sister who betrayed me, an FBI agent who said he'd protect both my sisters and me, and he didn't and hasn't, and now you. Do you think I can believe anyone right now? Not on your life."

He stood and pushed in his chair. I smelled sweat and, as he exhaled, coffee.

"The policeman thought you were in danger from an aggressive drunk who seemed determined to enter your room. *That's* why I'm here."

Maybe it was as simple as that.

Prosper's cell dinged, and he excused himself for a moment, taking the call in the sitting area, his back to me.

When he finished talking, I asked, "Anything?"

"No, not yet. Maybe when I get back to the precinct." He headed for the door. "From what you've told me about tonight, I would say Agent Duvernet is having difficulty keeping the personal and professional separate."

"Yeah, well," I mumbled, thinking of Gerard's hands on my ass.

I wanted to tell him that I suspected Gerard was faking the drunkenness. Then I had an idea. "Wait. Is the policeman in the hall the one who saw Gerard?"

"Yes."

"Can I speak with him for a second?"

He called in the officer. "Ms. Porter wants to ask you a question."

The officer turned to me.

"The man you saw at my door this evening. Did you see him get off the elevator? And if you did, think carefully. How did he appear at first?"

The officer looked over my head for a moment before answering.

"Interesting you should ask that. Now that I think about it, he walked normally until he saw me, then he lurched."

"How close were you to him?"

"I stood about ten feet away on the other side of the hall until he approached your door and knocked."

"Could you smell anything alcohol?" So much for me not leading the witness.

"No. Nothing."

I glanced over at Prosper then thanked the officer, who returned to the hall.

"You think he may have faked his drunken state?" Prosper asked.

"Could be. Why he'd do that, other than having a lame excuse for kissing me, is beyond me right now. But I'll find out. You can bet on that."

"I'm sure you will." He tried not to smile.

All this bullshit about Gerard while my sister was in danger? Prosper should be out looking for her. But I knew how it worked. He had a team working leads, tracking down fingerprints and DNA, talking to witnesses and hotel employees. I stepped back into the hotel room, turned, and found myself two feet from Prosper.

"I need you to find Bibi." I swallowed hard. "I can't lose her."

"I will do everything in my power to get your sister back. It's just…"

"Just what?"

"It's tough when someone might be interfering with my work."

"You mean Gerard."

"Yes."

Detective Prosper headed toward the door. I walked with him and opened it for him.

He turned to me. "Get some sleep. See you in the morning, hopefully with some news."

I said goodnight and locked the door behind him. Then I hurried to the chair and dug out the phone from under the pillow. When I pressed the side button to open the burner, it was locked.

12

I woke to my alarm at eight o'clock, five o'clock Pacific time. I was still in my clothes and twisted up in the sheet and duvet. When I rolled over to shut off my cell's alarm, I knocked the digital bedside clock to the floor. My notebook, however, remained on the bedside table, and somehow, in my pre-sleep fog, I'd managed to jot down the number from Gerard's burner. When I stood, my head ached, and my insides cramped.

Damn. When was I supposed to meet Detective Prosper? Ten o'clock?

While I made a pot of coffee, my head got worse. I was scared to call that number, and I knew why—Gerard could not be trusted. I could call that number, but it wouldn't be to my benefit or Bibi's. He always seemed to be in control and one step ahead of everyone, yet he screwed things up for everyone around him. Nothing good could come of it.

I poured cream into my coffee and sipped then leaned against the counter. When Sophie fell in love with Gerard, he worked undercover for the FBI in the extortionist gang. He said he'd fallen for her too. But Sophie's obsession with him knew no bounds. She'd been so in love with Gerard that she'd seduced and slept with my husband to get into his business account and steal millions for the mob. That was how Gerard planned to prove himself to the gang. How could he do that? How could he possibly rationalize that act for the sake of bringing down the mob?

And my sister? She always made major mistakes when it came to men. It still stunned me that my sister screwed my husband out of love for someone else. Then Gerard disappeared for a while, telling Sophie he had to lie low to protect them both. He thought that Sophie would understand. That's when Betty's partner told her that Gerard had used her to get the money. So, Sophie hanged herself.

"Now tell me he wasn't responsible for that," I said aloud as if trying to convince someone. Or maybe myself.

A month after she died, a letter came from her, written to explain why she was ending her life. She not only carried the guilt of falling for yet another user, but her greatest guilt was for betraying Hank and me, the two people who had always stood by her and loved her.

I hugged myself, reliving all this. Sophie still didn't get it. Killing herself was yet another selfish act. She didn't have to face us. She didn't have to change. She didn't have to see what her actions had done to us. She didn't even understand how much danger she put us in. By not giving the mob the money and leaving it to me in a Maryland bank, didn't she realize that the mob would come after it? Didn't she realize they'd come after me? Sophie took no care of others' lives.

I felt sick. I was responsible for always letting Sophie off the hook. I blamed everyone but her. I knew why—I needed my sister, my only living relative. Our early home life had shaped us both. I was the protector. She was the beautiful, vulnerable, magical Sophie.

But Sophie was dead. I had to deal with Gerard. When I said he made mistakes, he made beauties. Gerard understood mob behavior. He should have known Sophie was vulnerable. But I've come to understand that he's as naïve as Sophie when it comes to people unless it has something directly to do with his obsession—finding the rogue FBI agent who was part of the mob. He was so obsessed I was beginning to doubt the very existence of this agent. Gerard was originally assigned to find evidence to bring down the mob. Somewhere it turned into a quest to find this rogue agent. None of that he ever explained to me.

I inhaled a package of crackers I found in the cupboard and added more cream to my coffee so my stomach wouldn't get worse.

Maybe Gerard had gone off the deep end, and no one knew it. Since he had thwarted my poisoning scheme in Paris—that piece of *merde*—I couldn't trust anything he did or said. No matter how much he confessed to loving my sister. No matter how often he told me he was there to protect me. No matter his supposed motive for any of his actions. I could not trust him.

The notepad with the number from his burner gave me a sense of dread. If I called the number, I feared another twisty, fucked up mess that might endanger Bibi. Was it meant to be called? Would it endanger Bibi more if I didn't call it?

When I finished my coffee, I showered. More procrastination, although I did need a shower. I threw aside khaki capris and a Hawaiian print blouse. Fine for Kauai, but here? No. I pulled on the comfortable jeans I'd worn yesterday and a clean, burgundy silky top, brushed my shoulder-length hair and slipped on my pumps. Detective Prosper better have some news about Bibi this morning.

My cell rang. I jumped. The hotel manager had two names for me: Kurt, one of the car attendants who talked about Bibi all the time, and Charmaine.

"Charmaine is our evening bartender at the Olivia. She knows everyone who comes in regularly, especially our residents. She's a native Floridian. She's good at details too, maybe because she's the granddaughter of one of our famous Hollywood mobsters."

I almost laughed at that. I wrote down their last names and personal phone numbers. She told me they said it was fine for me to call them at home. As I wrote, I wondered why she was so free with their names and descriptions.

As if reading my mind, she said, "I spoke with both. They've agreed to talk with you."

"Have they talked to the police yet?"

"Yes. But sometimes the police miss something. They don't know your sister as you do, so you might make more headway with Kurt and Charmaine."

I liked the way the hotel manager thought. However, I didn't know Bibi at all. My sister was a stranger to me, and I wasn't sure where her loyalties lay or even if she was involved with the Boston gang.

The manager asked about the room and if I needed anything else. I thanked her again and hung up.

Finally, I took my coffee to the desk and stared at the hotel phone. I had to make up my mind. It was nine o'clock. I was meeting Prosper at ten. I procrastinated and called Kurt and Charmaine. Although they both seemed to like Bibi, neither had anything to tell me that I didn't already know. Charmaine had only met Bibi once at the bar, and Kurt was effusive with how easy Bibi was to talk with. He seemed a little too effusive for someone who parked her car. I kept their names and numbers just in case. Finally, procrastination over with, I needed to make up my mind about the burner.

I had no idea who would answer, but I had to do it. Using the outside line, I pressed all the numbers except that last one. Would it belong to someone in the mob? Someone Gerard worked for in his undercover role? Could it be an informant? This was probably a setup of some kind. Should I give him back the cell?

No. If he'd wanted me to call the number, he had his reasons. I didn't trust him, but what was it my mom used to say? Did curiosity kill the cat? Whatever. I had to call.

I closed my eyes and spit out, "Screw you, Gerard. Just screw you royally."

I pressed the last number.

It rang once, then twice, then three times before there was a click and a voice.

"I'm OK. Did you find it?"

I jumped to my feet, knocking over the chair. "Bibi? Oh, my god, Bibi, it's me, Angeline."

There was an audible gasp, followed by silence. Then she hung up.

13

W hat the hell?

I tried the number again and let it ring for as long as I could stand it. I tried again. Same. Grabbing the overturned chair, I slammed it into the desk.

"Fuck, fuck, fuck!"

I rubbed my face so hard I scratched an eyelid. OK, I needed to calm down. What was going on? Why didn't she stay on the line?

I walked around the room. "Stay calm. Now you know she's alive. That's what's important."

In the bathroom, I splashed water on my face and dabbed it dry with a towel. Staring at my reflection, I wondered if this was why Gerard had dropped the burner. To let me know Bibi was alive? But he could have told me. So it seemed more likely that he dropped it by mistake.

As I used to do as a lawyer, I'd talk to myself at the mirror, posit questions to see how they would go over.

"Perhaps he positioned Bibi with the Boston gang so he could find the rogue agent."

Would he actually do that? My brain flooded with questions and possibilities. Could it be that simple? No. Something was amiss. Back in the sitting room, I stood listening to the steady traffic outside on Young Circle, the bleating of horns, the disjointed music from a passing car, the rumble of a train in the distance. I couldn't believe it.

"Bibi's alive. She was OK."

But why had she hung up when she heard my voice?

It could be another simple answer: she expected Gerard and didn't know what to do when I answered.

I shook out my arms and then hands, ready to figure it out.

The best way to do that was to write down every question I could think of that needed answering, then analyze the possibilities. I worked best that way. It kept me focused and unemotional. I flipped to an empty page in my notebook and started a list.

Bibi had said, "I'm OK. Did you find it?"

- That was meant for Gerard.
- Bibi was scared when I answered.
- Had Gerard tricked her into helping him?
- Did this mean Gerard was "managing her?"
- But why ask for my help so I'd come to Florida?
- Was she even safe?
- Was she with the mob right now?
- Did she volunteer to go with the mob?
- What happened after she left her apartment with Shawn?
- Was she playing me? Us? Why would she do that? No.

I TAPPED the pen on my chin. The only person who could answer any of this was Gerard, but then again, he might lie. He could be playing both of us. Maybe he'd planted suspicion in Bibi about me. But why?

I stood and grabbed my cell to call Gerard, then remembered I better not use my personal cell. I took a new burner from my stash and activated it, then called him to see if he'd answer a number he didn't recognize. Nothing. Screw that. I could leave a voicemail, but I was too angry to leave a simple message.

Bibi said she was OK. I should feel relief, but I didn't. I dropped back into the desk chair and wrote two possibilities in my notebook:

1. Gerard dropped it on purpose to let me know that she was OK.

(No. He could have just told me. AND he wasn't that selfless.)

2. Gerard accidentally dropped the burner.

She agreed to work for him, and he gave her a burner. But why?

She was with Shawn and only had seconds to talk.

I scared her when I answered.

I also put her in danger by calling back.

Damn.

The second one was most likely. But what about the evidence she'd hidden? Did Gerard know about that? When she said, "I'm OK. Did you find it," was she referring to that? Had she told him she'd hidden incriminating evidence against Shawn and her operation? If Bibi had, why hadn't she told him where it was? Was she suspicious of him? Maybe. She was smart. Maybe she felt safer with two of us having different parts of the puzzle. She probably didn't trust anyone. Who could blame her?

I poured two fingers of scotch and drank it. In all the confusion and craziness, I hadn't found what Bibi had hidden.

Neither had the police.

I gnawed the end of my pen.

If it had been in the apartment, the police would have found it—whatever it was. Then again, whoever ransacked her place could have found it. Then why would they need Bibi?

I wrote down a new question:

If Bibi was innocent, guiltless, why hadn't she told me where the evidence was when she knew it was me on the phone?

I PUSHED BACK my hair and groaned. It would only have taken a second. She could have sneaked it in before hanging up or getting caught, couldn't she?

Then another possibility occurred to me. I set down my pen.

What if Shawn had flipped Bibi, and Bibi was now part of the gang? Shawn could have made her believe I couldn't be trusted. Or maybe she told her I had been part of the gang and was now vying for control. Shawn could have told her just about anything. Bibi didn't know me. It wouldn't take much to even confuse her.

I stood and walked out onto the balcony. This was like being in a carnival funhouse of mirrors. I just kept seeing mirrors and no way out.

Back in the kitchen, I poured another cup of coffee. Breakfast couldn't come soon enough. I was seriously buzzed and burning through anything that came to mind. I'd be left with a smoldering ash heap of nothing if I kept this up. I needed to talk with someone. How about Detective Prosper? He had no skin in the game except for finding an abducted woman.

I checked the time on my cell. Nine-thirty-five. I checked my GPS to see how long it would take to walk to the cafe. Seven minutes. As I grabbed my satchel and threw my phone and the burner into it, another idea busted through.

What if Bibi was calling and Shawn was right there? What if Shawn had forced her to call so she could find out if anyone had uncovered the evidence? But why do that? No. That didn't work. If Shawn knew Bibi had that evidence, she would have forced Bibi to take her to it so that she could destroy it.

I headed out the door, feeling so confused, I didn't know what to do. How was I ever going to find Bibi? I needed an ally. I was ready to spill everything I knew to Detective Prosper. Whatever all *this* was went squarely back to Gerard and him dropping the burner in my room. He was at the center of it all. Hadn't he always been?

If I gave Detective Prosper the burner, he could open the phone with access to mobile device forensic tools, MDFTs. These had been used in several of my old law firm's criminal defense cases. What could be determined from the burner was beyond me. Technology changed so fast I sure as hell couldn't keep up, but it was worth asking Prosper. Right or wrong, it felt good to decide. I'd take it to the cops.

Outside, the sun already beat down, and the air was heavy, thick, and hot. The locals I passed seemed unaffected —fresh, smiling, some tan, some not. Christ, and it was only 9:45. I'd be a giant stinky armpit by noon. I fumbled for my sunglasses and slipped them on. Growing up in New Hampshire, I remembered the humidity and mosquitoes. Mom refused to use repellent because she said it was toxic, so I spent the summer covered in bug bites, calamine lotion, and a baking soda paste. The Northwest rarely had humidity or bugs. How I longed to be home in my new house with Tempest, having never heard of the Boston mob or Gerard.

14

I hustled along the palm-lined sidewalk, passing cafes and stores. Toward the Southeast, a dark cloud bank formed, a deep cerulean blue turning to black at the horizon. Tourists read menus hung in the windows of restaurants while locals rushed to work with coffee in one hand and a bagged breakfast in the other. I was already sweating from the humidity and hoped for a breeze. The weather might be different from Oregon, but the routines weren't.

Cafe Chocolada was squeezed in between an Irish pub and a Greek restaurant. The smell of cinnamon and maple syrup wafted from the doorway and plates of waffles. Under the cafe's red awning, I grabbed one of the last outside tables covered with a black and red faux leather tablecloth. The chairs were an uncomfortable metal and plastic wicker. I scanned the customers, looked for a server, then noticed the doorway. Painted Art Nouveau Mucha-style female figures framed the cafe's aluminum double doors.

I surprised myself by knowing the artist then remembered Mom used to have Mucha posters of the four seasons taped to the kitchen cupboards. No matter how many times we moved, the posters went with us. Those women in Mucha's paintings looked strong, the perspective of each seeming to rise from the ground like mythological goddesses. Or maybe they looked that way because I was a child. Yes, I once had been a child. Hard to believe. Hard to remember.

I shivered in the heat. Losing Mom and Dad so early had destroyed many memories of childhood. I never inherited family photo books or videos like most adult children did. When I worked at the law firm, someone once called me an orphan. I don't know what her point was or even why she'd said it, but when I got home, I broke down in a sobbing, sloppy mess. Hank asked me what had happened, and I told him, "I lost my mom and dad." He held me, somehow understanding the moment.

I stared at the one-level buildings across the street. A clothing store, a Ramada business center, a Thai restaurant. On the recent trip to New Hampshire to meet Bibi for the first time, I reunited with my mom's best friend, Kathleen, and discovered I wasn't an orphan after all. The secrets in my family came pouring out. My Dad couldn't have children, so he wasn't my biological father, as I'd been raised to believe. But he'd agreed to let my mother have sex with other men so they could have children. It was the 70s. They had no money for artificial insemination, if they even knew about that. But my dad's pride wouldn't allow that.

What I couldn't fathom is why would you keep this information from your children? I returned home to Oregon in shock, not knowing what to do with this news. My father wasn't my father. I had other brothers and sisters.

Then my half-brother Ian showed up in Oregon. He told me his father was my father too, and my father was still alive. He also said that my mom had been the love of his dad's life and vice versa.

Oh, damn! I'd forgotten about Ian. I was supposed to call him when I got to Florida. I wondered if he'd returned to Naples.

Then reality struck right at the moment—my father, my biological father, was alive and lived only two hours away from Hollywood. Two hours. Ian had sent me copies of our father's love letters to my mom and—

"Can I get you something to drink?"

I jerked around and looked up. It took a moment to remember where I was. The waitress, wearing black slacks, a black half apron, and a red t-shirt, had one of those welcoming open faces with a big smile, plus bright pink hair.

"Sorry, I'm a little jet lagged. Yes, please. I'd love some coffee with cream."

I told her someone was joining me and snapped into my professional facade for when Detective Prosper arrived. My cell showed he was ten minutes late. I was jonesing for a cigarette. The pleasant buzz from the scotch was wearing off.

When the coffee came, I poured in cream and, after tasting it, added sugar. I rechecked my phone. The memories of New Hampshire undermined my decision to involve Detective Prosper. But he seemed more trustworthy than Gerard. He kept his mind on finding Bibi and bringing anyone responsible for her disappearance to justice. Plus, he didn't trust Gerard either.

And he'd protected me. Even though it had pissed me

off at first, I'd come to a newfound appreciation of him this morning. I had to give the guy credit for working long hours and recognizing how dangerous the situation was.

But Bibi was still missing, and the case was a mess. How hard could it be to find a black woman who had been taken by someone who had been identified? But of course, I didn't have all the information. I wasn't kidding myself about Prosper. He said he'd share all, but I knew better.

I was hungry and grumpy. I snorted and whispered to myself, "Justice? How's that going for ya, Ang?"

In my notebook, I wrote a reminder to call Ian. But should I? Should I get him involved? Now that I thought about it, he wasn't Bibi's half-brother, so officially, blood-wise, it wasn't a family affair.

I pulled out my wallet and a five-dollar bill from my satchel, ready to pay and leave when the detective came rushing up the sidewalk. He dodged Jameson barrels in front of the Irish pub then tables under the awning, bumping into ours and plunking down in a chair across from me. He hailed the waitress by name. I'd never seen him so animated. I liked it. It was hard to imagine Gerard humming like that and sitting down with a smile.

I smiled back. "Good morning."

"So sorry. I was held up."

The waitress came over. Her name tag read "Kassy" with a K. "Hi, Art. How are you? The usual?"

"Yes, that would be great. Thank you." He looked at me. "Did you order yet?"

"No, I waited for you."

"How about lox and bagel? You look like you could use some nourishment."

My stomach growled so loudly that he and the waitress heard it. We all laughed.

"OK. Sounds good."

He ordered an espresso, orange juice, a Monte Cristo sandwich, and my lox and bagel.

After the waitress left, he jumped right in. "We met this morning about your sister. Our team is set up, and we've already found out several things." He stopped then said, "Sorry. How was the rest of your night? Were you able to get any sleep?"

I tapped my spoon on the table, feeling my nerves start to fray even though my mood had improved. I sat back and said, "I'm fine. What did you find out?" Then I met his eyes.

His gaze was soft and intense at the same time, as if he were sympathetic and trying to read my mind. He was easy to keep eye contact with, uncommon in my line of work. I still considered myself a lawyer though I'd lost my license. You couldn't take away years of knowledge and skills.

"We have an idea of what happened with your sister."

I clasped my hands under the table and waited.

"We've studied all the security footage from all the cameras. Your sister was seen walking willingly out of the hotel with a woman who fits your description of the person calling herself Shawn Diamandis. She had her arm through your sister's, and they talked as if they knew each other. There was, of course, no sound. She could have been instructing her as to how to act." He looked toward the door as if waiting for the waitress then back to me. "The man with them, unfortunately, was well hidden. Tall, over six feet. His face was under a baseball cap with no identifying signature, an upturned collar, plain dark clothes, no-brand shoes, a beard, and sunglasses. Overdressed for Florida, and most certainly a disguise."

His espresso came. He sipped, now staring into its dark roast. "I bet you have better coffee in Oregon."

"Did you find anything of interest in her apartment?"

"No. Right after your sister and Shawn left, her place was ransacked, and everything of importance was taken."

I was drinking my coffee and spilled it down my chin. He handed me his napkin.

"Who showed up on the footage?"

"We couldn't ID him, but he looked like the guy who left with your sister. He came up the stairs twenty minutes after your sister and Shawn got on the elevator. He carried a workout bag. We assume he's the same guy as the one who left earlier. Shawn doesn't seem to care about being seen on security footage. I can't figure that one out. We're trying to locate her and have a few leads."

The waitress came with our food. I waited for Prosper to continue, but he dug into his sandwich.

My instinct told me to tell the detective everything. He was already more straightforward with me than Gerard had ever been. Plus, he reminded me of Gus, the FBI agent who had overseen protecting me and who was killed on Kauai by Betty and one of her gangsters. I'd liked Gus. He was a good guy. I suppressed a grin as I remembered him dressed in his 70s rocker outfit when I met him at the Vintage bar in Portland. That seemed like eons ago.

I ate a few capers from the lox and bagel, then looked up. The detective seemed to be waiting for me to say something. When I didn't, he said, "Please call me Art, OK?"

I wondered if Prosper used this as a detective's tactic to make me relax so I would talk. Someday, I hoped, I wouldn't be so cynical. But calling him Art didn't sit well with me.

"I can't call you Art. I have you as Detective or Prosper in my head, like you calling me Porter. Working with law enforcement. Calling everyone by their last names."

He chuckled. After swallowing a mouthful of the sandwich, he said, "Fine. Call me Prosper."

We both laughed. It felt so good to be so at ease with someone.

I was ready to unload. I was tired of carrying this around, and wanted to trust him. "I'm going to tell you the whole, long, difficult story. I have no idea if this will help us or not, but I'm willing to try anything right now. But first—" God, I needed a cigarette. "—if Bibi was robbed after she left, then the whole thing was coordinated, and she knows nothing about the robbery and her dog being poisoned."

"That's true. Something else. We don't know if Shawn knew about the ransacking. It's also possible that the guy who left with them came back to the apartment independently. From the camera footage, we saw the man open the apartment door for Shawn and Bibi as they left, then jimmy the door so it wouldn't close and lock. It is possible that Shawn didn't know."

"Although highly unlikely."

"Right."

"So, the man poisoned Otto to safely search and rob the place. But the blood on the coffee table?"

"No match for that yet."

"And everything that he took could have been in the workout bag he brought with him. But how did Shawn and her guy get past the front desk?"

"The young woman at the front desk said the woman told her she was Bibi's sister, so she used your identity."

I groaned. Great. Just great. "But how did the male suspect get back to the apartment?"

"He was already in the building. He didn't need to get back in."

"Did the young woman give you a description of the man when they first came through?"

"Nothing except he was overdressed for Florida. She said he had a beard, baseball cap, hoodie, and the cap shaded his eyes. She said he walked around and looked at the art, so she didn't get a close look. Shawn told her he was an artist visiting from out of town. She signed him in as Anthony Thompkins."

"And Shawn signed herself in as me."

Prosper nodded.

My cell rang. When I looked at the ID, I said, "Sorry. I need to take this."

I stood and walked far enough away to be out of the detective's range.

"Ian? Sorry I haven't called. Can I call you back? I'm having breakfast with ... a friend."

"I'm nearby, in Miami. Work related. Can we get together later? Dinner, maybe?"

"I can't explain right now, but I can't plan anything. Let me call you back. OK?"

"Sure. No worries."

I felt a little guilty for putting him off, but I needed to think about whether to tell him about Bibi or not. I didn't want to complicate things more than they were.

Back at the table, Prosper asked, "Everything all right?"

"Just a family member checking in."

I nibbled the lox. Prosper finished half his sandwich and dabbed his mouth with the napkin. He had manners, kind of old world, and I liked that about him.

As we ate, he asked me a few questions about Oregon and my life as a lawyer. I told him I'd been disbarred and why. He picked up his coffee but set it down. "That had to be a tough call—keep your right to practice law or put a serial rapist away."

I shrugged. I didn't like talking about it. "Since my sister Sophie's suicide, my life has been a mess. The Boston mob responsible for her suicide needs to be shut down and the extortionists put away. I came here because Bibi has some pretty damning evidence that could bring Shawn and her cohorts to justice."

I sipped my coffee, trying to condense the whole story into a minimalist account so he could work with it to find Bibi. "Shawn told Bibi she needed to be at the next meeting of the 'organization.' Didn't give her a choice, said she was part of it whether she liked it or not. Shawn knew that Bibi knew something about the business." I waited and then pushed my plate to the edge of the table. "OK, here's the connection."

Someone bumped into Prosper's chair, but he ignored it and continued to keep eye contact with me.

"Back in Boston, the head of the mob, Betty, found Bibi on the street, took her in, became her patron, and became her godmother. According to Bibi, Betty wanted her to concentrate on her art and get a degree. Betty then connected her with all her wealthy friends. Even though Betty had family money, she created independent wealth."

Prosper checked my empty mug and motioned to the waitress. As she filled it, he ordered another espresso.

To me, he said, "An old-money rich woman as a mob boss. Interesting."

"Even more interesting. Betty picked up Shawn, another street urchin, only Shawn became Betty's lover. Betty truly loved Bibi while Betty kept Shawn around for sex and the cocaine. But the cocaine took over. Soon Bibi found herself shut out of Betty's life because of Shawn."

"This the same Shawn that showed up here?"

I nodded. "Only, before when she was Betty's lover, she wore grungy outfits and looked like she came from the street. This time, she showed up in Bibi's apartment all high end from nails to makeup, from clothes to shoes."

"Hmm. I wonder who she is. Hopefully, we'll be able to ID her. What happened to Betty?"

"She died on Kauai last year. After that, Shawn disappeared. Bibi didn't know what had happened to Betty until a few months later when the body was found at the bottom of a cliff."

"Do you think Shawn killed Betty?"

I drank some water.

"She didn't."

"How do you know?"

"I was on Kauai at the same time, hiding from Betty's gang and using a false ID."

"You know who killed her?"

I said nothing. He didn't need to know that part of the story. "Agent Duvernet knew where I was. When I was of no use to him anymore, he left me alone. After Betty died, he ran Bibi's DNA through the database. He wanted to know where she came from and if she was Betty's actual daughter. That's how he discovered Bibi and I were half-sisters. That's when I became valuable to him again."

"He sounds like... Never mind. So, you didn't know you had a sister?"

"No. Gerard said he'd give me the details if I agreed to help him with his case again. I agreed, met him in San Francisco, got the details about Bibi, and left right away to New Hampshire so I could meet her. He was upset. He wanted to do things his way. I was done with that. It wasn't until he found me in New Hampshire after I met Bibi that he told me

Bibi might be involved with the Boston operation. See what I mean by complicated?"

Prosper paraphrased everything I told him beautifully. He hadn't missed a thing.

"I'm impressed."

"I'm a good listener."

Among other things, I wanted to say.

He finished his espresso then sat back, looking quite content. "So, what do you think, Porter? Is your sister in this mob or not?"

I thought about it a bit before answering. "Honestly, I don't know. I don't think so. She might pretend to go along with Shawn if she feels threatened, but she texted me before she disappeared, saying if anything happened to her, would I please take Otto. She also said she'd hidden evidence that would bring down the gang. That's why Shawn wants her. I'm scared they might torture her, and she'll tell where she's hidden it. What I'm hoping for is that she'll string them along until we find her."

"What if she finds out about Otto being poisoned?"

"Then I doubt if she'll keep her cool. That was clever on their part not to poison Otto with her there. She's tough and would have died before telling them anything."

Prosper took the last bite of his Monte Cristo. "Aren't you going to eat anymore?"

I shook my head. "I'll take it back to the hotel to eat later." People around me talked and laughed and leisurely enjoyed the morning. Even under the awning and protected from the glaring sun, I felt perspiration gather at my temples and trickle down the back of my neck. I had no idea what to do next. "I need to do something to help find her."

"Right now, I have someone trying to locate Shawn's whereabouts, and maybe once we know whose blood that is, *if* the person is in our system, we'll have something to go on. We've also interviewed everyone at The Circ who knew your sister or had contact with her."

I was drained yet wired on the coffee.

Prosper's cell rang. After he listened to the caller, he said, "OK, keep me informed."

"Any news?"

"The team finished their searches of Bibi's belongings, including a storage unit and her car. Nothing." He looked defeated. "I'd better get back." We paid our bills. He had a cruiser coming for him. We said our goodbyes. He never offered me a way to help with the investigation, but I didn't expect he would. He knew I'd do what I wanted, what I felt I needed to do.

As I walked back to The Circ, I decided to check on Otto. Then I realized I still had Gerard's burner. I hadn't given it to Prosper. If there was any way for him to find Bibi's location from the burner, he needed it right away.

But should I give him the burner? If I did, Bibi would no longer have a way to communicate with Gerard unless he'd given her a backup of some kind. Had I put Bibi in more danger now that she had no access to Gerard? I hurried to the hotel. What the hell should I do? Maybe I could make a deal with Prosper to get the burner back when he was finished with it. No. He wouldn't do that. It was evidence. But what if Bibi decided to call me back? From what I know of her, she won't. She'll think either Gerard has abandoned her or...

My head hurt. I called the hotel and asked for my car to be brought up.

Other possibilities. Gerard has her burner number. He can still connect with her. Plus, wouldn't he have a backup plan if she couldn't get to her phone? That was another thing. Why hadn't he put a tracking device on Shawn's car? Wait. What if he had? That would mean Gerard knew where the mob was housed and where Bibi was.

My car was out front when I walked up to the entrance. Would I or wouldn't I give the burner to Prosper? It came down to this—who did I trust most. I sat for a bit before pulling out on the circle, then drove to the precinct.

15

—————

I left the burner and a note for Prosper with the front desk. He'd know what to do with it. I'd made up my mind, so there was no going back. At least Prosper would use it to find Bibi, not use her.

On my way to the veterinary hospital, the detective called. He thanked me for the burner and said it could give them the break they needed. I doubted it but call me a cynic. There were too many possibilities. As I drove into the parking lot, I thought of another one. What if Bibi had been part of the mob all along and agreed to work with Gerard to identify the rogue agent in exchange for any charges against her being dropped?

"Stop it!" I said it so loud I made myself jump. I was so tired of this guessing game.

Inside the animal hospital, they let me see Otto. I dropped to the floor in front of his cage as they opened it. He was the size of a Shetland pony, but he acted more like a lapdog as he put his front paws over my legs and licked my hand as I patted him. I liked this big oaf. This made me homesick for my house and my own dog Tempest. The vet said the toxicology reports should arrive in a few days. I rubbed behind Otto's ears and told him I'd find Bibi, not to worry.

The vet asked me questions about Bibi and walked me out to the front office. She seemed concerned about where Otto would go if he passed all the tests.

"He'll go with me, I guess, if that's all right with you."

Then her expression changed. "What if he has been irreparably damaged?"

"What does that mean?"

"If the poison destroyed his stomach lining, liver, and kidneys, he wouldn't live long, and he'll die in pain."

My hand went to my mouth.

"Would you be willing to give us your approval to put him down if he doesn't get better?" The vet's forehead wrinkled.

I felt sick. "He'll be fine," I said with little conviction. Nothing was going right, and this was just one more thing that made me want to kill Gerard and anyone in the gang. I felt for my gun in my satchel.

"Oh, just a minute," the doctor said. She went back behind the office and came out with a dog collar. "Here. It's Otto's collar."

I took the collar as if being handed a box of ashes. "Why give it to me?"

I caught the vet's expression, one of sympathy and concern, as if I weren't facing reality, but she quickly smiled and said, "We always ask our pet family to take personal items home with them, just as they do at hospitals for human patients. When Otto passes his tests with flying colors, you can bring it with you to take him home."

Home. Hopefully, to Bibi and her apartment. In the meantime, if she weren't found, I'd need to figure out what to feed him and how to feed him. I wondered if I'd be let into Bibi's apartment for his food.

In the car, I held the heavy, thick red collar in my hands. It was one of those with the pointed metal grommets. I hated them. Bibi must have wanted Otto to intimidate people. But I guess that's what she expected. Protection.

If I ended up inheriting Otto, the collar would get trashed. I threw it on the passenger's seat with my bag and wondered what to do next. I should call Ian back. I should talk to people who met Bibi. I should figure out how to trace Shawn. I should. ...

Head spinning, I drove to the beach instead.

I parked along the Broadwalk, as the locals called it. The wind off the ocean felt harsh, and the water was choppy. Few people were down here. I stood on the sand and let the wind whip me, sand embedding in my clothes and hair. I had a feeling that Bibi was all right for the time being. At least that's what I told myself.

The wind tired me fast. I slipped into Hedy's, a small shop along the Broadwalk, where I bought a few clothes to get me through the Florida heat—two cotton tops, straight striped pants, and a light pullover.

On the way to the car, the wind blew sand in my face. Then the rain came down in a torrent. Inside the car, I patted my face dry with napkins I'd saved in my satchel and brushed back my wet hair. I was soaked, but I didn't care. I was headed back to my hotel room to regroup.

Just as I was pulling out, my cell rang. I dug it from my bag and didn't recognize the number. I answered. It was Gerard.

16

M y pulse went into overdrive.

Fucking Gerard.

"Where's my sister? And where the hell have you been?"

"Meet me at 219 North 21st Avenue. It's a Peruvian restaurant. I'll be there in ten minutes."

"You tell me where—"

He hung up.

"Asshole." I thought about going back to the hotel, but I had to know why he wanted to meet. I punched the address into GPS.

The restaurant wasn't far away, but parking along the street was a bitch. At least the rain had let up. I slammed the car door, stubbed my foot on the sidewalk, and walked a block to the place, swearing under my breath.

I had no idea why he'd chosen this place. Runas Peruvian Restaurant was a boxy two-story building with striped awnings not far from Young Circle. The place looked ordinary and a lot like other joints I'd seen, although this one was conspicuously unimpressive, not like the colorful ones along Hollywood Boulevard. Two men sat outside under an awning, smoking cigars. One whistled. They gave me the eye. I gave them the finger.

When I stepped inside, my jaw dropped. Stamped metal ceiling over the long brass bar, white Gothic chandeliers, photos and drawings of Hemingway, and a large, intricate, stained-glass piece above the door, again echoing Mucha-style women. Above me in the entryway, the mirrored ceiling made me somewhat dizzy. Ahead, the bar ran the room's length and looked like something from a pulp novel. The bartender, a looker, was drying a martini glass.

Gerard sat at a corner table in the dining area, this time not so Miami Vice. Just jeans and a plain shirt. On the way, I'd fantasized in gory satisfying detail kicking his ass, but what good would that do?

When I sat down across from him, he leaned in and said, "How'd you get a sunburned nose so fast?"

I wanted to smack him. Gerard was drinking a bottle of Pilsen Trujillo beer. The waiter approached, and I ordered a Pisco sour.

After the waiter left, I leaned across the table and glared. "Where's my sister?"

"She's with Shawn and the others."

Gerard seemed off like he'd had a rough night's sleep.

"You know that for sure?"

He nodded.

"Then why aren't you rescuing her?"

"She's there for a reason, Ang."

"Don't give me that crap! The cops are looking for her. You need to get her out before something happens." I shook out my napkin then twisted it, eyeing Gerard. "You're using her, aren't you?" I kicked him under the table. "You are and don't lie. How else would you know where she is?"

"She's helping with the case."

"I knew it! What the hell was that all about last night. Why'd you drop the burner at my place?"

He flinched. "You have the burner?"

I sat back and stared at him. "You're not serious? Yes, I have the burner." Not technically, but it *had* been in my possession.

The waiter delivered my drink, and I ordered a second one. This was going to be a brutal meeting.

I threw back half my drink then drummed my fingers on the table. Gerard was unusually quiet, which confirmed that he was either hungover or knew he'd screwed up.

"You dropped the burner in my bedroom."

That got his attention. "In the bedroom?"

I smacked the table. "Oh, come on! Don't tell me you don't remember. I suppose you don't remember what you did either?"

He leaned over the table and clasped his hands together so tightly that his knuckles turned white. "Ang, I remember leaving the Olivia bar downstairs and getting on the elevator. After that, I remember nothing. *Nothing.* I woke this morning with no memory of the evening after that one drink."

"No fucking way," I said under my breath.

"My whiskey was spiked."

Could I believe him? Who would do that and why? What would be the end game? "You kissed me and pushed me on the bed."

He looked horrified.

"Nothing happened."

"Thank God."

Thank God? Trying hard not to lose my temper, I

grabbed his wrists. "Forget that. Tell me how to get my sister out of there, wherever there is."

"I can't."

"Bullshit! You're the reason Sophie died. You put me in danger. Now you're using Bibi. Sometimes I wish I'd succeeded in poisoning you in Paris." I pointed at him. "You'd damned well better tell me. She's in danger."

"No, she's fine. If everything goes according to plan, she'll be safe, and the others will be arrested."

"Oh? You've been slipped a mickey and don't remember coming to my place, assaulting me, and dropping your burner. All part of the plan, Mr. On Top of It? Christ, Gerard! They're on to Bibi. You need to get her out."

"How do you know that?"

"I called the number on the burner. Bibi answered with, 'I'm OK. Did you find it?' I was shocked. I told her it was me, and either she disconnected, or someone hung up for her. I kept calling, but she wouldn't answer."

The color drained from his face as he clutched his beer bottle. I'd never seen this sunken expression before, and it worried me more than anything.

"What aren't you telling me?" I clutched my satchel with the gun in it. I had to keep my wits about me. "Tell me and be straight. What's happened?"

He took a long swig of beer and cleared his throat. "Your sister had the burner so she could call me if anything didn't go smoothly. Probably when she heard your voice, she thought something had gone wrong. I don't know if she hung up out of fear or if Shawn hung it up."

"Fuck." My chest constricted, and I tasted bile at the back of my throat. I downed my drink. "Tell me where they are."

"The outfit owns a house in Victoria Park." He reached

across the table and put a hand over mine. "Ang, Bibi just panicked when she heard your voice. She probably ditched the burner. I've heard nothing from the house to assume otherwise."

"You've heard nothing?" I rubbed my nose and felt the sunburn. "If Bibi is gone for more than one day, she will try to get back to the apartment because of Otto."

"Ang, I told Bibi that I'd have someone take care of the dog. If she knew they tried to kill it, she would have turned on Shawn and the others. They wouldn't hesitate to kill her."

We were on borrowed time. My eyes filled with tears. I pulled my hand away, crossed my arms over my chest, and glared at him. "Can you please tell me what your end game is? What can she possibly do that will help bring these people to justice? I don't get it."

"The 'end game' as you call it is for her to gain their trust, play along, and when possible, get access to one of Rena's or Ralph's computers to download the entire files."

"But she has evidence on them hidden someplace. You could have asked her for the hiding place, and, boom, you'd have your evidence."

"Your sister told me what she has. It isn't enough to convict. We need copies of their current files, everything. They've expanded internationally. That's why they've moved to Florida."

"Bibi told me she moved to Florida to get away from them. Or did she come down here after she heard they'd moved because she was going to help you with a sting operation?"

He didn't answer. Either that was a *yes*, or he didn't know.

"What I don't understand is why she'd want me to find

the files. She knew she was in danger. Now, from what you've said, it sounds like she's hanging out with Shawn and the gang as an insider and that the files I find won't be worth a damn."

"Have you found the files?"

I didn't like the expectant look on his face. I also had a gut feeling he wasn't telling me the truth about the importance of the files. "If I'd found them, from what you say, what would it matter?"

"If you have them, you need to give them to me."

Not happening. I finished my drink. "So, you don't remember what you did in my apartment? You don't remember assaulting me?"

"Assaulting you? Did I ...?"

"No, you didn't. I stopped you."

"Did I hurt you?"

I shook my head.

"I'm so sorry, Angeline." His face sagged, giving him about ten years. But it was the sadness in his eyes that got me. I think he was sincere, but I had doubts.

I pushed my chair back. I was done here—except for finding out the truth. That's what was missing. Why would Bibi go along with this? She had to have an emotional stake in what she was doing to put herself in so much danger. Was there something I was missing?

"Gerard?" He looked up at me. I kept my voice neutral, non-accusatory. "I think Bibi's hidden files are enough to arrest these people."

No reaction.

My brain fired fast, and so did my mouth. "Bibi wouldn't go along with your plan unless she had an emotional stake in it. That's the only reason she'd put her life in danger *and* leave Otto in someone else's care. My guess is you told her that Shawn killed Betty."

He sat back, his face impassive, unreadable, but his left eye twitched once.

I thought of his fingerprints found in Bibi's apartment on the wineglass. "When did you and Bibi talk about this plan? In-person or on the phone?"

"We met in her apartment."

"If Bibi is caught with the burner, she's as good as dead."

Gerard stared over my head, somehow gone for a second. He hadn't denied any of this, but he wouldn't. He was trained for this. But how the hell did he live this way?

"Who do you think might have drugged your drink?"

"I don't know."

"Think. Who has a motive to drug you? Why? Are you the only one working this case?"

"You know I can't talk about any of that."

"Christ, Gerard, where'd you get your degree in 'undercover?' Between the sheets?"

Now he looked livid. "Stop, Angeline. This is not a joke."

The waiter delivered my second Pisco Sour plus a bowl of ceviche. I pushed it toward Gerard, who was tapping his foot under the table. He looked like he needed something to eat and a good twelve hours of sleep.

"Angeline?"

"What?"

"Did you find Bibi's information?"

"No."

"If you don't turn it over to me, you would be interfering in an FBI investigation."

"I guess it's a good thing I haven't found it then. I could always let your superiors know that you lied to Bibi to gain her cooperation."

He took a swig of beer, his face now hardened. He didn't

deny it. He leaned toward me and said, "Would you rather I tell Bibi how Betty died?"

I backed away. "You prick."

"You don't know everything, Ang. We've been tracking and watching this gang for a long time. We had information that Shawn was moving to take over the family business even *before* Betty went to Kauai."

He finished his beer, and his eyes no longer looked kind or sympathetic. The ceviche sat there, uneaten.

"Gerard, we need to get Bibi out of there."

Gerard's jaw clenched as he said, "Leave it alone, Angeline. Let me and those on the case take care of this."

Oh, how I wanted to spew a few good retorts to that. But I stayed calm. If he wasn't going to answer me, I needed to know how to contact him.

"I need a number where I can call you if I find the information."

He nodded. "Do you have a burner?"

"A couple."

He took my hand and wrote a number on my palm. "Don't wash it."

Then he put a fifty-dollar bill on the table and left.

17

I had no idea what to do next. I needed a shower. I needed to change my clothes. The hotel manager had given me the name of two employees to talk to about Bibi, but what good would that do? Some quiet time in my hotel room might jog loose some new ideas. While I let my brain wander, I made notes and tried to figure out where Bibi had hidden the stash.

Back at the hotel with Otto's collar, I made coffee. The two cocktails had zapped my energy. I sipped the coffee while staring at Otto's collar, praying that the big guy would make it. I took another burner from my stash and saved Gerard's number. I wish I knew what happened to Snoop, my hacker. Another victim of this fucking case. Why didn't I ask Gerard about her?

As if I'd get a straight answer.

I was forgetting many things. I couldn't remember when I'd last eaten. Oh, wait—breakfast with Prosper. But I'd forgotten to bring home the leftovers. That reminded me of Ian, his call. I hadn't called him back. Not that I wanted to. I was too tired to deal with a half-brother and the knowledge I had a biological father just a few hours away.

Slow-motion took over. I drank coffee, hoping for the buzz, and examined Otto's collar, reading the tags attached, praying that he'd be all right. I did not want that dog to die. As I checked the tags, I noticed a small incision in the rugged, woven material. I put my fork down. Something hard was inside the collar near the buckle. I couldn't get it out with my fingers, so I used a knife. Out popped a small flash drive.

I jumped up. "Bibi! Damn, girl!" Was this really it? It had to be.

I grabbed my laptop.

With my laptop humming, I stuck the flash drive into the USB port. Hundreds of excel files appeared. Shivers streamed up my arms. I randomly opened a file. The spreadsheet columns made no sense to me as they seemed to be in an alphabetized code. I opened another. The same. But the amounts were off the charts. After opening a few more, I changed the interface to lines of files with dates. The dates went back about ten years. Would any of this make sense to the FBI?

The main question was—should I give this to Gerard? My gut said no. What if I made a swap? Get Bibi out of Shawn's grip in exchange for the flash drive.

I ejected the flash drive and deleted the Excel history on my Mac. The best storage—back in the collar went the info.

"Smart place to hide it, Bibi."

Then I remembered her message: "...promise you'll take care of Otto. You know what he's like. He's sweet and needs his ugly striped afghan. He also knows a lot."

He knows a lot.

Stupid me! I didn't get the hint.

My cell rang. Ian. Damn. Not now. But I couldn't keep ignoring him.

"Hey, Ian, sorry about—"

"I'm downstairs in the lobby. Want to catch a bite to eat at Olivia's? It's on me. I'm super excited about seeing you again."

If he only knew. But I needed to eat, and maybe it would do me some good to see someone not connected with all this.

"That's great. Give me twenty minutes, OK?"

In the time that had passed, I'd decided to tell Prosper about the flash drive. If anything, I could tell him what was going on, and maybe he could get Bibi out of there. Fuck Gerard's rogue agent. At least get rid of Shawn and the major players.

I called Prosper.

"Hey, Porter. We've made progress on the burner."

"You have? What?"

"We have some satellite positions that could lead us to an area where she is."

"Finally." But something stopped me from telling him about the flash drive. Gut instinct, I guess. "I just talked with Gerard. He mentioned Victoria Park."

"Really? Where'd he get that?"

I decided to ignore that question. "What's Victoria Park?"

"An area known for Russian mobsters. I wouldn't put it past the Boston group to team up with them."

"I think it's a recent move. You might check newly purchased houses and rentals."

"Good idea."

I remembered Ian. "I have to meet my half-brother downstairs. He's been waiting for me."

"Call me when you're done."

We agreed to meet later, place to be determined.

18

I an stood as I walked toward the table, his grin wide, his face flushed. He gave me a hug and a light kiss on the cheek. I felt stiff at first but then relaxed. It felt damn good—someone happy to see me who wasn't law enforcement or FBI.

"You're my sister." He said this as if trying to make it sound real.

I laughed. "You said that the last time I saw you."

But his saying that dredged up doubt. Did he look like my biological father? Did I have proof he was who he said he was? I couldn't help being suspicious of him. I was suspicious of everyone. But he'd shown me photos of my mother's love letters to his father. He had to be the real thing.

When I sat down, I struggled to maintain my energy. "Sorry I haven't called you." How much to say to him? Why am I in Florida? I could give him something to explain why I couldn't concentrate on him. "My other half-sibling has gone missing."

"Oh, no, I'm so sorry to hear that. That must be terrifying. Is there anything I can do?"

"Distract me, please." I tried to smile. "It's about the only thing anyone can do." I paused. "And please excuse my appearance. I've had no time to take care of the usual."

"What happened? Can you tell me?"

"I really can't."

"I have lots of contacts here in southern Florida. I know a terrific private investigator who has good relations with the police."

"Thanks so much, but it's already in the hands of the police. But if nothing happens in the next forty-eight hours, I might take you up on that." Hoping to drop the subject, I scanned the menu and chose. With the satchel in my lap, I could feel the gun inside. In case Prosper called—or Gerard—I placed my cell on top of the bag.

The waiter came, and we ordered. After he left, I asked Ian, "Did you tell your father about me?"

"No. I want to talk with you first about how you'd like to approach him. But that can wait. You have too much going on right now."

"Thanks for understanding."

"Of course."

My coffee came. I glanced at my phone. I felt so useless and desperately wanted to be moving, to be actively engaged in finding Bibi, not sitting here, eating with Ian.

His cell rang, and he excused himself to take the call. I squirmed in the chair, uncomfortable, wanting to run off. I remembered the last time we had dinner. We'd met on a plane on my way home to Oregon, and I enjoyed his company. But he was too pushy about dinner and meeting me for coffee. I thought he was after me for a date. He was wearing a similar sports jacket when I finally did meet him for dinner. When he left the table to answer a call, I checked his coat and found a notebook full of details about me. It freaked me out. That's when I demanded he tell me who he really was.

It was a relief when he apologized and said he was my half-brother. By this time, I knew all about my mother's affairs, my mom and dad's agreement that they'd have children via her getting pregnant by other men.

Ian had told me he didn't want to connect his father with me unless I brought something positive to the family. I thought it was a scam at first until he sent me photos of love letters between my mother and his dad. Mom ended their love affair. She sent him all his letters because she didn't want them around and was afraid "dad" would find them. He was a troubled, violent man with bipolar disorder. He was also an alcoholic. I knew some of this as a kid, but Mom getting pregnant by other men? In the letters, she said she had to stay with her husband because he needed her. How many times had I heard that from other women?

Those letters gutted me. Ian's father deeply loved Mom. She was the love of his life. I still can't get those letters out of my head. Even my husband Hank never wrote letters like that to me.

"I'm worried about you."

I jerked up to see Ian standing over me.

"Are you sure you're OK? You seem like you're on another planet."

I smiled. "I was thinking about your—our—father's letters to my mother. Did your mother know about them?"

He sat, shifted side to side in his chair, and didn't look at me.

"Sorry," I said. "I should let you tell me everything in your own time."

He shook out his napkin, draped it over his lap, and sipped his drink, his eyes finally landing on mine. "Thanks.

But right now, I want to talk about you. This is major what you're going through with a missing sister."

As cliché as it sounded, I felt good that he wanted to focus on me. Everyone else seemed only to want me so I could help them. I wanted to find my sister, but I didn't want Ian involved. There were already too many people in the mix. It would be nice to have someone who knew nothing but was there for me. However, the offer of a PI was tempting. No, the more people involved, the messier it would get. He was saying something, but I didn't hear it. Ian had to understand that I was a lawyer, not a damsel in distress.

I cleared my throat and interrupted him. "Ian, thank you. It's good to know I have you on my side. But for the time being, I'm letting the authorities do their job. But, believe me, if I need you, I'll call."

"OK, no worries. As a former lawyer, I'm sure you know what you're doing."

I needed a prop, so I picked up my fork for something to hold. "Tell me about your dad. What's he like?"

"You mean *our* dad?" He grinned. "This must be hard knowing after all these years your real father is alive."

My cell vibrated with a message, and I glanced down. Prosper and our TBA info. I looked up. "Uh, I ... I don't think it's sunk in yet. I mean, yes, it's hard. Maybe once I meet him."

My calamari starter and a small dinner salad came. So did Ian's linguini mare.

"No wine with dinner?" Ian said. "It's my treat. Live large."

I laughed. "I'm living as large as I want to at the moment."

As I ate, I asked him about growing up and how his dad treated him. Their relationship sounded so normal.

"Where does he live?"

"Half time in Naples, a new condo downtown. The rest of the time, he lives in Boston. That's where he is now."

Boston? "Was he originally from Boston?"

"Yes, the whole family was. Mom and Dad used to have a place on Lake Winnisquam in New Hampshire, but once they both retired, they sold that and bought the place in Naples."

Lake Winnisquam was where we lived when I was young, so Mom and Ian's dad must have met there somehow. "What did he do? Obviously, something that made enough money for two places."

"Dad was a doctor, a surgeon at Boston Medical Center. Plus, there was family money."

"You said you're a chemical engineer, like my late husband?"

He nodded and finished a mouthful of linguine. "I should be in China now, but there's a problem near the site, and we can't go until it's cleared for safety."

As we ate and talked, I noticed his elegant hands, just as I had when we'd first met. Still no manicure, nails a little ragged, something that had impressed me then as now. He was still tan. He was dressed casually in slacks, a basic belt, a light-blue button-down shirt, and the navy-blue sports jacket. His tall, slender body carried his clothing well. He wasn't wearing a pierced earring this time as he had in Oregon. I wondered if his head of thick silver hair was genetic from his ... our father. I wondered if our father would accept me as a new daughter.

There were so many questions I wanted to ask him, but the questions flitted in and out of my head like the lights of a police cruiser.

I finished my meal before Ian. I only had forty-five

minutes until meeting Prosper at Micky Finn's Irish Pub on Hollywood Boulevard.

"Look, Ang, let me call my PI friend. It's obviously causing you great concern. I can see it on your face. And please, if you must go, I understand. I think I'm holding you up from something, right?"

This guy paid attention like a good cop. Or maybe chemical engineers were also observant. Hank was a chemical engineer, but he hadn't been interested in people. I exhaled. "I'm meeting the detective on the case."

"Then go, for heaven's sake. But I just want to help you find your sister while she's healthy and unscathed."

I shivered. Healthy and unscathed? Jesus.

I thanked him for dinner. We stood. I slung my bag over my shoulder. When he hugged me again, I realized how tall he was as his chin came down on the top of my head. I hurried away but glanced back. He no longer smiled. He seemed to be glaring. He was not happy. However, when I waved, he broke out in a broad smile and waved back. He was exasperated with me. I was distracted, had refused his offer of help, and kept dashing off. I felt bad. I'd make it up to him later.

19

Micky Finn's was what you'd expect from the name, but not what you'd expect from Southern Florida. More like being dropped into a pub in Ireland. A soccer game was on the "telly," and the place was dark wood, packed, and rowdy.

I stood inside the door, letting my eyes adjust to the low light. A man came up to me and introduced himself as Mark, the owner. I noted the Irish accent. When I told him I was there to meet someone, he said, "Art described you well, but he didn't say what a looker you are."

I felt the heat rise in my cheeks and laughed. "Ah, the Irish gift of flattery."

He grinned and pointed to Prosper, who sat in a booth at the far end of the room.

At the booth, I said hello, and Prosper said, "Sorry. I forgot it was soccer night."

I shrugged and sat. He was drinking a Guinness and had bought me one too.

"So, catch me up," I said as I sucked down the head of

the beer. "Anything more on the burner?" I leaned in to hear him.

"Not yet."

"Did you get an ID on the blood left on the coffee table?"

"Unfortunately, no. It's not in our database. And that acrylic nail? Nothing in our database on that either. It's like these people don't exist."

I swallowed my impatience. So why had he summoned me? "You're telling me we don't know who poisoned Otto and stole everything? Plus, you can't ID Shawn from the acrylic nail?"

"No. Sorry. We can't even say the acrylic nail was from Shawn. Both are dead ends." Prosper seemed curt and not his usual self.

"Everything OK?"

"I heard from your friend Duvernet. He wants us to back off from finding your sister. It could interfere with his case."

I gritted my teeth. FBI usually trumps any local law enforcement regarding extortion and kidnapping, but this was a missing person's case. When Prosper didn't continue, I faked a smile and said, "I hope you told him to go 'f' himself." It was tough to swear around someone who didn't swear.

He waved at a man who recognized him but kept his attention on me. "I told him that I'd be willing to work with him."

I couldn't read his face.

"What?"

He leaned back for a minute, considering what to say next. I waited, fed up to the teeth with Gerard and now Prosper.

"Spit it out!"

He took a drink, licked some froth off his upper lip, then

leaned forward on the table. "Porter, he said it would be best to let him handle it. It seems your sister went into this voluntarily. I'm not sure I can now continue with the investigation because she's not missing."

"She was abducted."

"No, not according to Special Agent Duvernet."

Damn Gerard. "You only have his word that Bibi wasn't abducted. Besides, how do you define missing or abducted?" I almost spit. He didn't answer. "And you only have his word that she volunteered for this. Besides, even if she 'volunteered,' it doesn't mean she wasn't coerced into it. My sister might get killed. Doesn't that mean anything to anyone?"

A loud whoop went up from the crowd, followed by cheers. Now I was shouting.

"Did he tell you where she is?"

"No. I told him we needed to meet. He agreed."

I had to shout above the crowd's cheering. "Gerard won't tell you anything. Think about it. Has he told you about the case in detail?"

When he didn't answer, I said, "See? He's just looking for what you know."

"Porter, I need to know what he knows. I've worked with the FBI before. This is not unusual. I'm concerned about your objectivity. I understand you're worried about your sister, but you need to let law enforcement work the case."

"As if I haven't let law enforcement work the case? You said you'd let me know about progress in the case. I've given you vital information. Now you're saying you and Gerard are working together? Well, good luck with that. Let me know how that goes."

I was done. I was being shoved aside, pushed out of the investigation. Fuck both of them.

I swung from the booth and strode to the door, pushing

past two big guys and people blocking the doorway. The sidewalks were crowded with people as I headed to the hotel. Latin music played from a place nearby. Fairy lights circled the palm trees along Hollywood Boulevard. People were laughing and enjoying themselves. I wanted to scream.

Prosper caught up with me.

"Angeline, stop!"

Calling me by my first name made me stop, and we banged into each other. I crossed my arms over my chest and waited.

"I've only agreed to meet with Duvernet. I need to make up my mind about him." He paused and made me look him in the eye. "Look, I get what you're saying. He could be playing me, too. But I won't know until I hear what he has to say."

"It's your call, but I have history with Gerard, and I don't trust him. You should check anything he says with me." I shifted from foot to foot, watching his face, waiting to see his reaction.

"I told Duvernet I had to talk with my superiors. But I came to you first. How about you tell me everything you know and suspect so I can have that in my pocket when I meet him? I understand that he has a different motive in dealing with your sister. But he also has power and resources."

I considered this.

"You were a lawyer once. You know how this works. Technically, in this investigation, you are only a 'concerned party,' a member of the missing person's family, and that's all. If my captain knew you'd been disbarred for taking the law into your own hands, you'd have never been allowed anywhere near this case."

He was right. He *was* being straight with me. And I appreciated that.

"All right. Let's go to my hotel room. I need a real drink and someplace private. It's a long story."

At the hotel, a different cop stood outside my door. Prosper said hello, calling him by name. The cop handed me a message.

I opened the hotel envelope and pulled out a piece of stationary.

"Don't talk to Detective Prosper until you've spoken with me."

"Who delivered this?"

"Someone from the front desk."

Gerard. Screw him.

20

Inside my hotel room, I balled up the note and threw it away. Prosper watched but didn't say anything. Why had Gerard left a note when he could have called my burner? Oh, shit. He didn't have my burner number. I had his. But he could have called on my personal cell—unless he thought someone was tracking us.

Did it matter? Not really. I poured a scotch for Prosper and me and deliberately took the club chair, so Prosper had to sit on the couch. To me, the couch was always a weaker position when questioned by a policeman or detective.

"Was that a note from Duvernet?" Prosper asked.

"What makes you think that?"

"The way you reacted like someone was giving you an order that pissed you off."

I laughed. Gerard would never have picked up on that.

"Yes, and yes. It was from him, and it pissed me off."

He sat back, legs crossed, nursing his drink. "He's trying to keep you from cooperating with me."

I raised my glass to him. "Affirmative."

He studied me. "Is he succeeding?"

"Let's just say I'm weighing my options." The scotch had gone down easy. I kicked off my shoes and rubbed my feet. "Since he wants to talk to me before I spill anything to you, tell me why I should tell you everything I know."

"Because I want to find your sister and get her out alive from wherever she is."

"I know that already. But what makes you think *you* can do that?"

"I had some experience with this in Canada. Plus, I'm not hot-headed and have no ulterior motive."

I nodded, staying silent so he'd continue.

"We have access to two fine hostage negotiators if it comes to that. I won't go in with guns blazing." He rolled his glass between his palms as if considering what he would say next. "Here's what I think. I think Duvernet has personal motives for keeping her where she is, and I don't think he'll put your sister's welfare ahead of whatever he's after."

A chill went up my spine. Damn, this guy was good, but what he said was precisely what I feared most. I stood.

"Let me ask you this, Porter."

I turned to look down at him.

"Will it make it worse if you tell me what you know? Is there anything you tell me that will put your sister in more danger?"

I'd already thought about that. "My hesitation is two-fold: *how* you plan to get her out when you find her and how Gerard could screw it up."

He cocked his head as if he couldn't believe I'd said that. "First of all, I don't know yet how I'd get her out because I don't have all the information." He stood, and now he was the one looking down at me. "Do you know what Duvernet is planning? Do you think you could find out?"

"I honestly don't know. Maybe."

Prosper was so close to me now that I could smell him, like a mixture of lime and gunshot. I backed away, not because it repelled me. Just the opposite.

A silence descended on us except for the rattle of the air conditioner.

"What are you thinking?" Prosper finally asked.

"What if I talk with Gerard first? Straight out, ask him about his plan."

"And if he won't tell you?"

"I'll tell you what I know."

He swallowed the rest of his drink in one gulp, then took his glass to the kitchenette and put it in the sink. I followed him and decided to find out if he was trying to cut me out of the equation by giving him the option to do this, not that I'd take it or go along with it. I just wanted to know where I stood.

"Look, Prosper, maybe it would be best if you cut me out of the case. Work directly with Gerard. Just the two of you."

He turned to face me. His clenched teeth made the scar on his neck throb.

"No, Porter. Not happening. You're the key to this. He knows it. I know it. I'm just not sure what you have that we don't."

That knocked me sideways. The key? The one thing I had was Otto's collar with the flash drive.

"I think you give me too much credit. If you've worked with the Bureau before, why not now? Combine info and forces. If Bibi *did* join the mob to find something Gerard needs, then maybe she's not a hostage. Maybe she's free to come and go like the rest of them."

"I don't think so," Prosper said. "That's my gut talking after years of experience. She'll be watched, tailed, accompanied wherever she goes, even when she leaves the premises." He shrugged. "Besides, it's too late to back down now. Like it or not, you're at the center of this thing."

Prosper stood so close I could feel his body heat. I rubbed my chest, poured another two fingers of scotch, and walked to the balcony door to stare out and get my thoughts together. One thing had been made clear with this meeting with Prosper—I trusted him. He had one objective—to save my sister. Everyone else played a shadow game, maybe even Bibi. What did I honestly know about her?

Prosper came up and stood beside me.

I gestured to Young Circle with my glass. "We're going in circles, just like that traffic circle out there. Only we don't know which exit to take."

"I can make this easy for you."

"OK, go for it."

"Before you tell me what you know, find out Duvernet's plan if you can. Then I'll see if I want to play ball with him or not. I think you'll get better answers than I will."

He was right. I lifted my glass. "Agreed." For better or worse, I'd thrown in with Prosper.

I slugged back my drink. Damn right I'd get the answers. I knew exactly how to get Gerard to talk. I doubted if Prosper would agree with my method, but it didn't matter. I knew Gerard's weakness.

21

Prosper left around eight o'clock. Before he left, I talked him out of one of his cigarettes. When the door closed, I poured more scotch and held the cigarette but didn't light it. Out on the balcony, the night sky hung heavy with rain, but the evening sounds of people seemed oblivious to it. My shirt quickly clung to me from the humidity. Melancholy notes from a saxophone played somewhere in the park and floated above the sound of people buzzing to and fro. Intermittently, I caught a flash of light reflected off the sax but couldn't see the person playing it. When I finally had a good buzz going, I went back inside and called Gerard.

He didn't pick up, but I knew he wouldn't. He didn't recognize the burner number. I left a message. He called right back.

"Angeline, thanks for calling." He was being courteous? Nah.

"The detective just left. We need to talk. Can you come up?"

"I'm about twenty minutes away. I'm leaving now."

"I want to know what's going on, Gerard. All of it."

But he'd hung up. I shook my head, beyond caring about his rudeness. Tonight, I would do whatever it took to get him to tell me about his plan to find Bibi and bring her to safety. I also wanted to know the whole story about him and Sophie.

I changed into the only dress I owned, one I'd hauled around with me for ages. It could have been left over from Paris, but I doubted it. I remembered throwing most of those clothes away. The humidity made my hair frizz but screw it. I put on a minimum of makeup, not that he'd notice. He'd guess what I was up to no matter what I looked like. I'd either hook him or not.

My bottle of scotch was getting low, so I called downstairs for another. I found a station on Spotify, some soft sexy jazz, and played it through the hotel's iPhone player. Then I waited.

Twenty minutes later, Gerard arrived with a bottle of Glenmorangie, a scotch that cost over two hundred dollars. Could he write it off on his Bureau expenses? My next thought was who was seducing whom? He handed me the bottle.

"Who'd you steal this from?"

"As Americans love to say, 'No big deal.'"

That sounded funny with his accent. I'd often forget he was French American until his accent was accentuated— usually when sex was in the air. Damn Frenchman.

He looked me over and said, "You're wearing a dress. You're not going to try to kill me again, are you?"

I couldn't help but laugh. He remembered I didn't like dresses except in Paris when I went there for revenge. "Depends on whether I get what I want or not."

I held out my glass. He poured.

As he poured, I noticed his pupils were dilated. My heart lurched. Dilated pupils in this low light? I only had one lamp on besides the kitchenette overhead. The only reason his pupils could be dilated would be drugs. Had he been high from being drugged or from using when he nearly assaulted me?

I tried to think of what to say to him as I sipped the scotch and rolled the liquor around on my tongue. He watched me. I tasted notes of espresso and chocolate. I guess he knew what I liked. Maybe he *had* been paying attention. I nodded in appreciation. The stuff was damn good. I needed to thank him—and also bust him on the dilated pupils.

We clinked our glasses together and sat on the couch, each taking an end where we could turn toward the other. Interesting that he'd dressed casually in a green, short-sleeve shirt and jeans as if not expecting anything—or expecting everything.

I dove in. "Two questions, Gerard."

"Fine. Ask."

"Are you using an amphetamine of some kind?"

He seemed unperturbed by the question. "I took a drug to counteract the one slipped in my drink last night. The side effect includes sleeplessness, but I need to be alert and awake."

"You've been awake all this time?" He looked pretty fresh to me, but that too could be pharmaceutical speed. The armed services gave good drugs to their soldiers when on an extended mission, so why not the FBI?

"What's your second question?"

"What's with you telling me not to talk to Prosper before I talked with you?"

He stretched out one leg on the couch and held his glass

to his chest. "You need to know what Bibi is doing for us. Prosper has a different agenda, and it interferes with ours."

So now he's speaking for the FBI? Before I could ask, he continued.

"Angeline, Bibi is safe. We have officers watching the house. She's working the case for us and doing well."

"You know where she is. What's the address?"

He didn't answer.

"Let's back up a minute. Did she agree to work for you?"

"Yes."

"Why?"

"She wanted to stop the mob. Remember? She hated Shawn and what she did to her godmother...Betty."

"Yes, I know who her godmother is."

Just hearing that woman's name made me grit my teeth. I hated Betty, but I felt guilty about killing her. Still, it was either her or me.

"You're telling me she wanted to help? No coercion on your part?"

"She suspects Shawn killed Betty."

We locked eyes for a minute.

"Again, what is Bibi supposed to do for you? Get files off the mob's computers? I need clarification: why aren't the files she secreted away enough?"

"We need everything we can to bring the suspects to justice. We need an airtight case. I know what's on the flash drive won't be enough. It's too old, files from Betty's reign. I told you that."

I ignored his jab. "If all that's true, why won't she tell you where she hid the other files, and what's in those files? That tells me she doesn't trust you."

"We'll find the files eventually."

"'We?' Meaning you and me? Not happening."

I waited for a reaction.

When it didn't come, I decided on a different tactic. "Did you promise Bibi that you'll put Shawn away for a very long time? Just what did you promise her?"

He held my gaze as if trying to make me uncomfortable or back off. I stared right back.

Finally, he said, "Bibi knows that we'll do the best we can and do even better if she gets us more evidence."

"She could have told you where this other evidence is. That could be enough."

"Did she tell you? No. Your sister doesn't trust *anyone*."

"Ouch, Gerard."

"You asked about the files she hid. I think they're more recent and have specific banking information that shows the illegality of their operation. Bibi wants to make sure she has something specific to put Shawn away." He paused, then shrugged. "So that's what we need—recent files." He sipped his scotch.

"That's bullshit. That's not what you want, Gerard. You want the rogue FBI agent. That's all you've ever wanted."

He didn't respond. Then I noticed the tick of his left eye. OK. That's a tell.

It was time to get tough. He'd never seen me in a courtroom. I got up, nabbed the bottle from the side table, and filled my glass. I knocked his leg off the couch and sat down again.

"Do you even know if this rogue agent is male or female? That's what you really want, right? For Bibi to find out who it is. Does this person have a hidden tattoo that reads 'Rogue FBI Agent?'"

Gerard chuckled. Then our knees touched. He looked down. I pulled away. We were playing a cat and mouse game, and we both knew it.

I wanted to threaten him, tell him I'd partner up with Prosper or take up my brother's offer of a PI if he didn't tell me everything. But I didn't have to.

He sipped his scotch, then said, "We believe the rogue agent is Shawn's partner, as in lover. We know the agent is a male, and we have Shawn's real identity. She's the weak link. She likes Bibi, and Bibi's turned out to be a good actor. It's obvious from their interaction. They drink and laugh together. Bibi said they act like fast friends. Bibi's done a good job of helping them identify wealthy targets. She even offered to put herself up as a liaison to hustle wealthy men."

That surprised me. Why would Bibi go to such lengths? Or was she liking this new role?

"How did you convince Bibi to do this and put herself in danger? When I was in New Hampshire with her, she didn't want any part of this."

His lips were a few feet from mine. I inched in. If I had to fuck him to get honest answers, I would. I needed to appeal to his emotional and physical sides.

"Gerard, I can't lose another sister. Sophie made mistakes. She was always picking the wrong men, and she should have never had anything to do with you. If she'd never met you, she'd be alive today."

I finally had a reaction. Gerard looked like I'd punched him. He swallowed hard and looked down into his glass. "I loved her. I've told you that." His voice was so low. I almost couldn't hear him. "But I finally had a lead on the guy I'd been hunting for years."

I managed to sit still and keep my voice steady. "You sacrificed my sister."

"No. I would have never done that."

"Then what happened?"

"The strategy didn't work. And..." Gerard tugged at his ear.

"And what?"

He looked around the room as if he were trapped. But it was a self-imposed trap, one he'd have to admit to sooner or later.

"It was my fault. I didn't communicate clearly or enough with Sophie. I didn't realize that she needed regular reassurance that I loved her. I thought she knew that. But a month was too long to leave her without any communication. I told her why I needed to be gone that long, but ... I loved your sister, Ang. I planned to leave the FBI after I'd extracted both of us from the organization. She didn't realize it had to be done in a certain way, and well, never mind. I should have told her the plan."

"You screwed up, Gerard. That's what you did. But it wasn't because you miscalculated. It was because you were obsessed with finding this rogue agent."

Gerard knocked back his scotch and refilled his glass.

"This current strategy?" I asked. "It sounds a lot like you're willing to sacrifice Bibi."

His head jerked toward me, and his eyes narrowed. "*No.* Bibi is safe. She will be safe. If everyone would just work with me."

"Work with you? What the fuck, Gerard! You haven't been honest with anyone. You haven't told us what and why you're doing what you're doing. And now you want us to work with you?" I snorted, fed up. "Why didn't you want me to talk with Prosper before I talked with you?"

He squinted, and his nose twitched like he was smelling something rancid. Then his face hardened, and he glared at me.

What the fuck? I jumped up and walked away. When I

turned, I threw my glass at him. The glass hit him in the head and then bounced to the floor. His hand went to his forehead. A trickle of blood slid down his temple. He wasn't glaring anymore.

He stood, looked at his bloody hand, and slowly walked to the bathroom. I grabbed the bottle of scotch and took a long swig.

When he returned, he sat down and dabbed at his forehead with toilet paper. The cut was superficial and had already stopped bleeding. His eyes drooped, and his mouth had gone slack. He looked like a man buried under too many secrets, someone who had lived a lie most of his life. But I was done feeling sorry for him. He'd screwed up, and Sophie had died. He wasn't getting my other sister.

I was so pissed I wanted to scream. Instead, I stood over him and said, "What the fuck is wrong with you? Your job is to save lives, you asshole. What gives you the right—"

"You don't believe I want to save everyone on this planet?" Gerard jumped up. "I care, Angeline. No matter what the hell you think, I care."

I glared up at him, locking onto his accusing eyes. My heart raced, and I felt light-headed. We were both itching to hit each other.

Then he grabbed my arms, pulled me to him, and kissed me. Kissed me hard and full on the lips.

I shoved him away.

"Oh, no. You want me? Then you're going to tell me everything." I swept back my hair. I was ready to fuck him— if he told me everything. That's when I knew what I wanted, had always wanted. I *did* want him. But I wanted the truth about him and Sophie even more.

I sat down shakily, wiped my lips with the back of my hand, and said, "What happened to you and Sophie?"

22

Gerard paced as he talked. He seemed far away as he spoke.

"My original job was to infiltrate the Boston crime operation so I could detail their chain of command, establish where they operated and how they planned to expand, then find out how they hid everything in a legal business. That's how it started, anyway. But I could never get past Sam, aka Link, to insinuate myself in the business end. I was just a pretty face to lure wealthy targets."

My hands shook, so I shoved them under my armpits.

He glanced my way. "You all right?"

"Fine. Go on."

"As you know, I teamed up with Sam, the second in command to Betty." He paused but didn't look at me. I knew what he was thinking—*the guy you killed.*

The guy I killed in self-defense.

"I had to accompany Sam everywhere, me, the perfect bait to lure wealthy women."

He said all this in a flat voice that broke every so often. I didn't dare speak.

"We met your sister at a Florida business conference. She bragged about you and your wealthy chemical engineering husband. In the evening, we went back to Sam's room, where he drugged both of us, and we ended up in a threesome. He set it up, so I seemed as innocent as she was. I was. I didn't know he would drug us both and take a video. When we came out of the drug, he showed it to us and threatened to release it if we didn't do what he wanted."

He turned and looked down at me. "I want you to know that Sophie wouldn't betray you. Her exact words to Sam were, 'Go ahead, you asshole. It won't hurt me.' Then she turned and walked out of the room." He sighed and looked a little lovesick. "She was impressive, Ang."

I was near tears hearing this about Sophie.

Gerard took a few sips of scotch.

"Sam told me to go along with the ruse, pressure Sophie to get a million dollars somehow. Sam had researched your husband's business, so he knew what it was worth in liquid assets. I knew the bastard wouldn't stop there. I had to find a way out for us."

He paced again.

"What did you do?"

"I told Sophie that I paid Sam a million dollars for the video so it wouldn't ruin our lives and that Sophie needed to somehow come up with a million, too. I did not want to do that, but I'll tell you why I did in a minute."

I refilled our glasses. I couldn't tell if I was getting drunk, but I sure hoped so.

"Sophie flat out refused to rip off your husband's business. She said that even if Sam put the video online, she wouldn't do it. I told her Sam wasn't beyond killing us. She said, 'I don't care. I'll die first.'"

A chill passed through me, and I shuddered. For God's sake, get to it, Gerard. I couldn't stop shaking.

"Sam was no dummy. He'd recognized my feelings for Sophie. So, he double-crossed me. He secretly told Sophie he'd kill you and me if she didn't get the money. He told her to keep her mouth shut, not to say anything. Then he told me he'd kill Sophie if I didn't disappear for a month. 'I'll make your girlfriend disappear permanently if you don't.' So, I told her I had to go away on a job for a month, but she did need to get a million to him, or he'd never leave us alone. And that was true."

This all sounded credible, but damn! Everyone had been played. Gerard was a tool. "Why didn't you nab him on extortion then?"

"Because I couldn't make it stick until Sophie sent the money to Sam. Instead, she put it in a Maryland bank under a fake company name and, as I recall, made you co-CEO so you could access the account." He ran a hand through his hair. "Anyway, Sophie didn't have the password to your husband's online accounts. She *had* to seduce him to get the passcode."

"Sophie told me she was helping Hank with his computer. It was sluggish. She had the passcode to get access."

Gerard shook his head. "No, Ang. She needed the passcode to his *business* accounts."

Exasperated, I said, "I still can't see her sleeping with him to get that. She could have asked him for it, and Hank would have given it to her."

He shrugged. "We'll never know, will we?" He paused and stared down at his hands. "I thought once she stole Hank's money and gave it to Sam, we'd be free. Sam was smart. He never went back to the same source."

"But she didn't give it to Sam."

"Exactly."

"Why didn't you intervene?"

"She didn't tell me about that. She was waiting for the month to pass. She kept putting Sam off about the money, saying it got held up. Three weeks in, I was in L.A. when Sam told her I'd only pretended to love her, that it was all part of the setup, that I was gone and never coming back. But I'd *warned* her about Sam, told her not to believe anything he said. I'd even given her a burner to call me in case something went south. But she stopped answering my calls." He heaved a sigh. "That was my mistake. Underestimating Sam. He could be pretty damn charming."

I leaned forward. My voice turned tremulous as I spoke. "Sophie wrote me a letter. I got it a month after she died." I cleared my throat. "She was heartbroken. She thought you'd betrayed her. And I'm sure she was wracked with guilt about betraying Hank and me. That's why I think she hanged herself."

"No. It wasn't that."

We locked eyes. "Then what was it?"

"She was pregnant."

"I *know!*"

"By Hank."

I jumped up. "What?"

"It was Hank's baby."

Why was he doing this to me?

"You are such a piece of shit, Gerard. Why lie to me like this?"

"I'm sorry, Angeline. It wasn't me. I had a vasectomy over twenty years ago."

I wanted to throw up. I wanted to kill him. I whispered, "Why are you being so cruel?"

He walked over to me but was smart enough not to touch me. My mind raced.

I backed away. "No! If my sister had been pregnant by Hank, she would have definitely confessed. She knew I'd give her the choice of keeping the baby or letting us have the child."

"Ang, she didn't know about the vasectomy. She thought I was the father."

I closed my eyes and covered my mouth with my hand, the hand I wanted to hit him with. He had no reason to tell me this—unless he wanted to weaken me for some reason. The one-two punch. Throw something at me that would throw me off balance. But to what purpose?

"If you're telling me this to make me weak, to distract me, to not answer my questions, I *will* kill you, hear me?"

He gave a slight shake of the head. "You asked me to tell you everything, and that's what I'm doing. I want you to trust me. Sophie ended up hating me." He cleared his throat. "Just like you do."

I didn't care what he thought. My sister had been carrying Hank's child. *Oh, Sophie, you stupid, stupid woman.*

Gerard was still talking, but I was too shocked to listen. When I finally focused, he seemed to be on a rant.

"... dealing with evil people here, not just extortionists. They have several law enforcement under their control. I haven't been able to do anything without them knowing about it and passing it on to Shawn. Then Shawn tells the guy I'm after who is, unfortunately, extremely intelligent and has no conscience."

I bit my lip and tuned him out. Did I want to hear the rest—if there was anymore? After hearing this, how *could* I trust Gerard to get Bibi back for me safely? But even if Bibi could be brought to safety, she wouldn't stay safe. She knew too much.

I walked over to Gerard and slapped his face. "I hate you. You, you ... stupid son-of-a-bitch ... you—" I pounded on his chest.

He grabbed my wrists. "I'm sorry, Angeline," he whispered. "I'm so sorry." Tears filled his eyes.

"I still hate you."

"That's OK."

"No, it's not. None of this is OK."

He pulled me toward him, his hands on the small of my back.

"No, you're right. None of this is OK. We've lost too much. It has to end."

"Yes, it does."

I knew what was coming. Two lonely, sad, and frustrated people, victims of loss, ensnared in an FBI mission and entanglements of the personal kind that seemed to get worse. It wasn't love. It wasn't even making love. But I needed to be held. How much I longed for it.

We kissed tentatively at first, and just the human touch made me want to cry. He kissed my neck, my temple, and whispered, "OK?" I nodded.

No romantic words, no endearments. Gerard was right. It didn't matter how we felt about each other. We were two humans in the here and now who needed each other at this moment. I took his hand and led him to the bedroom. Before Hank, I'd had one-night stands purely for sex. But this was going to be loaded with darkly woven, confused feelings and history. I didn't care. For now, at least. I wanted a body, someone who had their own screwed-up reasons for wanting sex.

We undressed each other. All my anger and hate—gone.

None of it mattered. I wanted him. I needed him. I wanted to lose myself in sex and be someplace else for a moment in time. After our clothes were off, he held me. Just held me. For a short, painful moment. Two vulnerable people, holding on.

I laid back on the bed, and he straddled me. He was muscular, his chest waxed, and he had a coppery, meaty, earthy scent. We ran our hands over each other. Drunk and unnerved, I shivered when his fingers trailed over my breasts, nipples, and belly. When he cupped his hand between my legs, I shuddered and closed my eyes.

We kissed. The kisses grew longer and sometimes made us so breathless that we were forced to break away. Our lips and tongues searched for something that words couldn't say. I ran my hands through his hair, down his neck, over his shoulders, and spine to his ass that tightened as I squeezed it.

"I hate you," I whispered in his ear and felt him harden against my belly. We kissed more, and I arched upward as I sunk my nails into his forearms.

When he pulled back, his lips looked bruised. His eyes glistened. He had that fierce, wild look men have when they want nothing but a woman's body. He held my face between his hands as he finally entered me, forcing me to look at him, so I wrapped my arms and legs around his body as if I could squeeze the life out of him.

23

After he fell back on the bed, we lay there staring at the ceiling. As my body began to cool, I shivered. For once, we had nothing to say.

Finally, I broke the silence. "I need a cigarette."

It was so cliché, we both laughed.

I threw on a hotel robe and found the cigarette Prosper gave me. Gerard pulled on his jeans and set up the coffee maker.

Outside, the lights of Hollywood burned in the distance. The palms outside my window swayed to the salsa music coming from downtown. I pulled back my hair and lit the cigarette on the kitchenette stove, grabbed my mug of steaming coffee, and sat on the balcony, sharing my smoke with Gerard. I felt relaxed and empty, something I hadn't felt in a long time.

But I still hated him.

The smoke curled up from the remains of the cigarette, and after I stubbed it out on the concrete balcony, I called down to Olivia's for something from their mozzarella bar and flatbread menu.

In the bedroom, on opposite sides of the bed, we dressed. That's when the doubts crept in. Could sex be part of his role as an undercover agent? Had it been real or something that was part of his strategy? As part of my strategy, I'd gone into it, and he told me what I wanted to know. But what about him? What had he wanted out of it? What was his game?

Room service knocked. The food arrived, and Gerard went to answer the door, but I stopped him. When I opened the door, I said hello to the cop stationed outside. News of Gerard being in my apartment was sure to get back to Prosper.

"Can I pay for the food? I have an expense account," he told me.

Now there was an awkwardness between us. I said, "Maybe I could charge you for the sex, and you could write that off."

I waited for him to laugh. When he didn't, I blurted out, "Oh, my god. You've done that before, haven't you? You've written off the cost of a prostitute!"

He half grinned. "I can't talk about my cases."

"Oh, come on. Seriously?" I laughed. It didn't surprise me. Undercover agents had to do drugs to be believable when working with drug dealers. I shrugged. But all of that didn't matter. I remembered one issue we hadn't talked about—Prosper.

We ate while standing at the kitchenette counter.

"Why did you tell me not to talk to Prosper before I talked with you?"

"Prosper has a mole. He doesn't know it, but someone is passing particulars onto Shawn. I don't have a name yet, but I will."

"That's another reason for you and Prosper to sit down and talk."

Gerard said nothing. He bit into a cracker, crunched loudly, and stared into space. I was not going to keep at him. He would or he wouldn't. I'd made my point. As I watched him chew, mouth closed, I couldn't help but notice how much better he looked than the last time I saw him in New Hampshire. I had to ask.

"Hey, why'd you look so bad when I saw you at the airport in Manchester."

He poured himself a glass of water and washed down the cracker he'd been eating.

"Insomnia. I'd never had it until after Sophie died."

I nibbled at a piece of flatbread and licked butter off my bottom lip. I hesitated before asking, "Are you sure it's not the drugs you're taking?"

He stopped eating and leaned against the counter, rubbing the back of his neck, looking down at the floor. "I've been hesitant to tell you about the rest of what I know because it's going to hurt, and I've hurt you enough."

I put down the flatbread I was about to eat. "Hurt?"

He searched my eyes. "You said you want to know everything. There's more. Are you sure you want to hear this?"

"How much worse can it be than finding out my sister was pregnant with my husband's child—then committed suicide?"

The look he gave me sent a chill down my spine.

After wiping his hands on a napkin, Gerard said, "Let's go sit down at the table."

We took our mugs of coffee to the table. Outside, sirens wailed, one after the other. The noise magnified. I couldn't hear myself think. Horns honked, people yelled, loud music streamed from cars on the traffic circle. I jumped up and closed the balcony door, my heart banging in my chest. When I sat down again, I stared over at Gerard, gritted my teeth, and wrapped my cold hands around the steaming coffee mug.

He spoke softly. "I was in L.A. when I received a text from Sophie. She needed to see me asap. She was in danger. She'd received threatening notes on her door. I took a direct flight to Eugene and messaged her. She texted back, 'Hurry.' I rented a car and drove to her place. As you know, I'd been there before."

I could picture her duplex, a well-kept gray house that had been divided in two as rentals. Her half of the split front porch was strung with windchimes and had a high back white wicker chair with a floral cushion. She'd never saved enough to buy a home.

When I looked up at Gerard, he seemed locked in another time and place. I gently prodded him. "Then what happened?"

He was looking at me but looking beyond me. I turned cold.

"I knocked on the front and back door. She didn't answer. The back door was unlocked."

A numbness filled my body.

"I walked through the kitchen, calling her name." He cleared his throat. "I found her. Hanging in the living room." He drew his arms in tight to his sides. Tears pooled in his eyes. "She wore a blue dress. Pinned to the dress was a note." He pulled out his wallet and handed me a crumpled piece of paper that had been smoothed and folded. The note read:

"This is what happens when you fuck
with me, GD. You're just a grunt. Stop
hunting me."

MY HAND SHOOK as I handed it back. Gerard returned it to his wallet, rubbed his forehead, and ground his palms against his eyelids. "Sophie didn't send those texts saying she was in danger. They were sent to lure me to her place. I'm sure the guy I'm after did this. I'm sure he knows I'm FBI and undercover. He might be rogue, but he still has connections. Plus, the note was too personal, as if I knew who he was." He finally focused on me. "Angeline, Sophie didn't commit suicide. She was killed."

I pressed a hand over my mouth so I wouldn't cry out and alert the cop outside. Shaking, I forced back tears. When Gerard reached for my hand, I gave it to him.

This rogue agent had signed his death warrant no matter what it took.

24

H e pulled me to my feet and held me until my teeth stopped chattering. Then he blew on my cold hands to warm them. I was confused. None of this made sense.

After I pulled away, I walked in small circles, holding myself as if I could keep myself from falling apart.

I stopped. "Wait. That can't be right. Sophie left me a letter." I rubbed my temples, trying to remember what she wrote. "She said something like she'd miss me until we met in the afterlife. She *was* taking her own life. She *did* take her own life."

We locked eyes. Gerard looked as confused as I was. Then he said, "Maybe she did plan to do that." He paused. "Ang, maybe he went there to kill her. Maybe he was too late but decided to use it to scare me, not knowing she'd left a suicide letter. That makes the most sense."

We were talking about my sister's death, but I was numb. We might as well be playing Sudoku with Gerard and me discussing strategy.

"That has to be it," I said. "There were no signs of a

struggle, plus she wore that blue dress and made up her face. I doubt very much if he went there to kill her that she'd be dressed up that way."

Gerard sat down again. "Why didn't I take notice of all that? There was nothing out of place except the chair kicked over. You're right, Ang. He didn't kill her. He just took credit for it." His shoulders slumped, and his cheeks were sunken. "I was just too upset to notice."

Relieved, I sat next to Gerard. Sophie had beaten that rogue asshole to the punch. As horrible as suicide was, she hadn't had to endure being killed by someone who was ruthless and had no conscience.

"Why didn't the police follow up on the note?"

Gerard glanced over at me. "Because I took it. I couldn't have the police involved." He rubbed the back of his neck, stood, and walked over to the window to look down on the city. I joined him. In the distance, one neon light flickered, trying to stay on but failing.

"Why would the guy lure you to Sophie like that?" I thought I knew why, but I wanted to hear him tell me.

"He wanted to show me how powerful he was. He wanted Sophie out of the way. He wanted me to break. Maybe he wanted to turn me, force me to go rogue too. I don't know. He probably wanted to scare me, show me what happened to people who crossed him. Thank God that she … that he didn't kill her."

He still couldn't say the words.

"So does this guy run the mob? How can that be possible if no one knows who he is?"

"He was FBI and trained well. Nowadays, it's easy to run an enterprise from a phone and computer out of sight from the foot soldiers. He could meet with Shawn alone and in a safe place."

Gerard's usual ruddy coloring had turned to a milky pallor. We were a real pair. I bet he hadn't talked with anyone about this because talking about it made it all too real. I knew how that felt.

I stumbled through more questions. "Why can't the FBI identify him? Can't they determine who he is by his former handler? Why is this so difficult? He's an FBI agent."

Gerard snorted. "To keep a lid on his identity, he was handled by only one person, and no one knew who the handler was. There were other stop-gap measures to make sure his identity remained a secret."

"Shit! That's stupid. It's like giving an agent a free pass to do whatever."

"I'm sorry, Angeline. This is..." He couldn't finish.

My chest hurt from holding back tears. The reality that Sophie could have been brutally murdered, maybe even tortured, doubled me over. I felt as if I'd eaten ground glass. I poured my coffee down the sink.

While I waited for Gerard to have his moment, I straightened, and all my muscles tensed. This guy knew about me and my association with Gerard. I was in more danger than before, even more than Bibi. At least she was an operative, an asset. I was disposable.

I went over to Gerard and looked down at him. "Gerard?"

He looked up.

"I'm in bigger trouble than I thought."

He shook his head. "No more than you were before. I'm sure all along that your movements have been reported to Shawn."

I shuddered. "Why?"

"Because you're Bibi's sister, and she's a wealthy woman. They also have a grudge against you. You were difficult.

Right from the beginning, you wouldn't hand over the money Sophie stole. Then you went into hiding. They had to hunt for you. Then they had to send people to threaten you to get the money."

"They want Bibi for her wealth?"

"Of course. That and they want her computer skills."

"I thought they wanted her so they could find out where she hid the incriminating evidence."

"True. That too. They're multitasking."

I think he was trying to lighten the mood, but it didn't work.

"Clarify this for me," I said. "You're still undercover?"

"Not on this case exactly. I disappeared right after Sam was killed. He was the one I was working for and using for intel. Shawn didn't know me. She may have been told about me, but she doesn't know who I am."

"So, your whole purpose is to flush out this rogue agent."

"Along with keeping Bibi safe and protecting you."

"Protecting me?" I turned away, laughed, and went to the kitchenette for water. "Oh, Gerard. You have a lousy record for protecting people."

"You're still alive, aren't you?"

"Did you take care of Sam? No. Did you take care of Betty? No. You seem to show up right after I've saved myself."

"You don't know everything." He joined me in the kitchen.

I crossed my arms and watched his face closely. "Gerard, you only tell me things when I'm squeezing your balls."

"I can't tell you everything, Ang. You know that."

"Obviously. But your idea to put Bibi undercover with no training, no resources but you, nothing, is total bullshit. You do know that don't you? It's such a desperate move. I still think you have only one true goal—to take down the rogue agent. So how do you expect to get my sister out alive? What is your plan?"

I was shaking again, this time from anger. He had no plan. He was flying by the seat of his pants. With my sister! Was he going to get her killed too?

"There's a plan in place," he said in a calm, soothing voice. He paused. "That's why I don't want the police involved."

I threw up my hands. "Oh, for heaven's sake. It's police jurisdiction." I was tired to the bones. My pelvis throbbed from the sex, the food had turned into an acidic lump in my stomach, and I was beyond pissed. I was fed up.

Gerard looked rung out, haggard, exhausted. The drugs must have worn off. But he surprised me by taking me in his arms. He smelled of hotel soap. "Look, I have to go. I'll be up all night, and there are a few things I need to do."

I yanked myself from his arms, done with his evasiveness. It was 2:55 in the morning. I needed at least a few hours of sleep.

"What happens next? What is your big *plan*? Your *strategy*?" I asked. "Lawyers need to have a strategy, a pretty damn good one to save a client from prison. I'd expect one from you to save a *life.*"

He glared at me.

"Hit a nerve, did I?"

"Ang, you need to talk to that detective to see what he knows."

"Fuck you, Gerard. I'm not your go-between. You need to tell me where Bibi is. You owe me a sister."

"Leave it alone, Ang," he said, his voice harsh and demanding. Now he was back to being Gerard the Prick.

I snorted, a good derisive snort. Then reality hit. I got in his face. "You don't have a plan, do you? You're just hoping that Bibi somehow stumbles across your rogue agent's identity. You don't care!"

He pushed me against the cupboards. "I do care! I wouldn't be here if I didn't care. The rogue agent is my fucking *mission*, Ang. And Bibi is a lot tougher than you give her credit for. She's good. She knows what she's doing. *And* she went into this on her accord."

"Let go of me."

He did.

I walked to the door. Then I remembered something Gerard had told me. Reluctantly, I reminded him. "In the note pinned to Sophie's dress, the person used the word *grunt.* Only military people use that word. Unless, of course, it's become some crime syndicate or FBI vernacular."

Before opening the door, I decided to give it one last try. "Talk to Prosper, Gerard. There's strength in numbers."

"Maybe there is on the battlefield."

"This is a battlefield."

He sighed and shook his head. "I can't, Ang. He has a rotten cop or two working inside." He reached for the doorknob. "Plus, I can't rule out Prosper either."

"Then test it out. Meet with Prosper and give him some false information and see if it gets back to Shawn. Put Bibi on alert to it, and she can tell you if it got to Shawn or not."

"You've been watching too much SVU," he said.

"Hilarious, Gerard."

He took his hand off the doorknob. "Look, Ang, it doesn't mean it's Prosper. He has a team he works with, and he could tell them. There's no way to tell who the mole is— if there is one. That's why I don't want the cops getting anywhere near the place. I need Bibi to stay there until she's completed the mission."

Now I was pissed. "Completed the mission? No way, Gerard. You need to tell Prosper that the FBI knows there's a mole in his department. He's not your mole. I would bet my dog's life on it. You two need to share what you know so you don't get Bibi killed."

Gerard didn't say anything. When he left, I made a point of saying hi to the cop outside my door. That would get back to Prosper for sure. The FBI guy was there until 3:00 shagging the woman in Room 420.

I closed the door and dropped the phony smile. Fuming about Gerard again, I went to check my cell. Three calls from Prosper. I listened to his voicemail.

"We found Bibi. Call me."

25

P rosper and his team hadn't exactly found Bibi. They'd found a house that had recently been bought by a Boston business that had no public profile. The place seemed to be the perfect hideout with a high hedge, six bedrooms, a security system, a fenced and gated backyard, and plenty of parking. As he described it, I thought of the Corleone family home. Hank had loved the *Godfather* movies.

Prosper sounded edgy as he relayed all this.

"The rest of the houses around that area have been lived in for a while, so this is our best bet."

"But you've never actually seen anyone suspicious there?"

"She's there," he said coldly.

Obviously, Prosper knew Gerard had stayed at my place for hours. It didn't matter. I was overloaded and numb from all the info Gerard had laid on me. I rubbed an arm as I tried to think. Something could go wrong so quickly.

"OK," I sighed. "What can I do?"

"Tell me what your FBI agent told you."

"The cop stationed outside my door called you, right? And that was all for my protection?"

"Porter, I can't do my job if the FBI undermines my actions. If you have a personal relationship with him, you need to tell me now. I've been honest with you about—"

"I'm tired of playing the go-between. You two figure it out. Here's his number, Detective."

I waited while Prosper wrote it down. I needed a break from them both.

"I want my sister back, safe and in one piece." My voice was firm but shaky. "Good night, detective." I hung up.

A minute after I hung up, I felt terrible. Prosper was an OK guy, but I was tired, wrung out, and sore. Sore at being in the middle. Sore at not being able to get Bibi's whereabouts from Gerard.

Had I been stupid having sex with him? I didn't think it mattered to the outcome of the case, freeing Bibi, or even to him. Was it simply sex? No.

I undressed, climbed into bed, and pulled the sheet up to my chin. I could still smell Gerard on my skin, taste him, hear him whisper in my ear.

I was exhausted but couldn't sleep. I'd often been like this with significant cases where I worked 24/7, drank a bathtub's worth of coffee, and caught an hour's sleep here and there, but it had been a long time since I'd done that. And I wasn't getting any younger.

I felt guilty too. Guilty for having sex with the man Sophie had loved. Jesus, was this ever going to end? This emotional flip-flopping?

I tossed and turned, hating having no power to move this case forward and get my sister out of the gang's clutches. I could thank Gerard for that, the bastard.

The bastard I'd fucked.

The bastard who'd gotten my Sophie killed.

Killed.

I turned onto my back and stared at the ceiling. If Sophie hadn't hanged herself, the rogue agent would have done something horrible to her. I was sure of that.

Now I understood what drove Gerard. Using Sophie's death to threaten him explained why Gerard was obsessed with finding the guy.

But screw Gerard. He'd lost a love interest. *I'd* lost my sister. Being constantly engaged in this criminal debacle kept me from any possible closure. If there was such a thing. Now I had to deal with the idea that Sophie's death would have happened no matter what. She'd died because she'd become ensnared with the mob and was a threat to the rogue agent. I rubbed my face until it was hot. What the hell do I do with all that?

Nothing. Not now. Sophie was gone. I couldn't bring her back. Revenge? I'd tried that, and it hadn't worked. Going after the gang? On my own? I didn't want to die yet. And I wasn't going to get any help from either Gerard or Prosper. I'd screwed one and pissed off the other.

I needed to concentrate. Sophie was dead. I needed to figure out what to do about the living one. Right now, the goal was to get Bibi to safety.

I sat up and called Gerard. Surprisingly, he answered. His voice was husky, and he said, "What's up?"

I slipped out of bed. "Prosper called me right after you left. His guard outside my room called him."

"No surprise." He paused. "Anything new?"

"I'm setting up a meeting tomorrow morning. The three of us." He didn't say anything. "Prosper has zeroed in on a house that may be the mob's headquarters." I gave him the description that Prosper had given me.

Gerard swore under his breath, using French words I'd never heard before.

"We need to meet so Bibi doesn't get killed."

"He can't raid the house now, not when we are so close to identifying our suspect." He blew out another exasperated French word. "Where and when?"

I gave him Chocolada's address. "Six o'clock. The sooner, the better."

"An uncivilized hour, but yes. Ang? What else did he say?"

"Nothing. He just wasn't happy about our ... relationship."

"He said that?"

This time I hung up without saying goodbye.

26

After shaking hands with Gerard, the first thing Prosper did was ask for his FBI badge. He looked it over, seeming to recognize it as authentic. After that, we sat down. The tension was as thick as the Cuban stuff they served as coffee. The waitress chitchatted with Prosper for a bit, and then he ordered a breakfast burrito and coffee. Gerard ordered just coffee. I ordered coffee and a piece of toast.

Prosper jumped in. "Agent Duvernet, Porter here thinks we need to coordinate our strategies to get her sister back safely."

Gerard glanced at me and raised an eyebrow.

Prosper continued. "My objective is to bring her sister home safely. What is your objective?"

Gerard poured cream into his coffee. I pictured last night, and it took all my effort to keep my face neutral, but I felt the blood seep into my cheeks. Gerard sipped his coffee and said, "I'm sure you understand that I can't tell you. As an FBI case, it would be of great help if you would let us take over."

Prosper kept his cool. "You do understand this is our jurisdiction. That you have to consult with us about your case if you want cooperation."

"This is an FBI case. If you intervene, this could ruin work that's been ongoing for a long time."

I stared at him. "Gerard, tell him, or I will."

Prosper put his arm out like he was holding me back in a speeding car. "No, that's fine. I get it. Can I ask a different question?"

"Please."

"Is your objective the same as mine?"

"No."

Prosper surprised me with, "Then we have nothing else to discuss."

"But we do, Detective. You see, this is not an abduction case. Bibi is there of her own free will to help me with the case." Gerard drummed his fingers on the table. "You no longer need to pursue this as an abduction."

Prosper seemed unfazed. "I only have *your* word for that, Agent Duvernet. Usually, the FBI contacts us right away when an incident occurs, and they have agents involved. No one contacted us. You didn't come forth. In fact, Porter here," and he nodded in my direction, "had to convince you to speak with me."

Gerard said nothing.

Prosper let that last bit sink in before he said, "Bibi Brackston may have left willingly, but she never came back. The evidence points to abduction as she left her dog, an animal she dearly loved, and has never been back to care for it. Plus, after she left, her dog was poisoned, her apartment ransacked, and things were stolen. Blood was found on the coffee table. It's not kidnapping because no one has demanded a ransom. It's a missing person's case."

"It's an FBI case." Gerard made it sound like that was the final word. Knowing Prosper, I knew it wasn't. And I was having trouble keeping my mouth shut. Does anyone care that it's my fucking sister?

The food came, and Prosper dove into his burrito, seemingly unfazed by Gerard.

Gerard leaned back. "Look, Bibi left willingly. We planned that. I told her that I would take care of the dog and put him with a reputable sitter. She knows nothing about her apartment because that happened after she left, and I didn't want to upset or alarm her."

Prosper said, "You told her you would care for the dog, but the dog was poisoned."

"As I said, that happened *after* we made the deal, and she'd already left. This is still an active FBI case. You know how this works."

"Yes, I've worked cooperatively with the FBI before."

This was such a pissing match, and I was sick of it. I said to Prosper, "He told me that it would put Bibi in danger if you went in to bust these people and free her. Gerard's objective is to find a rogue agent."

"Is this true, Agent Duvernet?"

"I can't confirm that."

Prosper looked back and forth from Gerard to me. When my eyes met Prosper's, I had to think like a lawyer again so I wouldn't go off half-cocked. "Poisoning the dog means something. It's not as clean as Agent Duvernet would like it to be. The head of this organized crime group lured her away, then sent a man back to the apartment to toss the place, looking for evidence that Bibi has that could be used to indict people in the organization. Both sides are using her. I'd like to know from each of you what your plan is to safely free my sister."

Prosper motioned to the waitress and asked for a to-go box. "Porter, I understand your concern, but first, I need to locate your sister, and it would help to have the FBI's assistance with that."

Gerard leaned toward him. "I will safely extract Bibi when the time is right. In the meantime, I would suggest holding off on raiding the house when you find out where it is. That would get Bibi killed."

I grit my teeth, trying hard not to say anything more.

Prosper paid the bill, stood, turned to me, and said, "Thank you, Porter. Now I know what I'm dealing with." He seemed genuine when he said it.

I stood and shook his hand, thankful that he also had been professional. "Please call me if you need anything."

After he left, I looked down at Gerard. "From now on, don't expect anything from me." I shoved in my chair. "We're done here."

As I walked away, nudging through the morning coffee crowd, anger gave me a momentum I hadn't had before. Anger at myself for having sex with him doubled down on the momentum. I now felt powerful enough to free Bibi.

And while I was at it, I'd find the rogue agent, too.

27

A s I hurried back to the hotel, I left a voicemail for Prosper to call me.

I didn't get it. What the hell was Gerard doing? It made no sense for him to piss off Prosper and me. The night before, at my hotel room, he seemed to want our assistance. Or maybe that was an act.

But I'd had an objective for having sex with him, so why wouldn't he have one? Nobody involved in this mess had pure intentions. I had to keep that in mind. So, it goes back to *What was Gerard up to?* It made no sense to torch a working relationship with Prosper. What motivated that, and why agree to a meeting?

I rubbed my tight jaw. I had to admit that Gerard's chilly geniality left me feeling betrayed. After this morning, if I found anything of importance, he'd be the last to know. There was also the matter of the flash drive. According to what Bibi said about its contents, Gerard determined there wasn't enough evidence to arrest any of the gang's members, never mind identify the rogue agent. Even a computer geek like Bibi couldn't possibly determine that. If I were Gerard, I'd want a forensic accountant to have a go at it.

Someone on a bicycle brushed my arm. I stopped and hugged my satchel to my chest. The bike did a wheelie, and I found myself face to face with the naked man I saw the first night I arrived, only this time he wore colorful bathing trunks.

"Didn't mean to scare ya. Just remember where it's at. That's all I gotta say." He had that stoned drawl. "Art. It's all about the artistic, man. That's where it's at."

I stopped. "What?"

He turned his bike toward the street, a pink flamingo bobblehead bobbing on the handlebars. He waved and peddled away, the cannabis aroma floating in his wake.

Coming from Oregon, I was no stranger to the likes of Bicycle Man. "This is your brain on drugs." If Sophie were here, she'd remind me that some cultures revered people like Bicycle Man, even considered them shamans, soothsayers, or mystics, a human bridge between worlds.

I needed a break. Lightheaded, I needed to eat. I hadn't even eaten the toast I'd ordered at the cafe. If only I could go to the beach for a few hours. I hadn't been to a beach since Kauai, and this one was a short drive. I could sit on the sand, listen to the waves roll on, watch kids throw beachballs, and build sandcastles. I'd raise my face to the sun, dip my feet in the water, feel the ocean spray. Maybe I'd even buy ice cream from a passing vendor. Warm water, sun, and ice cream. So unlike Oregon beaches.

My cell rang. It was Prosper.

"I called the Miami FBI SAC."

SAC was the Special Agent in Charge.

"And?"

"I told him about your friend and gave him the badge number."

"You memorized it?"

"I have a photographic memory. Just wanted you to know I was checking him out and will get back to you soon."

"Fine with me. He screwed us both."

Oh, God, why'd I say that? Thankfully, Prosper didn't chuckle or snort.

"It bothered me," he said, "that he was able to go from state to state. Usually, FBI cases are passed on to agents in the field offices. Duvernet was not known in the Miami field office, and they were reluctant to give me information. Probably because I told them my source said he was undercover."

My source? OK, fine, but I should have remembered about jurisdiction between states. I was slipping. "I'll be interested in what SAC says."

"By the way, I'm sorry, but I had to pull my officer from outside your hotel room. I couldn't justify the expense anymore."

"I figured that would happen."

"Where are you?"

"Walking back to the hotel."

"Better hurry. There's a storm coming."

Storm? I'd been so much in my head that I hadn't noticed the sun had disappeared. Behind me, a black blanket hovered over the ocean, the wind blowing the city's detritus and palm fronds ahead of it. I ran to the hotel's entrance, covering my head with my hands, getting caught in the first spits of rain.

Inside, I pulled a sliver of something green from my hair. I waved to the desk clerk and walked down the hall, headed to the elevator, passing a bank of windows. Rain sluiced down like a waterfall, creating a closed curtain to the world outside. So much for my beach getaway.

On the eighth floor, I hurried down the hallway, looking behind me, my footsteps echoing in its emptiness. I dropped the room card key twice before getting inside, locking the door, and dumping my satchel on the counter. My heart pounded as thunder boomed and lightning zigzagged across the sky, lighting the city in sharp black and white. I could almost feel the electrical charge in my body.

Since I was a kid, I'd loved lightning storms when mom and I would pull up a chair at the window and drink lemonade while watching the sky. She would swaddle Sophie and hold her on her lap. Sophie would laugh and cry, trying to be brave as the thunder boomed. I sighed and wondered if Bibi liked lightning storms.

In the kitchenette, I picked up the half-finished bottle of scotch Gerard had brought last night—was that only last night?—and dropped it into the trash. I didn't give a fuck how expensive it was. Gerard was a piece of shit. Prosper would find out just how much of a shit Gerard was when SAC called him back.

With no cop outside my room, I felt like a target. I made sure the door was securely locked. Then I pulled my Glock from my bag, checked the magazine, the safety, and laid it on the table within reach. One of my cells vibrated through the satchel's leather. I pulled out my personal cell—a message from my lawyer and another from my financial advisor. Tempest's dog sitters left a cheery voicemail. Good. Someone was happy, and Tempest was safe.

Ian had also left a voicemail, calling to make sure I was doing all right and asking if I had any time to get together. He ended the call with, "I'm still scratching my head and saying out loud, 'I have a sister!'" I felt horrible that I wasn't as excited about having a brother. It seemed that these new siblings had me enmeshed in their worlds and look where that got me—scared for Bibi and trying to keep her from getting killed. Plus, I had to avoid Ian because I didn't have the juice to give him.

As I wasn't going anywhere until the storm passed, I raided the mini-fridge for bottled water. My only experience with Florida's tropical storms was when Hank and I had gone to the Keys for our fifth wedding anniversary. We chose an old-fashioned beachside hotel on Islamorada, something that harkened back to the 50s—quaint, peaceful, perfect. Until a cocaine-fueled movie crew took over. Gone were the romantic nights we planned, the sleeping in, cocktails, and reading on the beach. We left early then ran into one of those wicked storms that beat against your car so hard you can't hear each other talk, gives about ten feet of visibility, and causes you to crawl along, afraid of a multi-car wreck.

A hardball of grief lodged in my chest. I missed Hank.

Prosper seemed to be a lot like Hank. Level-headed. Patient. Guileless. That's when I decided to wait on Prosper's intel from the FBI before I made my plans to find and save my sister. I sensed I could trust him.

For now, I needed a diversion. Ian's call reminded me that I had a father. I sat at the table and opened my laptop. I knew my biological father's first name from his love letters to Mom. I Googled "Dr. Michael McKnight, Naples, Florida," and he was listed, but I had to pay to get his address and phone number. After adding that to my contacts, I checked Boston, Massachusetts, but nothing.

If Snoop, my hacker, were still in action, she would have found him instantly. My chest filled, and I pressed palms against my eyes. Someone else I possibly could have lost. I had no idea what had happened to her or him or they. Hopefully, she was still alive, but I feared she'd been arrested and jailed, and if that were true, I had no doubt Gerard had a hand in it. Tick another box in the jerk column, not that I was keeping track.

"Fuck," I growled, jumping to my feet. I turned to the Marilyn Monroe-Warhol painting reproduction on the wall. "Hey, Sis, can you help me out here? Can you send a big Florida-pink arrow, so I'll know where to go, what to do? She's your twin. Can't you somehow tune in to her and send me her coordinates?"

Sophie via Marilyn smiled back at me.

I shook my head. So much for my sanity. Bicycle Man had nothing on me.

I paced again, feeling claustrophobic, cut off from the world. No matter what I did, Bibi might die. I couldn't give up. I kept thinking about that damn flash drive. Who said it was unimportant? Gerard had never seen the files on it. He only had Bibi's description of its contents. His lack of curiosity and concern was a red flag.

Something was wrong. Why wouldn't he want to have at least a forensic accountant take a stab at it? Sloppy work or a deliberate choice?

Of course, I only had Gerard's word about any of it. Now I wondered if I'd made a big mistake. Was Gerard legit? His Lone Ranger approach wasn't the way the FBI usually handled this. But that wasn't true. I didn't know everything about how the FBI worked. If he were still undercover, he would act on his own or at least appear to act on his own. And he wasn't doing anything for Bibi's sake. It was all about the rogue agent. So why the obsession? Was it only because of Sophie, or was something else at the heart of it?

I finished the bottled water then made a cup of coffee.

Now what? It was only eight in the morning. I couldn't call back to talk to the dog sitters because it was five o'clock in Oregon. I couldn't check on Otto because the veterinary hospital didn't open until nine. I poured extra cream into the coffee to save what was left of my ravaged stomach and continued pacing, trapped by time and the actions of others. At least I was getting some exercise, even if it was only taking laps around my hotel room.

I stopped in front of the Warhol, remembering what Bicycle Man said. "Art. It's all about Art, man. That's where it's at." Goosebumps covered my arms.

Click. The thieves had stolen everything of value. They had taken down Bibi's framed computer art, pulled it from the frames, looking for something hidden, and finding nothing, left the digital prints. And I had the odd one out. My gut said an important one. I went to my closet where I'd hidden it in the false bottom of my suitcase.

28

Outside was inky black, and the unrelenting rain slashed at the windows. Headlights smeared the blackness as cars drove past. Lounge chairs inched their way along the balcony, aided by the wind. The daytime sounds were muted, almost silenced, overcome by drumming rain and, at times, whistling wind. It might rain in Oregon, but never with this ferocity.

I flipped on all the lights and put the odd digital piece on the table where I studied it. Why frame this? Why even create this digital image? The man in the painting stood so formally that he looked like a mannequin except for the eyes, small piercing eyes that had been enhanced to look as if they were boring into you. Perhaps the gentleman had sentimental significance in some way to Bibi. I sat with it.

"Are you important? Who are you?"

I would think if it were important, Bibi would have left what? A clue to its meaning? But then again, if she were hiding something, why not in plain sight? My gut said that this was significant, and to find out what it meant, I needed to think more like her—if I could.

I checked the back of the piece and found nothing. How could digital art be used? I wished Sophie were here. She'd been a whiz at anything digital, web-based, had even created extremely complicated games. Then I remembered something Sophie had taught me, something relatively simple.

I Googled "How to Reverse Image Search on iPhone" and followed the directions. When it said, "take a photo of the image," I did and then scrolled to find the search results.

It seemed to take a long time. I drummed my fingers on the table. Then it happened. The algorithms matched the digital art to a photo. I gawked. No way. The results read "Otto P. Snowden." I Googled the name.

Otto P. Snowden (1914-1995) was an influential 20th-century leader in Boston's African American community. Otto and his wife founded Freedom House in Roxbury, Massachusetts.

BIBI NAMED OTTO the Dog after this activist. But what did that have to do with this case? With Shawn? With anything other than she admired this man?

"Oh, my God, Bibi, you're brilliant! Why didn't I think of that?"

I held up the digital print and examined it. I laughed. Bibi's last text to me had said, referring to Otto, *He's a good boy and needs his ugly striped afghan. He also knows a lot.*

"He also knows a lot," I said out loud, almost too loud, and I slapped a hand over my mouth. I should not be so excited. But I was. Then it occurred to me: it might be noth-

ing. It could be another ruse. Unimportant. Waste of time.
Like the flash drive.

According to Gerard, the info on the flash drive would
not indict Shawn and her crew. What was I dealing with? A
couple of McGuffins?

No. My gut said this Snowden piece held the incriminating evidence or the path to it. Just like those QR codes
that send you to websites, I figured something was
embedded in this print. Now all I had to do was figure out
how to decipher it and what it would lead to. I brushed
goosebumps from my arms.

I took a quick photo of Otto Snowden then put it back in
the false compartment of my suitcase while I weighed the
pros and cons of whom to give it to. Before I'd made up my
mind, my cell rang.

Back at the table, I dug it out of my satchel and
answered.

"Hello, this is Doctor Clemente at the Hollywood Veterinary Hospital. Is this Bibi?"

My hand went to my throat. I couldn't tell from her voice
if it was good or bad news.

I told her who I was and reminded her of my situation.

"Have they found your sister yet?"

"No. Is Otto all right?"

"That's what I'm calling about."

I held my breath.

"I'm happy to say that Otto is much better and can go
home now. He has no lasting effects from the poison but will
have to be fed a special diet for a while."

I sighed with relief. "Oh, thank God." I almost cried, but
now I had another problem on my hands. What to do with
Otto? "Right now, I can't have him with me. I'm in a hotel,
and my sister is still missing. Do you have any suggestions?"

"I'm so sorry to hear about your sister." She paused. "We can keep him one more day, but I'm afraid after that you'll have to make arrangements for him." She covered the phone and said something to another person. To me, she said, "This might be too early to suggest this, but one of our volunteers here said she'd love to adopt Otto."

The heat swept up my neck and face. I snapped, "Yes, it *is* too early to suggest that."

She apologized, then I apologized for snapping at her. "It's been a hard day. I'm sorry, but would you please keep him another day?"

She agreed to that. "Maybe the person who offered to adopt Otto would agree to care for him until they find your sister."

I sat down at the table, head in hand. "I'll call you tomorrow. Is that all right?"

After we hung up, I doubled over. I wondered if I was getting an ulcer. It felt like little piranhas eating away my stomach lining. But then I remembered I hadn't eaten since … I couldn't remember when.

I called the front desk and asked if there was a good place to order lunch nearby that delivered. She asked if I liked Peruvian food, gave me the number for J28 Sandwich Bar, and suggested I try either the pan con chicharron sandwich or quinoa bowl. I knew what quinoa was but had no idea about the sandwich. I didn't care. I just needed something to eat. I called, ordered both, asked them to deliver to the hotel, and paid over the phone. After dumping the coffee down the sink, I found a can of ginger ale that I poured into a glass and sipped, the bubbles going up my nose. I tore open a packet of crackers and ate those, washing them down with the ginger ale. For a moment, I thought of my mother, *our* mother, and how she fed us soda crackers and ginger ale when we were sick. Did Bibi have that growing up?

After my insides calmed down, I was changing my clothes for no reason when my phone rang.

Prosper wasted no time. "I know why your pal Gerard—"

"*Please* stop. He's not my pal. Now, what about him?"

"Miami SAC called back. There's a good reason why he doesn't want to work with us—or anyone else. Duvernet is on official leave. He was told to take time off after the incident with your sister. He'd become obsessed with her death and this mob and the idea that there was a rogue agent involved."

My shoulders sagged at that news. "I suppose they didn't indicate if there was an actual rogue agent?"

"No. I was lucky to get that out of them. Tell him he needs to report in."

"I can't tell him to do anything. You should know that by now." I waited, my body feeling old. I rubbed my arms to get the blood pumping. "Are you and I OK?"

"You need to stay away from him and the case. Let us handle it. I'll be working with the Miami SAC from now on."

"What about my sister?"

"We'll do everything we can to get her out of there safely. In the meantime, as I said, stay away from Duvernet. The Feds will pick him up sooner or later if he doesn't report in."

One of the two burners in my satchel buzzed. "Look, I have to go. I'll keep in touch."

I swallowed hard. If it was Gerard, I wouldn't answer it. Now I wondered about his mental health. Could the rogue agent be someone he'd created to explain why he couldn't bring down the Boston mob? I sighed, reached into my satchel, and pulled out the one that vibrated, the one I'd used to call Bibi. My voice cracked as I answered. "Yes?"

"Ang, it's Bibi," she whispered. "I need to get out of here."

"Oh, shit, Bibi." I scrambled for a notepad and pen. "Give me the address."

She did. I heard something in the background. My heart raced. "What was that? Bibi?"

"I can't get away right now, but the next time I call or message you, I'll meet you at the corner of the block. It might…"

I didn't catch the last part. "What?"

"Wait," she whispered. She yelled away from the phone, "I'm in the bathroom! Fucking chill!"

"Bibi? I didn't get that last part."

Someone banged on her door again and yelled, "Get your ass out here."

She hung up.

Oh, Jesus. My fingers gave way, and the burner fell to the floor. I tried to scoop it up, but my fingers were like cooked noodles. Finally, after I had control of my hands, I picked it up and put it on the table, then rubbed my chest.

When my heartbeat slowed, I called Prosper.

29

No answer. I left no message. My first impulse was to jump in the car and rush to the address Bibi gave me. I'd wait nearby for whenever she called. But that was impulsive. The need to act was like a thick rubber band that had snapped my body. I rubbed my arms, my neck, then shook myself from head to toe, releasing all the pent-up emotional energy.

Think. Be rational.

I replayed the call in my mind. Bibi called me on a burner from the bathroom. Just how did she get a burner inside that place? Sure, Gerard gave her one, the same number I'd called. But Shawn would have tight security. So how then? I'd had my doubts about Shawn believing that Bibi wanted to join the mob. Maybe Shawn was smart and let her in even though she knew Bibi was a plant. That way, Shawn could keep an eye on her, neutralize her, feed her only what she wanted her to know.

No matter how Bibi got the phone, she wanted out now. Maybe she was done helping Gerard, or she'd found nothing to identify the rogue agent. Maybe Shawn was getting suspicious. Maybe the Russians had scared her or asked her to do something for them.

I pinched the bridge of my nose and groaned. I didn't know a damn thing about what Gerard was up to. He needed to tell me about his setup with Bibi and what he had for backup plans to get her out. Now that I knew he wasn't working for the FBI, I had no problem calling him to ask him questions. He wasn't working on a case. He was out for revenge. Nothing good could come of that.

Still, he wanted justice for my sister's death, and I admired that about him. He put his profession at risk just as I had. Maybe if he knew that I knew he was on leave and shouldn't be on this case, he would work with me to get Bibi out. Not that he'd be happy about it. Not that he'd even answer my calls. Maybe that's why he'd cut ties with both Prosper and me. He had to know that Prosper would call the Miami SAC to find out about him.

But what about Bibi? Did she know about Gerard? I hadn't been objective about her. She might know he was working on his own. What had he told her? He played the revenge card with her, giving her the motive to bring down Shawn: Shawn had killed Bibi's godmother.

I grabbed my notebook to slow down my thoughts and start another list.

- Who did Bibi interview with at the FBI in Boston? Not Gerard.
- Why didn't Gerard's status come out during her interview? Or did it?
- Maybe she's known all along Gerard was on his own.

- Gerard never gave me the interview transcript because he never had access to it.
- What did he tell Bibi about why he was acting alone?
- What if he was lying to both of us to get us to work with him?

THAT LAST ONE gut punched me. I needed a cigarette.

Of course, he could have lied to both of us. Or I should say *manipulated* us.

What if the rogue agent's note on Sophie was a lie? What if Gerard told me that to get me on board with finding the rogue agent? Had he manipulated me, or was he mentally unstable and there was no rogue agent?

I just couldn't believe Gerard was mentally unhinged. Maybe the FBI didn't want him out there talking about a rogue agent. Maybe there was one, but that wasn't Gerard's mission to catch that person or ID him or her.

What else? Maybe he lied to Bibi. Maybe he didn't tell Bibi that Shawn killed Betty. Maybe Gerard told her the rogue agent killed Betty, but he couldn't bring the mob to justice until he knew who he was. He needed someone inside to ID the guy.

But it made more sense emotionally that he'd have Bibi thinking Shawn killed Betty. I could see her going for that. But why not just kill Shawn? Why hang out with her and pretend they were pals? Because Bibi seemed sensible. If she played her cards right, she could get evidence to convict Shawn and bring down the entire gang.

Whatever the mission or strategy, Bibi was in danger.

And Gerard could be manipulating both of us. Unless we got to the truth, neither one of us was safe.

Outside, the storm raged on. I rubbed my temples and wished I were home walking Tempest and breathing cool, dry Northwest air.

I closed my eyes. What was I missing? As I let my tired brain rest a little, I listened to the rain washing the balcony clean, and a final question popped up: why had Bibi called me instead of Gerard?

I opened my eyes and rubbed the tiredness from my face. I paced. This was so screwed up. I wanted to call Prosper. I wanted to talk to someone who was involved who had a level head. But what if Gerard was right about a snitch in Prosper's department? My mind looped with questions but no answers.

I craved a cigarette and called the Olivia bar to see if they had any. Nada.

"Is there someone who can go to Publix for me and buy me a pack?"

The girl said, "Let me switch you to the front desk."

Someone knocked on my door. I disconnected. I'd call her back.

I lunged for my gun, my hand sweaty. Then I remembered my food delivery. At the door, I said, "Who is it?"

A young female voice said, "Food delivery from J28?"

After shoving the Glock in the closest drawer, I opened the door to a figure covered in rain gear and dripping on the carpet. The smell of food made my stomach rumble. I thanked her, gave her a large tip, and looked up and down the hall as she walked away.

With the door locked again and the gun back on the counter, I put the quinoa in the fridge, sat down at the table, and unwrapped the sandwich. As I ate, lightning lit up the room opalescent white, and thunder cracked so loud and nerve-wracking that it rumbled through the floor and up my legs, causing my heart to boom in my chest. I drew in air and exhaled a few times until I could breathe easily, and my nerves relaxed.

When my hands stopped shaking, I picked up my sandwich. It dripped and fell apart, so I ate it piecemeal, small pieces that I chewed slowly as my mouth was so dry that I found it difficult to swallow. After finishing most of the sandwich, I washed and dried my hands, drank a glass of water, then another, not having realized how thirsty I was.

After clearing the takeaway box and paper bag, I stretched and then checked my phones. Nothing.

Once the food hit, I felt better, and my brain began to work again. The nasty nerves and paranoid thoughts dissolved, and a possibility about Gerard became clear.

I had to face the possibility that Gerard was the rogue special agent.

With my notebook open to a new page, I picked up my pen and tapped the table.

Staring at the Marilyn picture, I forced my mind to look at Gerard from an evidence-based position. From the very beginning, he'd been deeply involved, working undercover in the crime outfit, luring rich people to rip off. That's when and how he met Sophie. After Sophie died, the mob came after me for her hidden money, and I fled to Kauai, where he showed up *after* I killed Betty in self-defense. When I went to New Hampshire to meet Bibi, he'd followed me there too. When Bibi texted from Florida to say she was in trouble, he was already there and told me not to come. Something else: not once had I seen him with another FBI agent, or one I could attest to. Of course, that was undoubtedly due to him being AWOL from the FBI. I didn't want to believe *he* was the rogue agent, but I needed to look at the possibility anew and objectively. I had to reimagine what our history meant if he were indeed the rogue agent.

Starting from the beginning, I wrote an alternative story-line for Gerard as Rogue Agent using the "what if" method.

- What if Gerard killed Sophie because she found out he was the rogue agent?
- What if Gus suspected Gerard of being rogue so Gerard had Betty kill him?
- What if Gerard didn't come to the Kauai cliffs to rescue me, but to see if I was dead? (Makes sense. He showed up at the cliffs *after* Betty tried to kill me. That's why he looked surprised when I walked into view.)
- What if Gerard told me not to come to Florida because he didn't want me screwing up any plans he had.
- What if me coming to Florida and teaming up with Prosper blew his cover? (Which it did.)

Even though this alternate Gerard was a major possibility, why would he be so stupid to pretend he was hunting the rogue agent?

Unless he used this as a diversionary tactic.

I chewed a cuticle and made it bleed. All of it could be true. But one of my beliefs trumped everything, and it wasn't even rational. Gerard loved my sister. I felt it in my gut, even my heart. Therefore, he couldn't be the rogue agent, could he? No.

I was scribbling on a page in the notebook when I

remembered Sophie's suicide letter. She'd written that Betty's partner in the mob had threatened to kill Gerard and me if Sophie didn't steal the money. Why would Sam, Betty's partner, threaten to kill Gerard if he worked for the gang? I breathed a little.

My cell buzzed. My financial advisor. I ignored it.

So, again, why did Bibi call me instead of Gerard?

Maybe I'm naive, but we're blood. Perhaps she just didn't want to be Gerard's spy anymore. Perhaps she'd found out something about Gerard.

I shoved my gun back in my bag and called Prosper. Screw the snitch in his department. It wasn't Prosper. I was sure of that. He answered this time.

"I can't tell you everything right now, but Bibi called and wants me to pick her up near to where she is. I have an address. She said she'd text me when she slips out. I'm going to need backup." I gave him the address and a description of my car. "She wants me to be on either corner of the block in my car so she can sneak out, and we can quickly get away. I'll call or message you when she gives me the go-ahead."

"Porter, keep your phone on record so we can have evidence if something goes wrong."

"That's encouraging."

"I don't mean it to be discouraging, just practical."

"Where should I take her?"

"Take her to headquarters. We'll find a safe house for her until the FBI round up the organization's members."

If Gerard was telling the truth, I wasn't taking her there. Maybe to another hotel under an alias. I grabbed my keys and bag. When I opened the door, Gerard stood there.

30

G erard pulled back the hood of his rain jacket. "Can we talk?"

He was a mess again—unshaven, unkempt, dark circles under his eyes as if he'd been up for days, which I bet he had.

I hoisted my bag to my shoulder and crossed my arms. Sweat built up at the back of my neck. With a long fake sigh, more to calm me than show irritation, I moved aside and motioned him in. His lack of sleep was catching up with him.

I leaned against the island counter and kept a hand on the outline of my gun in my satchel. "What do you want?"

"I need to explain why I acted the way I did this morning."

When I didn't say anything, he rubbed his nose then shoved his hands into his pockets. I noticed his jeans seemed a bit baggy, and he wore a belt to cinch them. He had to be doing drugs to keep going like this.

"Ang, at breakfast, I was ready to tell Prosper what we

were doing for this case, but something happened to stop me."

I'm sure he wanted me to ask what it was, but I wasn't playing this game. I kept my eyes on his face, waiting for his explanation or excuse. He tilted his head like he was surprised I was acting this way.

He said something in French I didn't understand.

"Damn it, Gerard. Spit it out."

"Just before breakfast Bibi sent me an image of Shawn meeting a man in a car outside the house they use as their southern headquarters. It looks like Detective Prosper."

"Oh, stop. That's enough." I spun around, went to the door, and opened it. "I want you to leave."

He didn't move.

I closed the door in case someone overheard us. "Come on, Gerard! As if Prosper was involved in that gang. Even if he were, he wouldn't go there and draw attention to himself like that. Give me a break. He's too smart for that. If he *were* the police snitch, he'd be using a burner and calling her, not driving up in daylight." I figured I'd better go along, pretend to listen, and then get him the hell out of here so I could be ready for Bibi's call. "When did this happen?"

"This morning before breakfast. He must have gone there before meeting us."

"If it *was* him. How did Bibi catch them, never mind photograph them? She's in a house where she's being watched. When she called me—"

Oh, no. I blew it.

"Called you? When did she call you?"

"I want you gone. Now. No more. That's it."

He walked up to me, so close I could smell his body, perspiration and something metallic. I stepped back.

"Angeline, this is important."

I shoved him away, but he gripped my right arm. I looked down at his hand around my arm and said, "Let go."

He did.

Bibi's voice came back to me, her urgency, the fear. I was the only one who had a pure reason to get her out of there.

He cleared his throat and, in a quiet voice, said, "Tell me why she called, Angeline. What did she want?"

I didn't answer.

"Angeline, please." His voice broke as if he were choking back tears. A vein in his neck throbbed. He was not in good shape. As if *he* were the one who had something to lose.

But I needed to hear what he had to say, so I said, "Not until you tell me the real reason why she's there and how she's helping you."

He rushed ahead with his explanation. "The mob has used their time here in Florida making connections with the Russians. Someone on my team is working for the mob and feeding them info about what we're doing, so they've stayed one step ahead of us."

His team? He didn't know I knew yet. "The rogue agent you've been talking about?"

He nodded and then coughed, a ragged rattling in his throat. "Shawn's smart. But I'm sure she's taking orders from someone higher up, and I think it's our man."

Irked, I said, "So you don't think a woman could run the mob?"

"I don't think she's running this one."

I let it go. The idea that Bibi could even take a photo of Shawn talking to someone outside in his car was ludicrous, not after what I heard when she called me. Someone was always watching her. Unless. ...

Could that call have been a setup?

"Gerard, you need to be honest with me. Could Bibi be part of the mob? A real member and only be pretending to help you?"

Then I thought, *No. She would have never left Otto this long. She knew nothing about him being poisoned.*

"No," he said. "She's not a member. She hates them."

I felt a clock ticking in my head and looked up at Gerard. "I don't believe Prosper is in on it. He might have someone who is, but my gut says he wasn't the one Bibi saw talking to Shawn."

He pulled out his cell. "Here's the photo she sent me."

"You have the photo?" I looked at it, enlarged it, and tried to make out details. "What's the baseball cap he's wearing?"

"A Maple Leafs hat. It's a hockey team."

"That's meaningless. Could be anyone."

Gerard said, "Except he's a Canadian from Toronto."

While I had the cell, I forwarded the photo to my phone. "Besides, why wear a hat that can implicate him? And he wasn't wearing that this morning. Someone is impersonating him, someone who knows he's from Canada. It could easily be the agent you're after."

"I thought of that, but I had the car license traced, and it belongs to the Hollywood precinct."

"Someone stole the plates."

"Possible," he admitted.

"Still doesn't confirm it's him."

"Then someone is good at screwing with us."

I laughed. "No shit, Gerard. It's an organized crime syndicate." Something else occurred to me. "Exactly how do you know this group is talking with the Russians?"

He looked at me as if I were stupid. "Bibi, of course. They've been to the house."

I was done. Gerard exhausted me. His interactions with me were patronizing, and none of this was helping. I wanted to be back in Oregon, living *my* life. It was time to get tough and not wait on anyone else.

"Tell me," he said. "Why did Bibi call you?"

"No, Gerard. You need to stand down. You're not even on this case anymore. You're on leave—supposedly."

He didn't flinch, move, or even blink. In a flat, unnatural voice, he said, "So Prosper called SAC."

"He wouldn't be doing his job if he didn't." I stepped up close to him. My eye twitched as I suppressed my anger. "And you should have never put my sister inside because you *have no authority*." I concentrated on letting this sink in. "You need to back off and let the police get her out."

"I can't do that."

"You're acting rogue, Gerard. You know that, don't you?" This was the voice I used with a defiant client. "Are you trying to kill another one of my sisters because if you keep going this way, that's what's going to happen?"

And as with defiant clients, he didn't like being told what to do, even if it was for his own good. "Your sister was already in danger. Someone found out what she knew and passed it on to Shawn or the guy I'm hunting."

That did it. "Hunting?" I said and snorted. "Gerard, listen to yourself. You're a mess." I opened the door again. "Get some sleep. Lay off the speed. And SAC said you better report in."

He looked down at me. "I'm only trying to do what's right, Angeline."

"You've put another one of my sisters in danger, Gerard. I can't forgive you for that."

There it was. We locked eyes. He went to say something but didn't. I stepped back.

He walked out and down the hall, past a housekeeping cart, toward the stairwell instead of the elevator. I felt terrified for him, but now even more so for Bibi.

31

At the bar downstairs, I fought an urge to run to Publix and buy cigarettes as I sipped tonic water with a slice of lime, needing to stay clear-headed as I waited for Bibi's text or call. If I'd had to stay in my hotel room one more minute, I'd be climbing the walls. In all the drama, I'd forgotten about Otto Snowden and the digital art piece. But I couldn't do anything about it right now. Whatever was on it would have to wait.

I pulled out my cell and enlarged Gerard's photo again. Was that really Prosper in the picture? Noting the head size and shape, I couldn't tell without more detail.

Then I pulled up Google maps and tapped in the address Bibi had given me. I looked at the street view to visualize the house so I'd recognize it when I drove by. The house had a circular driveway, but foliage almost wholly hid the entrance. If Prosper or whoever had impersonated him pulled up in front of the house, he'd be near the front door. There was also a path to the back. Bibi could have slipped out the side and taken that photo. I just hoped she didn't get caught. But how could they not know she had a burner? So much didn't add up.

I assumed she had a plan. As for getting out without someone noticing, she obviously thought she could escape to the corner of the block where I would pick her up. I planned to call Prosper right after she called me.

My mind kept going back to the Russians. If the Boston mob threw in with them, both of us were in grave danger, and I needed to get Bibi out ASAP. As I memorized the directions to their headquarters, the bartender glanced my way and asked if I needed something. I must have been repeating the directions aloud. I apologized. "No, just talking to myself."

As I glanced at the photo again, I zoomed in on the hat and then called Prosper again.

"What's up?"

"Do you own a Maple Leafs hat?"

"No. I'm not a hockey fan."

Boom! "Someone is impersonating you." I told him about the photo, then sent it to him.

"Not good," he said. "Have you heard from your sister?"

I explained how I'd taken the photo from Gerard's cell. He didn't say anything or ask any questions.

I said, "Any idea who it is?"

"No. But we knew plates had been stolen."

"One of your people?"

"Could be an outsider. Not hard to find out I was Canadian. And someone could have stolen the plate when the car was off the premises. The question is 'Why?' To throw shade on me, therefore keep people from working with me on this case?"

"Sounds about right. Gerard is insisting that you have a mole."

"Duvernet is going to get someone killed. Where are you?"

"The Olivia bar."

"You're not safe there. Get back to your room."

"I'm not safe in my room either."

"You're a hell of a lot safer there than the bar."

I smiled. Now that I knew it wasn't him in the photo, I felt a kinship with the guy. "You care," I teased.

He laughed. "Yeah, Porter. Plus, it doesn't do my reputation any good to have innocent bystanders get killed."

This was the kind of good-natured sniping I was used to with cops. I hung up and gathered my various phones while the bartender kept eyeing me. I smiled, left him a hefty tip, and put my forefinger to my lips. He slipped the twenty into his pocket and winked. It was always easy to get people to believe you were having an affair versus doing something ... well, dangerous.

As I turned, I bumped into Ian and was startled. "What the heck, Ian?"

"What's going on, Angeline?"

"Ian, please. I'm sorry, but not now."

"You told me your sister's missing, but it's more than that, isn't it?"

"Look, I don't have time. I need to go. Let's visit tomorrow, OK? Let me pass."

Instead of doing that, he pulled out his wallet and laid out every piece of his identification on the bar—license, med cards, insurance card, gym membership. Then he held up a photo of a couple. "These are my parents. Here's your dad."

That stopped me. I looked at the photo of the couple, then remembered to focus. I looked at the IDs.

"What more can I do to convince you that you can trust me?"

"Oh, maybe ten or twenty years of knowing each other." I pulled back my shoulders.

"Tell me what's going on, Angeline. I'm not losing a sister when I just found her."

I said nothing.

"You need my help," Ian said.

I covered my face with my hands to keep from screaming at him. Finally, with hands to my side and through clenched teeth, I said, "You don't know what I need. Frankly, you need to stay away from me. You have no idea how dangerous this is."

His eyes narrowed. "And you don't know what I am capable of. I bring my own skill set."

"Skillset?" I almost laughed.

His demeanor changed from a brotherly helpmate to something a little frightening. "It's no laughing matter, Angeline. I'm a 6th-degree black belt in Krav Maga."

I blurted out, "I have no idea what that is."

"Let's just say it's a martial art developed by the Israeli military."

I let that sink in for a minute.

OK, that was impressive. I had to respond. "So, your strategy is to kick their asses?"

My burner buzzed before he could answer. I dug it out, expecting Bibi.

I said to Ian, "You need to leave. Now."

He didn't budge.

I answered. "Bibi?"

It wasn't Bibi. It was Shawn.

32

I shoved Ian aside and hurried out of the bar. "What are you doing with Bibi, Shawn? Tell me."

"Calm down, Angeline. Bibi's fine. And she'll stay fine as long as you give me the flash drive you found on the dog's collar."

I stood in the hotel lobby, trying to move away from people, then headed for the ladies' room, where I shut myself in a stall. "In exchange for Bibi."

"Of course."

"And everything you stole from her apartment." I thought of all her artwork on the computer and external hard drive.

"We no longer have that."

My chest felt like a belt tightened around it. "OK, meet me across the street from the hotel in the park."

"No. Meet us outside that Peruvian restaurant that your FBI agent likes."

"What?"

"You know the one. The one where you met Agent Duvernet. What's the name of it? Runas?"

I choked back a string of curses. "How do you know that?"

"As if we haven't had eyes on you, Angeline?"

The thought of that made my jaws clench. For how long and what did they see?

Shawn chuckled. "Oh, come on, Angeline. It's not as if we didn't know why you came here. And it wasn't as if we weren't watching everyone who came and went from Bibi's apartment and your hotel room. You've had quite a time here, good and bad."

What a bitch. I lowered my voice to sound calm. "Shawn, is Bibi all right? Have you done anything to her?"

"No, of course not. We'd hoped she'd join us, but that's just not her style. Speaking of style, you should really take her shopping. She's so 90s."

"Well, Shawn, what style should she follow? Your coke-ravaged slut style or your latest cheap Kardashian style."

She chuckled again. "Very clever." She paused. I waited. Then I heard a groan in the background.

"Was that Bibi?"

"I'll call you when it's time to meet across the street from Runas. Just you. No one else."

"Have you hurt her?"

"And don't call your lover. It's a simple exchange. Flash drive for your sister's life."

She hung up. I let out a strangled groan. So much for the content on the flash drive meaning little to nothing.

I left the stall and leaned against one of the sinks, hugging myself. Then one of the toilets flushed, an older woman stepped out, glanced fearfully at me, and darted for the door.

After I slipped my cell into my bag, I splashed water on my face. Damn. I had no idea if I could trust Shawn, but at this point, if there were a chance I could get Bibi back, I'd do it. Who could I trust not to botch the whole thing when I'd already done a good enough job of it? My bad for underestimating organized crime. They'd known my comings and goings since the moment I bought a ticket to Hollywood, Florida. Of course they did. They still had me in their sights, had all along. How myopic had I been?

I'd call Prosper as soon as I put Bibi someplace safe. I'd do this on my own. I had to.

33

Taking the elevator to my hotel room, I was drenched with sweat, not from the Florida heat and humidity, but fear and mixed feelings. Could I carry this off?

Ian was nowhere to be seen, thank heavens. I couldn't deal with him right now, someone so eager and ready to fight. And a little pushy. Skillset or no skillset.

In my room, the AC was on full tilt, and in a minute, my beaded sweat evaporated and chilled me. I turned the temp from sixty-four to seventy, and the air conditioner kicked off. After changing my clothes again, I packed a few things in an overnight bag. I thought I'd take Bibi to another hotel. Maybe in a different city. If I took her to the cop shop, Shawn would think we ratted on her. If we proved we were getting out of town, they might leave us alone. But I couldn't count on that. The gang relentlessly went after anyone they deemed undesirable or a threat.

Sighing, I turned off all the lights except one in the kitchenette, grabbed my things, and opened the door, where

I was met with Gerard's raised fist, about to knock. I gasped and jumped back.

"Fuck, Gerard!"

"Sorry to scare you, Ang. Can we talk?"

I glanced up and down the hallway. With my heart in my throat, I grabbed his arm and yanked him inside. I dropped my satchel. My heart beat insanely fast. I folded over, hands on knees, and feeling dizzy.

He squatted down in front of me and calmly said, "Easy. Breathe slowly, deeply, from the diaphragm. That's it."

Finally, I stood up and rubbed my chest. "You almost gave me a heart attack."

When I looked up into his eyes, he gave me such a look of concern that I couldn't help but step back. I swayed. He reached out and led me to a chair. After I sat down, he poured a scotch and handed it to me.

"Pills for me, scotch for you," he said, as if this were funny. "Look, right now we have our crutches, OK? We can dump them after this is over."

I kept rubbing my chest. "Will this ever be over?"

"Yes, it will, Ang. Believe me. It will end."

I didn't like the way he said that. "Hopefully, it will end in our favor."

He smiled. "With liberty and justice for all."

This time I laughed. I couldn't help it. Sometimes I liked this guy.

He pulled a chair up in front of mine and sat down. Now what? What happens if Shawn calls while he's here?

"Ang, what can I do to make you believe that I only care about making you and Bibi safe?"

"Why should I believe you—about anything? You've admitted that your main objective is to take down the rogue agent. You've lied to me even when you didn't need to. I mean, 'Who are you?'"

He leaned forward. "Tell me what you want, Ang. What can I do to prove that I want what you want?"

"Bullshit, Gerard. Since when?" I snorted. "I want Bibi, and you want the rogue agent."

He ran his fingers through his hair, looked over my head, and heavily sighed. "Ang, neither of you will be safe until that criminal is behind bars or dead. You both know too much, you've spent too much time with me, and he will never rest until this situation is mopped up and his group is out of danger."

"Is 'mopped up' what I think it is?"

"Yes. He wants us dead."

I knocked back the scotch. "Well, that's *so* comforting."

"What can I do to make you trust me again?"

I thought about it as the scotch warmed its way through my body. Maybe there was something he could do for me, something important, that could put me ahead of the mob.

"How about giving me back Snoop, my hacker?"

"What makes you think I have her?"

"Well, I know you don't have her, but the FBI does. If you have any influence at all, I want her released."

He raised an eyebrow. "Seriously?"

"Yes." I thought about the number of times she'd given me info that saved my life. Who knew what she could do for me in my present situation?

He shook his head. "That's out of my hands."

"I doubt it. You might be on leave, but you still know people in high places. Where is she?"

"I can't tell you."

"Of course, you can. You're going to lose your job with the FBI anyway."

He flinched. After he thought about it for a second, he said, "Ang, I'd be calling in some of my last favors."

"Do you want me to trust you or not? It's Snoop or no dice."

My cell rang. Crap. Gerard looked at where the ringing came from.

"Do you need to answer that?"

I stood. "You need to leave. Now."

Surprisingly, he stood and walked to the door. I was dying to answer my cell but not while he was here.

He turned and said, "I'll see what I can do." As the door closed behind him, the phone stopped ringing. I stared at the door, then the floor, and wanted to cry. Gerard seemed to be trying so hard to stay connected with me, but I still wasn't sure why. Right now, I was so confused about him. Why would he come back just to gain my trust again?

From my bag, I pulled out the burner and held it. A few seconds later, it rang again. It was Shawn.

34

I arrived at Runas fifteen minutes early and parked across the street. Sitting in the driver's seat waiting for Shawn and Bibi, I rolled the flash drive between my fingers and listened to "Rebel Yell" on my phone to keep up my courage. Thank heavens they didn't know about the digital painting.

The overnight bag with toiletries and extra clothes sat on the back seat. My satchel hung across my shoulder so I'd have my gun close at hand. I had second thoughts about my decision not to call Prosper. Maybe I should have. But even though he said he wouldn't arrive, sirens blaring, cops had protocols. Even if he hadn't used sirens, there was no way the police could intercept without Shawn knowing. Bibi would die.

In front of Runas, the same two Latino men sat at a cafe table smoking cigars, the ones I saw when I'd met Gerard there. One talked and pointed a cigar in my direction. I'm sure they wondered why I was sitting there. I wanted to warn them to go inside just in case something happened, but I wasn't getting out of my car.

To the West, the sky was black as the storm retreated. The thunder and lightning had stopped, but the air was thick, as heavy as wet wool. I turned on the car engine for the air conditioning and checked the time. Ten minutes.

I squirmed in my seat. The street was unnaturally quiet, and I jumped at the slightest noise. The two men in front of Runas played what looked like dominoes. If Bibi and I were at my house, the two of us could sit on my couch, dogs at our feet, and watch a soapy melodrama like I used to watch with Sophie, who cried like a baby during the sad parts. But Sophie was gone, and I doubted that Bibi would ever make it to my home as we seemed so far apart in so many ways. I just wanted her to be safe from everyone who wanted a piece of her. I owed that to her. My father dropped her off at a fire station when she was just two days old because she was born from my mom's illicit affair with a black man. We may never be close, but right now, I needed to get her out of Shawn's hands. Period.

I checked my rearview mirror and then my cell again. Seven minutes to go. Maybe I should have confided in Ian. He was blood, and he seemed determined to help. But Krav Maga? That was an Israeli form of martial arts and the deadliest one. Why had I turned that down? I felt nauseous. Second-guessing myself was not helping.

I stared out the windshield at the gloomy sky. Bugs flew around the hood of my car. My phone showed five minutes to go. I had to buck up. I couldn't pace the sidewalk or talk aloud as I usually did to keep myself calm, so I pulled down the sun visor, flipped open the mirror, and gave myself a pep talk like the old days when I prepared for a case.

"You did right not including Ian. You don't know him. He gives you legitimate concerns. Like why isn't he working? Why is he always around? Why does a chemical engineer need Krav Maga? That seems over the top even for law enforcement and criminals." My voice faltered. This wasn't helping. I cleared my throat, raised my chin, and spoke as if delivering a closing argument. "Consider this. Ian could simply have an interest in martial arts. Many people do. But what if he isn't a chemical engineer at all?" I took a lungful of air. "Ian could be a CIA operative, a mobster, or with Mossad. Being a chemical engineer would be a great front for any of those." I slammed the sun shield up. "Or even a rogue FBI agent."

I was spinning too much. I needed to focus. At this point, I wished I were back in my hotel room, writing in my notebook.

One minute to go. I wiped my forehead of perspiration and turned up the AC. As if Shawn would be on time. I bet she'd be late, happy to make me sweat.

But right now, I was sweating for another reason. I was pissed off at myself. I should have tested Ian. My dead husband was one of the best chemical engineers in the world and had owned hundreds of patents and licensed many of them. He'd often told me fascinating facts that only a chemical engineer would know, like why is what we pump into our cars not really gasoline? I could have asked Ian a couple of questions, say about elements or conversions. Why hadn't I?

And why the hell was I fixating on Ian when I should be ready for Shawn?

The answer was simple. I was losing my edge. I'd been out of the game too long. If you don't use it, you lose it.

I checked the time again. Shawn was five minutes late. Yup. Make me sweat. I needed this exchange to be over. After Bibi was in a safe place, I'd call Prosper. Later I would go someplace private and have a simple, short-lived, messy mental breakdown. Just to get it out of my system.

Yeah, good luck with that.

Tires crunched on pavement, and I jerked up in my seat. I glanced at the rearview mirror. A silver SUV pulled up about forty feet behind me. The vehicle's windows were tinted. My cell rang. I turned off the music and answered, "Shawn?"

"Yes. Please follow my instructions." She paused. "Step out of your vehicle and hold up the flash drive."

I wanted to laugh. She sounded like a TV cop. But I reminded myself not to underestimate her.

With my car's engine turned off, I shoved the flash drive into my pocket, slid from the seat, and stood by my vehicle, facing Shawn's SUV with the cell to my ear. She wasn't making all the rules in this exchange. And hopefully, she wouldn't discover that the flash drive held nothing useful until after I'd driven off with Bibi.

Using my authoritative voice, I said, "No flash drive until you get out of your SUV with Bibi."

Surprisingly, Shawn stepped down from the front passenger side and closed the door. She was dressed in a dark green t-shirt, camo capris, and black Doc Martin boots like she was going to war. *This woman likes theater. She's great at disguises.* Her brunette hair was pulled back in a ponytail, all very different from Bibi's description of her. She turned back to the car, opened the backseat door, and someone handed her a bag. It was a laptop carrier.

She slung the laptop bag across her body, then motioned to the man in the backseat. He had trouble squeezing out of the back. He reached into the SUV and pulled Bibi out by her arms. I hissed through my clenched teeth. She was fucking handcuffed. I reached into my satchel and felt for my gun. Damn them. Bibi seemed to go limp, and the guy held her up against the vehicle.

I blew a curse through my teeth and slipped the cell into my satchel as Shawn walked toward me. I met her halfway.

She held out her hand, palm up. "Let me see it, Ang."

I hated the way she said my name. "Not until you take the handcuffs off Bibi and let her walk over to me." I almost spit the words.

"Why would I do that?"

I wanted to smack the smirk right off her face.

"Look, Ang, I have no idea what's on the flash drive." She pulled a small laptop from her case and opened it. "I mean, like, it could be a copy of *Lolita* for all I know."

I wanted to say something snarky, but I kept my mouth shut. We might as well get this over with. Now I wished I did have police backup. With her laptop, she'd find nothing of use on the flash drive.

Shawn snapped her fingers, pissing me off even more. I pulled out the flash drive. She took it from me, stuck the flash drive into the laptop, and moved the cursor around. I looked over at Bibi and noticed that the big guy was having a hard time holding her up. Even though she was as tall as the guy, she seemed limp and folded over. Her head bobbed on her chest.

I reached out and shoved Shawn. "What have you done to Bibi?"

Shawn flinched and stepped back. "Don't touch me." She glared at me, but she was also smirking. I wanted to punch her.

"We gave her something to calm her down. She got upset when we handcuffed her."

"What did you give her?"

"Oh, chill. She'll come out of it in a few hours."

I took a step closer to her. "What. Did. You. Give. Her?" I didn't like the way this was going. "Shawn. Answer me!"

She shook her head as she turned back to the laptop.

"Let Bibi go. Now." I kept my hand close to the opening of my bag. How the hell was I going to get a drugged Bibi into my car once Shawn discovered there was nothing—

"You're dead," she said, looking up at me. She slammed the laptop closed, pulled out the flash drive, dropped it on the ground, and smashed it with a boot heel.

I gasped.

She shoved the laptop into its case and pulled out a gun. "Where's the real flash drive?"

"That was it. That was the one I found on the dog collar."

"It's garbage. Nothing but business spreadsheets."

"Then what the hell are you looking for?" I stepped back, slipped my hand into my bag. "Maybe there was something on that drive, maybe a hidden file, and now you've destroyed it."

Shawn's face burned red, and her eyes could cut metal. "Let's see if we can slap your sister awake and get some answers."

I had my hand on my gun and slipped off the safety.

"Don't try it, Ang, unless you want to die right here."

"You know someone has already called the cops," I said. She didn't respond.

Instead, she put her arm in the air and made a circular motion with her hand. The big guy let Bibi drop to the ground in a heap and put a gun to her head. I screamed, "No!"

The sound of squealing tires froze everyone. A silver SUV slid to a grinding stop next to Shawn's vehicle. The guy standing over Bibi pivoted with his gun. Ian jumped out, knocked the weapon from his hand, jabbed him twice, and the guy fell to the pavement.

Shawn turned back to me, but not before I smacked the gun from her hand just as it went off. She stumbled. I pulled out my Glock and aimed it at her. "On the ground. On your stomach."

Instead, she lunged for me, and I dropped the gun. I kicked at her as Ian charged us. Shawn and I both went down. I rolled away and grabbed my gun. Ian kicked hers into the shrubbery, grabbed my arm, and yanked me to my feet.

"Let's go."

I raced toward his vehicle. He'd already put Bibi in the back seat. I jumped in next to her. Gunshots hit the SUV as we sped down the street. We passed the two men at Runas. They lay flat on the ground, hands over their heads. Out the back window, I saw Shawn jump into her vehicle and take off after us just as a cop car arrived.

I held Bibi against me, then lowered her head to my lap. She was breathing, but her body felt lifeless. I rubbed her face and hands. She groaned.

"It's OK, Bibi. We got you out of there. Hang on."

And hang on we did as Ian drove like a stuntman on an action film. I held onto the back of his seat with one hand while hanging on to Bibi with the other. He had more skills than just Krav Maga. I glanced back. Shawn followed, but she didn't have the skill Ian did as he maneuvered around slow vehicles and pedestrians, took alleys, and shot through a tight pedestrian way between two buildings. When he finally slowed, he said, "All clear. We lost her."

I looked down at Bibi. Still out of it. I struggled to talk. Finally, I managed, "Where are we going, Ian?"

"I'm taking you to my—our—father's condo in Naples. You can't stay around here."

I tried to talk, but my pulse filled my head, and I thought I would pass out. I leaned my head against the door and closed my eyes.

"You OK?" he asked.

I couldn't answer. I rubbed my chest and arms, took ragged breaths trying to fill my lungs. Finally, I sat up.

Ian passed back an open bottle of water. "Drink as much as you can. You need to hydrate."

Right. This has nothing to do with almost getting killed.

I guzzled half the water. After my heartbeat slowed and I could think, I checked Bibi. She was still handcuffed with plastic zip ties. From my satchel, I took out fingernail clippers and hacked away at the locking heads. By the time I released her wrists, we were on Route 595 heading to I-75, Alligator Alley.

"Relax, Ang. We lost whoever was following us, and they don't know me or where we're going." Looking at me in the rearview, he said, "Now, are you going to tell me what's going on?"

As Ian drove, I told him the condensed version.

When I finished, his eyes widened. He started to say something, and then he just shook his head.

"What?" I waited. Nothing. "Go ahead. Say what you were going to say."

He swallowed hard. "I offered to help. Several times. But you pushed me away. Why? The only thing that makes sense to me is that you don't like me."

"What?" I snorted a laugh. "Damn, Ian. Liking you has nothing to do with it. I don't know you well enough to like you or not like you, never mind trust you." I pushed one of Bibi's braids from her face. She moaned. I took that for a good sign. "Look, I'm sorry. I just didn't want you to get hurt. These are dangerous people."

Being on the defensive only made me angrier. Plus, I was still shaken. Or I should say I was shaking. I caught Ian's eyes in the rearview mirror and said, "Thank you for getting us out of there. I don't know what would have happened if you hadn't come along."

"I do. They would have shot you." He shook his head like he considered me a moron.

Looking down at Bibi, I knew that was true. But they wouldn't have shot her until they tortured her for what she knew. I shivered with cold. "Is there any place to stop on the way to Naples?"

We were already on I-75.

"Miccosukee gas station. It's about halfway. I have lots of water, so no need to buy any." His voice softened. "Are you OK? Tell me the truth."

I didn't want to tell him I'd love a scotch. I swallowed hard, remembering Gerard saying, "Pills for me, scotch for you." So what? I hadn't taken my anti-anxiety meds for over a year, so with this kind of life, a little scotch kept me sane.

Ian reached down into a bag on the front seat, pulled out something, then handed me a bottle. I stared at it. "You're a mind reader too?"

"We all have our demons. Sometimes it's just best to roll with them for the time being. I've been watching you since you told me Bibi was missing, and I get it even more now that I know what you've been going through."

I wanted to ask, *Just how much have you been watching me?* But he kept talking.

"Whenever we saw each other, I could smell alcohol. And drugs. Smell is everything in determining how healthy people are. I've studied many ways to deduce the health of individuals."

He kept talking about what he had learned, from the health benefits of mushroom to micro-dosing as I held the bottle, trying to determine whether I'd drink or not, thinking I should keep a clear head, thinking about the overall warmth it would give me, the soothing medicinal lull. What did it matter now? We were on our way to Naples, to my—our—father's condo where we could crash and, hopefully, where no one would find us.

Ian adjusted the rearview so he and I were face to face. "That guy, the FBI agent who goes to your hotel room? I ran into him once as I was going up to see you. When I saw him knock on your door, I left, but not before I caught a whiff of him. He smells like someone who doesn't eat, drinks lots of coffee, and either snorts or pops the stuff the special ops give their people when they need to stay awake on long—"

"I get it, I get it," I said, having to stop him. "So, what's your vice? Or are you as pure as the newly driven snow?"

He laughed. That made me relax. Then something struck me. "Wait. So you just happened to have this scotch with you in case you ran into me? Or what?" The hairs on the back of my neck prickled.

"As I said, I've been watching you. Remember? I'm a chemical engineer. Everything is about observation. That's how we make our experiments and hypotheses. I deal in chemicals, remember? Chemicals usually have smells. Besides, you're my sister, and that's new to me. I wanted to ... well, I wanted to know about you. But you're so closed down that I thought if we could share a scotch or two at some point, you'd open up."

I unscrewed the top, took a long pull, and handed the bottle to him. He took a swig and smiled up at me in the mirror. "Thanks, Sis." He handed back the bottle and said, "But don't forget to drink your water. It's weird, but in Florida, as muggy as it is, as surrounded by water as it is, as close to sea level as it is, you get dehydrated fast." He paused. "And I'll bet you're not a big water drinker either, right?"

I had the scotch in one hand and the half-finished bottle of water in the other, having to hold them up over Bibi, who was curled up like a baby. I took another long draught of the scotch, followed by more water, then set the water in the bottle holder on the door, screwed the top on the scotch, and put that bottle in the seat pocket. My brain seemed to clear, and my nerves calmed. When I leaned my head back, though, I felt fuzzy, and my skin prickled. I closed my eyes, tired, whipped, a crash after an adrenal spike.

I shot awake when we came upon the toll station. We hadn't gone far. Bibi groaned like she was having a bad dream. Ian paid the $3.25, and we passed the gate.

I said, "I wish I knew what they gave Bibi. She doesn't seem to be coming out of whatever drug they gave her."

"Is she breathing OK?"

"Seems to be."

"Take her pulse."

I did. It was sixty-two, just fine. "I think I'll try to wake her." I rubbed her arm and said her name near her ear. She moaned as if trying to pull herself out of her doped-up state. I tried again, this time lightly shaking her arm. She curled up tighter, and her body shuddered. I whispered in her ear, "It's OK, Bibi. It's me, Ang." No response or movement.

"No luck?" Ian said.

I shook my head, drank more water, and had to force myself to stay awake. I felt so dopey. My mouth was dry too.

I managed to ask, "Hey, Ian, what were you doing hanging around the The Circ besides stalking me? Don't you have a job?" I noticed the puzzled look on his face as he looked up into the mirror at me.

"Don't you remember? I'm teaching in Miami until I'm cleared to go to China."

"Oh, right. Sorry." I'd forgotten. How had I not remembered? My brain was muddled.

"I'm just glad you're safe now. We'll be in Naples in about an hour."

I nodded. "It's weird, you know. Having a brother."

He had such a warm and happy smile that I wanted to cry.

"I never figured I'd have a sister, never mind one who got me involved with a bunch of gangsters." He laughed.

I drank more water to get rid of the cottonmouth. "Not the best way to get to know each other."

"You haven't known Bibi very long, right?"

I thought about that. "It's kind of funny. Whenever I've seen her, she's tough, street-tough, you know? But now she looks like a teenager." I yawned. "God, I hate this."

"Hey, take advantage of it. It's a long boring drive. But we'll stop at Miccosukee in case you need the ladies' room."

I yawned again, thinking an hour and a half was nothing compared to what we had to drive in Oregon. Other fragmented thoughts darted through my head: what did Miccosukee mean, Bibi could be part of the gang, how had Hank and I decided to go to the Keys for our honeymoon?

I pinched my arm to concentrate on my situation. But I couldn't keep my eyes open. Just before I fell asleep, I glanced back at the traffic as if I could identify someone following us. The last thought I had before falling asleep was about something Ian had said, but I couldn't remember what it was.

35

The loud hiss of a semi's jake brakes woke me. Ian pulled off Alligator Alley into a truck stop with a Tesla gas station. Another building housed the bathrooms. It was the usual semis, RVs, and cars. Families with kids sprinting to the store, some wearing t-shirts, and Mickey Mouse ears from Disney World.

My head throbbed, and the sun hurt my eyes. I rubbed my temples. Maybe I needed caffeine. Yes, coffee. I forced myself upright and tried to wet my lips, but my tongue was thick. I drank more water.

Bibi's eyes popped open. Her eyelids quivered, then closed. "Bibi? Bibi, are you awake? We've stopped. Do you need the ladies' room?" I pushed her braids to the side and noticed she'd lost an earring. My hand next to her skin looked as white as Styrofoam. Then I noticed a small place on her neck where there was a lack of pigment in the shape of a butterfly. Sitting in the backseat with her head in my lap, I'd never been this close to her before.

I tried again. "Bibi, it's Ang. Can you hear me?" I patted

her cheeks, but she didn't respond. Now I was more worried. She should be coming out of it by now.

Ian turned off the vehicle and turned in his seat.

"I don't like how drugged Bibi is," I said.

"When we get to Naples, we'll call a doctor."

I felt better with him saying that. "Seen anyone suspicious behind us?" I asked.

"Nope. Clear sailing. How are you feeling?"

"Exhausted, fried, too old for my age." I drank more water. "And I need coffee." I rubbed my face, trying to get my shit together, thinking about how good a bed would feel. "How do you want to do this?"

"How about you use the restroom first. I'll stay with Bibi. Then we switch?" He jumped out of the SUV and opened my door.

I slipped out from under Bibi's head, hoping she would wake. She didn't. In New Hampshire, she'd been suspicious, hard-assed, and shut down, grieving the loss of Betty, her godmother. She'd been unfriendly to me. She'd been tough. I wanted my tough sister back, someone who was fully in this with me. I didn't care if she liked me or not.

If she were awake, she could tell me if Detective Prosper was dirty. Or if she'd infiltrated the gang because Gerard had told her Shawn killed Betty. Maybe he told Bibi that the rogue agent killed her. Wouldn't that be convenient for him?

Then I was back to my own self-centered secret and motive to keep this under wraps—never wanting Bibi to find out that I killed Betty.

I raised my arms over my head to stretch and almost lost my balance. Ian caught me.

"Damn," I said. "Why am I so dizzy?"

"Sugar level, maybe? Heat?" he said as he pulled at his shirt to fan air to his skin.

I shrugged. "I just need coffee," I repeated as I flung my bag over my shoulder.

"Don't worry," he said. "When I go, I'll grab us something to eat and get your coffee. Get back here to be with your sister."

I smiled at him then walked away. Ian had saved my ass and Bibi's. He was almost too good to be true. And he was on our side. I hadn't felt this much relief in a long time.

As I headed to the ladies' room, sweat rolled down my back from the nape of my neck, and I shivered even though it was a sauna outside. I tried to hurry so we could all get back to the SUV's air conditioning, but my balance was off. I slowed down. Moving through this heat and mugginess was like swimming. But what did I expect? We *were* in the middle of the Everglades.

In the ladies' room, I looked in the mirror and almost didn't recognize my face. While sitting on the toilet, I fumbled with my cell and listened to five pleading voicemails from Gerard and one voicemail from Prosper insisting I call him. As I washed my hands at the sink, I tried to focus on what I should do about Gerard and Prosper, but I couldn't concentrate, my thoughts as slippery as. ...

I slapped both my cheeks and splashed water on my face.

"Snap out of it! Get it together."

Two chatty young women walked in, stopped talking, and stared at me. I dried my face then leaned on the sink. A fly buzzed my head. OK, what the hell was the matter? What was bothering me? It came in a flash.

Ian.

Ian was bothering me. But why? He hadn't made one wrong move. He'd shown me his ID, *all* his ID. He'd been there to make sure I was OK. Always patient, although a little pushy. Always available. That bothered me. Who does that?

But unlike everyone else, his only motive seemed to be to help me. Why? Because he was overjoyed to have a sister? Maybe he was bored with teaching. But you don't just walk away from teaching. Perhaps he was filling his time between that and his trip to China. And what about China? I mean, for God's sake, it was unnatural. We were strangers, yet he couldn't do enough for us, and all that without question? Yet, deep beneath that helpful person seemed to be a fault line of desperation.

Damn. I needed air, not this sludge of humidity. I needed to cool off. Ian was fine. He'd let me go to the ladies' room with my phone and gun and. ...

Fuck.

I hurried back to the SUV, my legs weak and my mind muddled. What if he was gone with Bibi? What if he was after Bibi for some reason? What if—

But there he was, trying unsuccessfully to get Bibi to drink water. He smiled at me, then frowned. "Sorry to be so cliché, but you look like you've seen a ghost. Sit down. When was the last time you ate? I'll get us some food." He helped me into the back seat, handed me the water bottle, said, "Drink," then headed into the gas station. I tipped the bottle, spilling water down my front, then stuck the bottle in the cup holder on the door.

Bibi was curled up on her side, and I was squashed against the door. It took all my strength to pull Bibi's head onto my lap and get comfortable again.She made a little cry like a child having a nightmare, and then she was quiet.

I leaned my head back, exhausted.

When Ian returned and said my name, I jumped. I must have dozed off. I hadn't realized it, but he'd kept the engine running so we'd have air conditioning. Plus, now he had sandwiches. How could I doubt this guy?

Ian squatted next to me, his hands full. He had a plastic bag and two hot coffees.

"I guess I'm not that great of an observer," he said. "I don't know how you like your coffee, so I got sugar and creamer packets."

"I could drink it black right now," I said. "Thank you."

"What sandwich do you want?" he said as he held out the bag. "There's turkey, ham, or roast beef. I also got dill pickles and brownies."

Too nice? What was wrong with me? Simple. I wasn't used to friendly people, not in my line of work.

I took the turkey sandwich and thanked him. Maybe I didn't know enough good men. He took my unfinished bottled water from the cup holder and handed it to me.

"Why don't you sit up front? There's nothing you can do for her until we reach Naples."

"I want to be here when she comes to." I finished off the water, and Ian took the bottle.

"Want another?" Ian said. "What about a brownie?"

I shook my head. "No thanks." I was past the point of being hungry, but I needed to eat.

Back in the driver's seat, Ian passed me another bottle of water then settled in with his beef sandwich and black coffee. I dumped a packet each of sugar and creamer into my coffee and sipped it, my face automatically scrunching from the bitterness. Then I nibbled on the dry sandwich. I watched Ian eat and noticed how he kept an eye on us and those around us in the parking lot, seemingly on hyper-alert. Would an engineer be so vigilant? He reminded me more of law enforcement or a security guard. Maybe to him, this was a lark. Without the adventure of being in China, he needed this to fill the void. But I'd told him how dangerous this was. Does someone learn Krav Maga because they have a yen for action or danger? I wrapped the rest of the sandwich and stuck it in my satchel on the floor.

As we headed back onto Route 95, he said, "Try to get Bibi to drink some water, even if you have to drip it into her mouth. She needs to stay at least hydrated."

I did and was relieved to see her lick her lips and swallow.

I dozed off. For how long, I didn't know. A car passed us, blasting its horn, waking me. My heart raced, and I looked out the window. We were no longer on Alligator Alley. Where were we? I tried to break through the brain fog.

Ian maneuvered through the traffic on a busy four-lane highway, swearing at some drivers. For some reason, I was relieved that he swore like everyone else. We passed golf and country clubs, restaurants, and a Publix market. The signs said we were on Davis Boulevard heading to Naples.

My satchel vibrated against my leg. Ian was busy paying attention to his driving, and the traffic was loud enough to cover any noise I made. Bending over behind his seat, I pulled out my cell just as it stopped vibrating. When I checked the number, I didn't recognize it. When a voicemail popped up, out of curiosity, I listened to it. It was Snoop. My Snoop!

The voice gave me goosebumps, one I've never been able to identify as male or female.

"Hey, Sistah! For some fucking rad reason, I'm free. You had something to do with that 'cause I was ordered to call you. So fucking call me back."

Gerard, you bastard!

You had to prove you could be trusted. He'd connected me with Snoop as I'd asked.

But now, it didn't matter. Bibi and I were safe, weren't we? I looked out the window. The traffic was insane, bumper to bumper, license plates from every East Coast state, a few from the Mid-West, lots of Canadians. People driving like maniacs. Everyone caught in their own lives, me escaping this one, but anticipating a new one with my brother and sister if we survived. I still didn't trust that we were out of danger. The Boston gang had hunted me at every turn. What made me think they wouldn't now? And now I had a brother and sister to think of.

Maybe I should send Gerard a text to let him know where we were. Before I could, another voicemail came in. Snoop's number again. I wondered what she was calling for this time. Maybe she missed me, and I smiled. I bent over and listened to this one too.

"Hey, I almost forgot. About your new brother. I tried to tell you before those asshole feds shut me down. The guy who *is* your half-brother? He's in China, has been for over a year. I checked again. Yup. Still there. So, the other guy? Fake." She waited, then said, "Angie, I'd stay away from him. Oh, and girlfriend, you need to change your life."

My hand shook as I deleted the voicemail. My mind went completely blank.

When I looked up, Ian was watching me in the rearview.

"What's going on?" he asked.

I held my stomach and pretended to act sick.

"Feel sick," I managed to say. "Dizzy. Feels like food poisoning. Maybe the turkey sandwich."

The look of suspicion left his face, and he looked concerned. Unbelievable how he could turn it off and on.

"We're almost at Dad's," he said. "Then you can lie down and rest."

Now I could see a slight glint of a different concern under his very professional acting facade.

My heart raced. My earlier instincts were right. He *was* too good to be true. And we were his captives.

oo good to be true.

How could I have been so stupid?

"Are you drinking your water?" Ian looked at me like he was my best buddy.

The water? It had been an open bottle when he handed it to me. That explained how dopey I felt, the brain fog, the dizziness.

Who the hell was this guy? I clenched my hands together to stop the shaking.

I needed to stop drinking the water, but I had to make him think I was drinking it. I held up the bottle so Ian could see me. "Doing it, Bro," I said with a smile and took a drink. When he wasn't looking, I spit it back into the bottle, then poured some of the water onto the SUV's carpeted floor. I did it two more times.

We passed a large carved wooden sign that read, "Welcome to Naples." Ian focused on his GPS.

Bibi mumbled something incomprehensible. Was she trying to warn me? Did she know Ian was a phony? My fake brother, the savior, drugs us then throws us in a room where we'd spill our guts about where the incriminating evidence was hidden. But was he in this with Shawn, someone else, or the Russians?

When Ian wasn't looking, I pinched my cheeks to make me look flushed. After a few shallow breaths, I started coughing and choked out, "I feel sick." I coughed again and caught Ian's face in the rearview. Was that a slight grin?

I put the water in the cup holder, my head back against the headrest, and said, "Are we almost there?"

"Almost. Maybe five or ten minutes. The traffic has been a bitch."

I gave him a slight nod and leaned my head against the window so he couldn't see me in the rearview mirror.

Ian slowed as he drove over a bridge. I noted Hyatt House on my right, Tin City Waterfront on my left. We passed 12th, 11th, and 10th street, then edged onto 5th Avenue, bumper to bumper along a busy street of shops and restaurants.

I rubbed my aching chest. I blinked and sucked down air, trying to clear my clogged brain. What the hell was I going to do? I needed to send the text to Gerard. I grabbed my stomach and leaned forward, head against the back of Ian's seat.

I expected him to ask how I was doing, but that part of the game was over. He seemed intent on finding "Dad's" place. I picked up my cell and ... low battery. I had to make this fast. "SOS. Ian not my bro. Use coordinates to find us." Then I hit send and dropped the cell back into my bag.

We turned onto a cobblestone street just off 5th. Bibi moaned and jerked. I rubbed her arm as I watched Ian in the rearview. *Think. Who the hell is he?* Even more so, what did he want? He couldn't want the same thing as Shawn.

Did he see Shawn destroy the flash drive? Did he even know Shawn?

If he's the rogue agent working with the mob, maybe that's why he has skills like Krav Maga. Then why not just grab me and take me to their headquarters? Maybe there's a major split going on. Maybe whoever had the incriminating evidence could hold sway over the Boston mob. Maybe this fake Ian was batting for the Russians.

Wait, I could text Snoop, have her contact Gerard. I looked up. Ian glanced at me in the rearview. I tried to put on a drugged look. He looked away. I was about to text Snoop when Ian stopped at a light and glanced back at me.

"What are you doing?" he said.

"I'm putting my head between my knees. It helps with the dizziness."

I thought Shawn and the Boston mob were bad, but now we were in the hands of a stranger who at one time probably trained with Mossad. If I wasn't sick before, I was now.

37

I an drove the twenty-mile-per-hour limit along a side street. I thought of jumping, but I'd definitely break my neck. This wasn't the movies. I needed to keep him in the dark until I could find a way out. The last thing I wanted was to be fed to the crocodiles.

Ian turned right and pulled up to a swanky, compact condo complex that faced a courtyard with a circular brick drive and fully flowering crepe myrtle in the center. I took everything in so I could describe it to someone or find a way of escape. My eyes were fuzzy, and I repeatedly blinked to clear them, trying to note everything along the drive. Across from the condo were a restaurant and salon where I could call 911 if I could escape. Red flowering bougainvillea climbed or dripped off every surface of the condo building, making it impossible to describe where we were. I'd need to look for a number on the building.

I had to remind myself to keep acting dull-witted and dizzy so Ian wouldn't know that I knew about him and his drugs in the water.

Ian jumped out of the SUV, smiling as he opened my

door. I wondered if this was my birth father's condo, or one Ian had rented. Probably my father's. Ian didn't do things halfway. Besides, he'd stolen the love letters between my mom and this man to convince me he was my brother. No wonder he was smiling. He'd pulled off a good one. Then I thought about Bibi. Was that why she was heavily drugged? Would she have known who Ian was? Damn. I'd been dripping the drugged water into her mouth, thinking I was helping her.

"You don't look good."

"Thanks a lot," I said, trying to stay in character too, but more to keep calm and not go running down the street screaming for help. I couldn't desert Bibi.

Ian was impressive, however, as he carried Bibi up the stairs. I grabbed my satchel and followed him. He was so confident that I wouldn't desert Bibi that he let me walk behind him. The stairs felt like a climb up to an execution. Who could ever find us here?

Ian unlocked a door. The foyer, filled with light and plants, led to another locked door he had to open too, all the while holding up dead-weight Bibi.

Two locked doors. How the hell would I get us out of there? Once inside the room, I glanced around for another way out. If not for Bibi, I'd pull my gun on him. But I wasn't that stupid. The guy knew tricks I didn't.

Inside, the condo was open-air design, well-lit, and spacious. All relaxing—if you weren't Ian's hostage. Or maybe we were kidnapped. I didn't know what Ian wanted yet, so it could be either one. I assumed he wanted information from Bibi, but then again, I didn't know what his end game was or whom he worked for.

He gently lowered Bibi to a couch long enough for her to stretch out. As he lifted her legs, she opened her eyes for the first time and tried to move. I rushed over, set my satchel on the coffee table, and dropped to my knees. Her eyes were closed again.

"She'll be fine," Ian said. "Can I make you some tea?"

"Can we get her a doctor?"

"Good idea. I'll call our family GP." Ian walked off to another room, supposedly to call a doctor. I could hear him talk but couldn't make out the words. If Ian wasn't my real brother, then everyone he threw at us was fake too.

I looked around, searching for an alternative way out. A private area off the living room seemed to be a painting nook with a built-in desk, a free-standing table, an easel, and a balcony. I searched for a way down but found none that wouldn't either break my neck or legs. As I turned back, a picture on the desk caught my attention, a photo of the doctor and his wife. Was that my father? He looked like the man in the picture Ian showed me when I was at The Circ. But that could be fake too. Ian, however, hadn't put up any photos of himself to pull off the ruse. Instead, I found a framed photo of a classic white Buick, next to one of the doctor. I picked it up and stared at it. This could be my father. Then again, it could be a prop. That seemed an apropos metaphor for my life lately.

"Ang?"

I hurried over to Bibi. "Hey, Bibi. I'm here."

"How's Otto? Is Otto OK?"

"Yes," I said, almost crying. "Otto is fine. But he misses you."

She smiled then closed her eyes.

"Bibi? Bibi? Wake up. You need to pull yourself out of this."

But she was out again. A shadow fell over us. I looked up.

"She'll be good as new in a while. The doctor's on his way."

Doctor? What doctor? "What's his name?"

"Smith, Dr. Benjamin Smith. He's our dad's GP."

Smith? Yeah, right.

"I've put the water on. Black or green?"

"Huh? Oh, black, I guess." I stood up. I was getting the shakes again. "Anything stronger?"

He grinned. If I didn't know he was a phony. ...

Ian seemed well acquainted with the place. He went to the liquor cabinet. "How would you like it? On the rocks or neat?"

"Neat, please." I sounded too polite, a giveaway. "I can get it. No need—"

"Nonsense." He filled a tumbler halfway and handed it to me. I took a healthy swig and walked around the living room.

"Are you still feeling sick?" Ian asked.

"Yes. It felt like I was going to throw up. But I feel better now that I'm moving. I'm not good at sitting for long periods." I turned to face him. "I'm sure you're the same way."

"True."

I needed to make him talk to get info out of him. "Ian, we can't hide out here forever. Sooner or later Shawn will come after us."

"What about that FBI friend of yours? Can't he do something?"

Ah, clever. Turn it around while digging for information. I'd need to be careful.

"Who? Gerard Duvernet? Forget him. He's useless. You saw what a mess he is."

Ian nodded. "What do you think they all want with your sister?" He motioned with his glass toward Bibi. "From what you said, wasn't her godmother the head of the Boston mob at one time?"

"Yes, but after Betty died, Shawn took over. Bibi was obsessed with art, so she didn't know anything about what Betty was up to."

"I find that hard to believe."

Ian had poured himself a tumbler, but it sat untouched.

"So did I at first," I said. "But the more I spoke with her, the more I figured it was true."

The less I said, the better. I stopped pacing and sipped my scotch.

Ian rubbed his chin. "What do you think Shawn wants? Obviously, you or Bibi have whatever she's after."

"I wish I knew. I thought the flash drive was it. But Shawn destroyed it, so that's that. She shouldn't have done that. Who knows what was hidden on that flash drive? It's possible there was a hidden file behind the obvious files."

"Would Bibi know how to do that? Put a hidden file on a flash drive?"

"She's smart and a digital artist." Stupid. I shouldn't have reminded him of that. I felt dizzy again, so I took a chair. "If Shawn hadn't been so whacked, she might have remembered that. Good thing you came along. I think she would have killed us."

"So maybe Bibi did know how to hide a file?"

"No way to know now if there was a hidden file. But maybe it's still there. I think Shawn downloaded its contents onto her computer, but I don't know if it would show up if downloaded. I know next to nothing about that."

He stood. I could tell he was distracted. "Sorry, but where's that doctor? He said he'd be right over. I'm going to call him again."

He left and went into the back room, which I assumed

was a bedroom. If he were connected to Shawn, I'd bet he was calling her to see if she downloaded the files. If he wasn't connected to her, I had no idea what he was doing. But it gave me time to figure out how to get us out of here.

I stood, still shaky, but getting my brain back. As I looked around, I considered my options. If I could find a way out, I couldn't go until Bibi came to and was reasonably coherent. Or possibly, I needed to break out alone and call for help. I ditched that option. I didn't trust what would happen to Bibi if I ran. Nothing mattered until I found a way to get past two locked doors. Maybe when the doctor came, I could run past Ian when he unlocked the outer door. I doubted I could slip the doctor a note, saying, "Help! We're being held against our will." Not any doctor that Ian brought in, that was for sure.

I took a chance, hunted in my satchel for my cell, and hoped Gerard had gotten my message. My hands shook so much I almost couldn't hold onto the cell. That drugged water had done something to my head and body, and I couldn't coordinate the two. I stared at the phone. Why was I looking at the phone? I sucked air into my lungs to get the oxygen flowing to my brain. That's why I'd been looking at my cell. I went to messages—a chastising one from Detective Prosper for going it alone and demanding to know what was going on. "ANSWER YOUR PHONE," he wrote in all caps. Nothing from Gerard.

"What are you doing?" Ian said from across the room.

I held up my cell. "Checking to see who's called me."

"Turn it off and put it away." His voice had changed. No warmth in it now.

I turned around. Ian held a gun at his side.

"Jesus, Ian, what's with the gun?"

"Angeline, if the mob is looking for you, they could use your cell's GPS to locate you. Turn it off."

There it was, Ian's actual voice—sharp, cold, impersonal, not the impersonation of my brother.

Shawn did have my burner number, but could she use it to track us? I stood, faced fake Ian, and pointed to the gun. "What's with that?"

He cleared his throat and looked down as if seeing the gun for the first time. He was back to acting. "It's our father's. I thought we might need it."

His voice had a tremor, as if mentioning our father touched him emotionally.

"OK, fine, but don't you think I know about my GPS? But I thought it might be helpful for the cops or Gerard to track us."

I was close enough to him to see his left eye twitch. He was not happy. I turned off my cell. It was almost dead anyway. But the burner was still buried deep in my bag, along with my Glock, not that I'd be able to use it, not with this guy.

I decided the best way to deal with this was to play along. "You look a little scary with that gun, Ian, like a gangster."

He laughed. "Yep, Chemical Engineer 007."

We both faked a laugh.

"Any luck with the doctor?" I asked.

"He got waylaid, but he'll be here."

I bet. He probably had to find a doctor's bag to go with his doctor's costume.

Ian crossed his arms, the gun dangling in his left hand. For the first time, I noticed he was a lefty—or ambidextrous. Yes, I was slipping.

He asked, "So how smart do you think this Shawn is?"

Interesting he should ask that. Did he ask to throw me off?

I set my cell on the coffee table, picked up my glass, and swirled the whiskey before taking a drink, all with one slow, seamless movement. "No clue, really," I said. "I don't understand why she enticed Bibi to join her in the first place. Why do that? Maybe she's big on the proverb from Sun Tzu about keeping your friends close but your enemies even closer?"

Ian paused, then laughed insincerely. He didn't know the expression.

"It's from *The Art of War.*"

Fake Ian squinted, giving me a look that said I needed to back off. He was losing patience.

To buy time, I walked around the coffee table, pretending to be deep in thought.

When I turned to face him, he was watching me with an intensity that made me swallow hard. I needed to keep him on the hook.

"Shawn wants something Bibi has, some evidence about the mob's illegal activities. I don't know what it is, but it must be something major, something that the Feds could use to bring down the organization." I put on a puzzled expression. "Shawn was pretty pissed when she found nothing on that flash drive." I rubbed the back of my neck. "But the cops found nothing in the apartment." I put on my best desperate expression. "Oh, God, I'm repeating myself. Sorry."

Actually, I *was* desperate. No matter if he found the evidence or not, I'm sure he planned to get rid of us.

"Maybe the evidence is phone recordings?" I ventured.

He stepped forward. "Phone recordings of what?"

Oh, damn. I'd landed on something. "I don't know." I paused. "Phone recordings of mob activities? I'm trying to understand why Shawn is after it with such vengeance. Why would she make the mistake of going ahead with an exchange in public in broad daylight?"

"Go on," he said, stepping closer.

I sidestepped around the table as if searching for answers. "It has to be something of enormous value to the Feds. If Shawn runs the operation like a business, transactions can be routed via legal means. Often those can't be traced or identified. There's extortion, that's definite. Is it possible drug trafficking, or maybe even trafficking people? So, what else do mobsters do?"

"Kill people."

The way he said it, so matter of factly, sent shivers down my spine. "You mean like arrange hits? Recordings of those?"

I did not like the direction this was taking.

Ian watched me like a cat playing with a mouse. "Maybe

Bibi recorded the arrangement of a hit with Shawn giving one of her men instructions."

"I guess. As I said, I have no idea. She never said a word about what she hid."

"If she were spying for the Feds, then maybe she didn't want you involved."

I shrugged like it didn't matter, but if Bibi had hidden this type of evidence, we would both be alligator food.

"I don't know why the Feds need more evidence. It makes no sense. According to the FBI agent, they already have evidence that Shawn had Betty, the former head of the mob, killed to take over." That, of course, was a lie, but I was willing to try anything.

"Oh, really."

The way he said it made me want to run. He knew it was a lie. Did he know that I'd killed Betty? No. There was no way.

Ian cleared his throat, set his gun on the coffee table, walked over to his chair, picked up his glass of whiskey, and finished it off in one swallow. I considered lunging for the gun, but I wasn't that stupid.

Outside, someone shouted, and a dog barked. The muffled constant flow of traffic sounded like the ocean's tide. Inside, the condo felt tomb-like. I had to keep the conversation going, something to keep us from the inevitable end of. …

"Ian, if you had a criminal mind, what would you do to get whatever it was that Shawn wants?"

He turned to me. "I don't have a criminal mind."

I almost laughed. "But if you *did* have a criminal mind. For example, why did Shawn set up that exchange that way?"

He seemed to be thinking that over.

I took a gamble. "Let's say you and Shawn are partners. Your plan is, first, for you to rescue us, get us out of town to what seems a safe place. That would instill my trust in you. After spending time with you and telling you about my history with Bibi, Bibi would wake and confide in you as to where the evidence was."

"That's way too complicated—and risky. And to what end? To get incriminating evidence?"

"OK, Chemical Engineer 007, then how would you find the incriminating evidence?"

He held his empty glass in two hands, looked up at the ceiling, and said, "Torture?"

"Oh, my god! Don't scare me like that." And that did scare me. Just hearing the word.

"Well, why go through all this long, drawn-out craziness? There are too many ways to screw it up. Torture would have worked, maybe not on your sis, but on you."

OK, so he knew that I knew that he knew.

A shiver darted down my spine, and I jerked. "I don't even want to think about that, thanks very much. And why do you think I'd crack, and Bibi wouldn't?"

"Bibi's been on the street, had a tough beginning, a fighter—from what you've told me."

I hadn't told him anything about Bibi. "You think I'd give up the evidence?"

"Yes, if a pro was torturing you."

Once again, I thought of his training in Krav Maga. Did that involve torture? Of course it did. This time, a full-body shudder. I downed my whiskey and held out my glass. He refilled my drink. I looked up at him and said, "But what if I don't know what or where the evidence is?"

He looked down at me. "Then you'd be tortured until you died."

I could feel my jaw hanging. I managed to mutter, "Not funny, Ian."

He stepped back and said, "Drink your whiskey, Angeline. If I were you, I'd turn over the evidence for yours and Bibi's sake."

I thought of the digital painting back in my room lying under the false bottom of my suitcase.

"Angeline, if you turn over the evidence, you and Bibi can go free. It's that simple."

"Go free? Really? What planet do you live on? This is real. Do you actually think Shawn and her goons would let us go?" I didn't want to say that we could easily duplicate the evidence we had, so it was a sure thing that once Shawn had the evidence, we'd be alligator food.

Bibi groaned, reminding us that she was still there. She rolled over and muttered as if wanting to say something.

From behind me, Ian said, "You're the one putting you and Bibi in danger. Give Shawn what she wants. You know the mob will continue in some form with someone at its head. It's even old-fashioned to call it a mob or a gang anymore. It's just plain business."

I whipped around, spilling some of my whiskey.

His eyes had turned a glassy gray, no depth, no brotherly love. Shit, here we go.

I returned the stare. "Ian, I don't have that evidence."

He shook his head and smiled. "Sorry to hear that."

He walked up to me and was so close that I smelled the coppery scent of gun bore cleaner. What the fuck? He'd cleaned his gun in the bedroom?

Bibi made a sudden move and yelled. I stepped over to the couch, kneeled next to her, cupped her face, and said, "Bibi, it's OK. I'm here. Can you talk? Can you sit up?"

Instead, she thrashed as if trying to get out of this

drugged state, as if fighting to wake up. I grabbed her hands and held them between mine. "Bibi, it's Ang. I'm right here. You've been drugged, but you'll be fine, OK?"

"I'll get her some water," Ian said.

I held her hands as she tried to unlock whatever place she was in, as if she could see and hear me but couldn't break through. That frightened me, and my fear rose to a whole new level. As I tried to calm her, I saw her as if for the first time. I didn't know this woman. I was a stranger to her. She might be my sister, but I had no idea who she really was.

Still, I rubbed her hands as if it would help me see her, feel her, connect with her, sharing one moment when we were important to each other. I ran the back of my hand down her cheek. She flinched, and I felt like yelling at her, "Wake up! Pull yourself together. Who the hell are you?"

After a few minutes, she yanked her hands away. I put my hands under my armpits to hide the shaking.

I felt Ian behind me and turned to face him. "What did they give her? What was the drug?"

He looked around as if searching for something.

"No more acting!" I cried. "What drug is she on, and why isn't she coming out of it?"

He locked eyes with me. "I have no idea. It's a cocktail, a mix of things."

For better or worse, the ruse was over.

"What else?" I asked. "What else do you know?"

"I know I'm hungry. That sandwich just didn't do it for me. How about I order some food?"

I don't know where the courage came from, but I slapped him. Hank always said I didn't know my own strength. "Who are you?"

He rubbed his cheek and said, "Was that necessary?" He was grinning. Grinning!

That really pissed me off. He was crazy.

I expected him to pick up the gun, but he didn't. Instead, he drank more scotch, held up the glass, and said, "You know, I don't even like scotch."

He was trying to make me angry. It took all my strength to calmly say, "Did you really call a doctor? And if so, is it a real doctor?"

"He'll be here, and yes, he's a real doctor." Ian went over to the small built-in desk and searched for something.

My burner! Did I have enough time? I sat on the edge of the couch and pulled my satchel toward me. It was light. I reached in for the burner. The cell was gone. So was my Glock.

A doorbell chimed.

"Here he is," Ian announced. "Stay there."

How the hell had he taken my gun and phone? While I was on the floor next to Bibi, trying to rouse her? That was the only time I'd had my back to him.

I turned ice-cold, my hands numb.

Who was this doctor he'd sent for? Definitely not the family GP.

Ian opened the door to a tall, lanky, middle-aged man who didn't look happy to be here. The man ignored Bibi and me as he whispered to Ian.

When they walked over to me, the man held out his hand. "Dr. Benjamin Smith."

Smith. Perfect. I ignored his hand and stayed close to Bibi. He checked her vitals. She moaned and flinched under his touch. When he looked up at Ian, who stood at the end of the couch, Ian nodded.

I choked out, "What? What's going on?"

From what looked like an actual doctor's bag, Smith pulled out a syringe and vial.

I pushed my way between him and Bibi. "No. No way! You don't know what drugs she's—"

Ian yanked me away. "I know what she's been given." I squirmed and tried to wrench out of his grasp. "Stop, Angeline! Smith is giving her an antidote."

I kicked at Ian and elbowed him, but his grip got tighter. As the needle went into Bibi's arm, I gasped. "You son of a bitch!"

Smith replaced the cap on the needle and dropped it into a plastic container marked "Hazardous Materials."

Ian let me go, and I dropped down to the floor beside Bibi. Smith closed his bag, and Ian let him out.

As I rubbed Bibi's hand, her eyelids fluttered, and she pointed her toes. Then her eyes popped wide open, and she bolted upright. "What the fuck?" She yanked her hands from mine. "Where am I?"

Ian's shadow fell over me.

I asked Bibi, "What's the last thing you remember?"

She scooted away and tried to stand, but she couldn't.

"Listen, Bibi." I urged her to make eye contact. "Look at me."

Her unfocused eyes brightened and bore into mine. "What am I doing here? Who the fuck is he?"

Ian crowded me. I looked up and said, "Step back." He did.

Bibi rubbed her eyes and then her temples. "My head. My head's killing me."

Ian said, "That will wear off as the drugs leave your system."

She squinted at him. "Who's he?" she asked. "*What* is he?"

I turned to Ian and said, "Yeah, you want to answer that?"

Ian stayed silent. I didn't like the look on his face, the I'm-all-business-now expression, one lacking sympathy, patience, anything good.

Screw him. I turned back to Bibi. "Bibi, look at me," I said. She turned from me to him to me. I waited for her to focus. When she did, I said, "You were kidnapped and drugged. Shawn wants the incriminating evidence that you gave to me. I gave the flash drive to her, but she said it was worthless. She was about to kill you and me when he. ..." I thumbed toward Ian "... supposedly rescued us."

Bibi white-knuckled the edge of the couch. "What do you mean *supposedly?*"

"Go ahead, *Ian.* Tell her." When he didn't, I said, "I'm guessing, but I think he's Shawn's partner."

Bibi shook her head. "No way. I've never seen him with Shawn. He's never been at the house."

Ian stepped closer. "I think it's time for you to answer some questions," he said, his voice now cold and threatening. "You've been with Shawn, acting like you want in. But Shawn knows you hate her and—"

"Fuck you!" Bibi jumped up, this time tense with anger. "Shawn was shoveling coke up Betty's nose and screwing her senseless. Shawn wanted to take over the mob, so she had Betty shoved off that cliff in Kauai."

I froze. Does Ian know the truth?

Ian ignored that. "You infiltrated our organization to get something on Shawn to put her away. We figured you were a plant."

I almost fell onto the couch with relief.

Ian cocked his head as if he were a lawyer in a courtroom, fishing for answers. "What we don't know is what you were looking for. Were you working for Agent Duvernet?"

Bibi sneered. "Like I'd work for someone? I wanted that bitch dead."

Ian gave that some thought. "OK, if you wanted the bitch dead, why didn't you kill her? You had plenty of opportunities."

"With all her goons around 24/7? And with what?"

"So why didn't you just give the feds what you had? The incriminating evidence?"

Bibi didn't respond. I noticed that she was trembling slightly, and like a balloon, all the air went out of her, and she dropped to the couch.

I shoved myself between Ian and Bibi. "Bibi?" I turned to Ian and commanded, "Get her some water. From the tap."

He didn't move.

"If you want the information, you better get her some water."

He hesitated before going to the kitchen. I sat next to Bibi, and she whispered, "How the hell do we get out of here?"

"I don't know."

I felt her forehead. She was sweating. She knocked my hand away.

"I had nothing to do with this, Bibi."

Ian returned and handed Bibi the glass. Bibi sipped, then guzzled the water.

I stood, faced him, and hissed, "She's not—"

"Sit down." His voice, low and guttural, gave me chills. I'd seen crazies like this while defending them. I waited a few seconds, then sat.

Bibi finished the water and held out the glass to Ian. "I need more."

"Your sister can get it this time."

While I went to the sink, Ian said, "Bibi, you fooled us with the flash drive."

She didn't say anything. When I brought the water to her, Ian had moved closer to her and had his hands in his pockets. I noticed the bump at the back of his shirt where a gun was shoved into his waistband. Was that mine? How many guns did he have?

When Bibi took the glass, her hand trembled. In a weak yet scoffing voice, she said, "As if I'd put anything of importance on a flash drive."

Ian swiped at her, sending the glass of water across the room to smash against the wall. I jumped, but Bibi didn't. She glared at him.

"Now," he said, "let's start over. You took something from us, and we want it back. What form is it in, and how do we get it?"

Bibi flipped her braids from her shoulder. Her dark skin shone with sweat. That's when I noticed that Ian's smack had torn the remaining gold loop from her other ear, and it was bleeding. She didn't seem to notice.

Bibi nodded in the direction of my unfinished scotch. "How about one of those for me?"

Ian picked up my glass. It had a few swallows left. He handed it to Bibi.

Bibi knocked back the scotch. "Did you honestly think I'd put important evidence on a flash drive?"

Ian's jaws tightened, popping his cheekbones. She needed to stop needling him if we were getting out of here alive.

As if sensing the need to lighten up, Ian said, "OK, so we fell for that." He pulled a gun—my Glock—from the back of his pants and set it on the coffee table. Then my cell. "You're smart, Bibi. Show us how smart you are by telling us where you hid the recordings."

So they *were* recordings. No wonder they wanted them.

Bibi closed her eyes and leaned her head back. I eyed my gun and started to move closer to the coffee table.

But Ian whipped around and said, "Stand over there where I can see you," pointing behind the couch and Bibi.

Strips of light penetrated the blinds, creating light bars across the wooden floor. I walked around the couch, wondering how we'd ever get loose. He wasn't leaving the two of us alone. Otherwise, we could plan on how to unlock two doors and escape. I stood behind Bibi.

"OK, ladies," Ian said as he sat on the coffee table facing us. "I'm assuming neither of you wants to die. But you will if you don't tell me where to find the recordings."

I put my hand on Bibi's shoulder for encouragement and said, "If you're going to kill us either way, why give it to you?"

Ian sighed. "Angeline, I never intended to kill you. If it were up to Shawn, she would have had you tortured. I'm not a fan. I saw enough of that in ... never mind."

"Are you the rogue FBI agent?"

He laughed. "So, there's a rogue special agent out there? Gotta love that." He shook his head like he couldn't quite believe it. If he were the rogue agent, he was brilliant at denying it. But I had seen his superior acting skills.

"Look, ladies, I like being reasonable. If you tell me where the information is, I'll let you go. It's that simple."

Who was he kidding? He reminded me of the politician rapist I put behind bars, the one who cost me my law degree and partner position in a law firm. Charming, so sincere. The rapist's defense was, 'Why would I rape anyone when women constantly throw themselves at me?' Well, the few who refused him and tried to escape were the ones he raped.

Ian stood and said quietly, "Bibi, I'm trying to be reasonable, but you're not cooperating. Help me out here. Tell me where you hid it."

My hands shot in the air, whether in surrender or wanting to bring the wrath of Zeus down on him. "Damn it, Ian! If what you say is true and you'll let us go, I want my cell and gun back." I walked over to the coffee table with more courage than I felt.

"Now, why would I do that?" he asked as he stood and blocked me from them.

"Because Bibi doesn't know where it is. I do. I have it. If you want me to show you where it is and give it to you, you need to show good faith and let me have my gun and phone. You need to let Bibi go. Then I'll go with you, and you can have it. No tricks. No subterfuge. Just a simple exchange of the recordings for our lives."

Bibi grabbed at the back of my jeans. "No, Angeline, no. I don't care if he kills me. I want Shawn and him to go down."

My neck twisted into a hard knot. "Well, I *do* care, Bibi. I've already lost one sister. I'm not losing you."

Ian considered this for a few seconds, then reached down and picked up my Glock, unloaded it, and put the magazine in his pocket. Then he picked up the cell and held them out to me.

"Don't turn this into a fight, Angeline. You'll lose." He pulled a gun from his waistband, a gun I didn't recognize, a much meaner gun than my Glock. After he slid it into the back of his waistband, he smiled as if he were entertaining me, not scaring me.

I tried to play it cool. "No worries. I watched you take

down Shawn's guy with two jabs. I don't intend to fight you in any way, shape, or form."

Bibi pushed herself from the couch. "Fuck you, white people. I'm so sick of this bullshit. All I want to do is do my art. I want nothing to do with you except to maybe dangle Shawn out the window of a high-rise window and drop her."

Oh, great. Why is she bringing this up again?

He glanced at me with a look that made my skin crawl. "You won't do that, Bibi." His tone didn't change when he said, "Because we'll hurt your dog. What's his name? Otto?"

Crying out, Bibi flew over the coffee table and head-butted Ian in the stomach. His gun slipped from his waistband. They toppled to the floor. Tall and muscular, Bibi wrapped her legs around Ian's waist and an arm around his neck. I shoved my cell into my pocket and ran for his gun as they rolled and overturned the table.

Ian escaped from Bibi's grasp and slammed her against the floor, knocking the wind out of her. I picked up the gun and aimed it at Ian. He jumped to his feet, hauled Bibi to hers, and held her in a headlock.

"Put the gun down, or I'll snap her neck."

Bibi went limp, causing Ian to have to catch her. She yelled, "Shoot him."

I pulled the trigger.

Nothing.

I pulled it again. He'd taken bullets from the magazine.

"I told you not to get in a gunfight with me."

As he lunged for the gun, Bibi jumped his back, and they barreled into me. The gun went flying. Ian threw her off. I fell hard on my side and crashed into the wall. Pain shot through me, and I screamed.

"You fucking psycho!" Bibi yelled as she picked up the

gun, fired at Ian, and this time the gun exploded but missed. Ian grabbed her before she fired again. She threw the gun, and it skidded along the floor. I crawled toward it, pain shooting through my side. Before I could nab it, I grabbed Ian's ankle. He shook me loose, kicked me, and was about to stomp on my hand when Bibi brought a large clay vase down on the back of his head. He howled, and bleeding, flung Bibi across the room. I grabbed the gun from the floor, yelled, "Fuck you!" and shot him.

For a few seconds, none of us moved. I sat on the floor, holding the gun with both hands, prepared to shoot again.

Ian struggled to keep his balance. Blood seeped through his shirt from the gunshot and down his neck from where the vase had hit him. Then he stepped toward me. I scooted back. "Don't! Don't come any closer!"

That's when I heard sirens in the distance and a loud banging on the outside door.

"Ang! Ang, are you in there? Open up. Police!"

Ian kept coming. I shot him again. This time he fell.

Bibi was on the floor, leaning against the wall, falling to the side.

Adrenaline spiked. I made it to the inside door, unlocked it, and flung it open. But before I could get to the second door, Ian was on me again. But he was weaker, and I heaved him away, lost my balance, and went down. I managed to keep hold of the gun.

Now Ian was on his knees. "I didn't think you had it in you," he said. Spit mingled with blood flew from his mouth.

I pushed up the wall to my feet, the pain excruciating. Bibi silently crawled across the room behind Ian. I didn't want him to look back and see her, so I held out the gun, hands shaking, ready to fire again. Ian got to his feet took three lumbering steps toward me. I tried to fire, but my hand was too slick with sweat. He lunged and knocked me down. I dropped the gun. Ian crumpled.

Bibi was at the door, fumbling with the lock. When she opened it, Gerard stepped in, his weapon drawn. He frantically looked around then saw me.

"Ang! Oh, God."

I looked down at my shirt. I had Ian's blood all over me.

"I'm OK, Gerard. I'm OK!"

Just as I smiled in relief, a gun went off.

My ears rang. I looked down at Ian. He had picked up the gun and used his last bit of fury to fire. I stepped on his hand and wrestled the gun from him, then he let go, fell back, and was still. When I looked back toward the open door, Bibi held Gerard around the waist and lowered him to the floor. His eyes were wide with surprise. I rushed over, gritting my teeth with pain, and lowered myself next to him. His eyes found mine.

"*Merde*, Ang," he said. "That wasn't supposed ... to ... happen." His eyes squinted, then closed.

"No, no, Gerard! Come on! No, don't!"

His fingers loosened from his gun, and I took it from him.

Oh, no, no, no.

"Gerard, don't let them win. Don't die." I took his hand, held it to my face, and looked at Bibi. She was crying.

40

I pulled off my shirt, balled it up, and tried to staunch the blood coming from Gerard's upper chest area. Bibi picked up the gun and went over to Ian. I thought she was going to shoot him a few more times, but then the police busted in.

Because Bibi held a gun, the police ordered her to the floor and took the weapon from her. When they finally let her stand, she kicked Ian a few times and called him names I'd never heard before.

The police checked the condo. Voices yelled, "Clear!" Someone led Bibi into the hallway, and as she passed, I reached across and brushed her hand.

I didn't know I was crying until my tears fell on my hands holding the bloody blouse. When the medics arrived, they draped a blanket around my naked shoulders and led me away from Gerard so they could do their job. I couldn't see what they were doing. Then he was put on a stretcher and taken away.

My entire body came alive, as if it had been sedated and

was just now feeling the pain. I yelped. My ribs. A medic asked me what happened, how I was hurt. I told him. "We need X-rays and check for internal damage with a CT scan or ultrasound."

I pointed to where Gerard was taken. "Is he alive?"

"Yes, ma'am. But don't talk. We have another ambulance that will take you to the hospital."

The pain in my side and back got worse by the minute. The medic gave me an injection which sent the pain from excruciating to bearable, making it possible for the detective to ask me questions. Right now, he was talking with Bibi. The medic pulled an armless chair from the apartment so I could sit down.

As I tried to get comfortable, Detective Prosper arrived. He eyed me as he spoke with a Naples detective. Bibi came over, sat on the floor, and leaned back against my chair. Two more medics arrived. Bibi leaned her head against my leg. "Sorry, Ang. I only wanted to find out who killed Betty."

My chest filled with a suppressed cry of pain. I reached out and placed a hand on Bibi's head. She would end up hating me when the truth came out.

She said, "I hope the agent lives."

I ran Bibi's braids through my fingers and mumbled, "Me too."

I wasn't hopeful. Gerard had taken a severe hit.

A female detective came over, accompanied by Prosper.

"I'm Detective Cindy Biboux. Can you tell me what happened here?"

I don't remember what I said. I do remember saying that I understood there might be an inquest about me shooting Ian—or whatever his real name was. I would also have to give an official statement. Prosper was unusually quiet, but it wasn't his turf. I'm sure he had a few things to say to me.

But I didn't care about any of that. I wanted to know about Gerard.

When the pain medication fully kicked in, nothing mattered. I barely knew my name.

41

I 'm at the hospital. X-rays reveal two cracked ribs but no internal damage. I'll be on pain meds for a while. Although Ian smashed Bibi a few times, she's fine, just bruised. The fake Ian was right. She's tougher than me.

Detective Biboux arrives to take my statement. I ask how Gerard is.

"Sorry, Ms. Porter. It's the Feds, and they're keeping his condition under wraps. Even from us."

After I give her a statement in the hospital and I'm released, I head to the floor where they have Gerard, but they won't tell me anything or let me in his room. An FBI agent stands outside his door for his protection. Or maybe for another reason. I'm sure it's protocol when something like this happens. I'm used to the FBI not being forthcoming. I take a seat in the waiting area and use one of the hospital's phone chargers for visitors. When I have enough juice, I call Bibi and leave her a voicemail. I tell her where Otto is and why. I give her an update on Gerard and me. She doesn't call back. I plug the cell back into the charger.

Later she sends me a text saying she's back in Hollywood

and has picked up Otto. She's had them reimburse me for the charges and has taken care of it. That's it. Nothing else.

I get it. I do understand. To Bibi, I represent as much trauma as Shawn does. She's still angry and wants to drop Shawn from a tall building. I'm not eager to talk to her about that. And I don't know how she feels about me, sister or not. I'm a white woman who has no idea what Bibi's been through, and unlike her, I wasn't dropped off at a fire station as a newborn because of my skin color.

My cell rings.

"Hi, Porter, how are the ribs?" Detective Prosper sounds chipper.

"Painful."

"Where are you?"

"Still at the hospital."

"OK if I come over? I thought I'd catch you up on what's happened. I'll be there in ten to fifteen." I tell him where I'll meet him. He hangs up.

At the hospital's Tree Top Cafe, I buy coffee and sit down with a Naples newspaper left behind on the table. But I can't sit still. The pain in my ribs is like the sun during a cloudy day. I know it's there, but it's hidden most of the time until the clouds part, and a sharp ray pierces the gray. Thank God for pain meds. As I walk back to the waiting area, I question why I even care about Gerard. I'll probably never see him again after this. Plus, I no longer hold him responsible for my sister Sophie's suicide. I didn't do any better at protecting her than he did. From my work as a lawyer, I know that people who have experienced trauma together often feel bonded. And damn, I *did* sleep with the guy. But that now feels more like it was a way to share our grief. Sex and death always seem so inextricably linked.

Back on the floor where Gerard is, I watch nurses swig

coffee or water as they walk past while checking their phones. Announcements are made using codes I don't know. When my cell is sufficiently charged, I call the two women who have Tempest, and they report that she's showing signs of missing me—hanging by the door, heaving long sighs, moping. My heart aches for the dog, but I'm also relieved. I thought she might forget me. Hearing she misses me makes me feel loved and wanted—at least by someone.

I'm just wondering where Prosper is when he shows up. I'm making a list on my phone of what I need to do when I get home when he walks toward me.

"Hey, Porter, how you doing?" He sits down next to me and hands me a latte and packets of sugar.

"Fancy! Thank you," I say.

He also hands me a brown paper bag. "It's a t-shirt so that you can get rid of that lovely tent top." When I arrived at the hospital, I was wrapped in a hospital gown. After I was examined, a volunteer gave me a gray t-shirt four sizes too big with a ZZ Top logo. But it was better than running around in a hospital gown with my ass hanging out.

From the bag, I pull out a t-shirt and hold it up. It's powder blue with a Naples logo, and it's women's style and just my size.

"Thanks," I say, feeling my cheeks flush.

After changing in the nearby ladies' room, I return and thank him again.

"Any news about Special Agent Duvernet?" he asks.

His respect for Gerard is noted. "No. I'm lucky, though. One of the nurses feels sorry for me and secretly gives me updates."

He nods, sits back, and places an ankle over a knee. "So, what are you going to do now?"

"Haven't any idea. After I find out that Gerard is going to pull through, I'll go home."

"And if he doesn't?"

Tears spring to my eyes. Jeez. The bastard's gotten under my skin.

"Sorry, Porter." He waits before asking, "You two have a relationship?"

I almost spit out my coffee. "Funny. You've already asked me that."

"I'm serious."

"We have a relationship, but not the kind you're referring to. Why?"

I peek over at him. He ignores my question and says, "So do you want to hear a few things we've discovered?"

I nod, eager to hear.

"Detective Biboux says the guy called Ian was loaded with professionally produced fake IDs—a license, car insurance, a medical card, a fitness gym card, even credit cards. Those could be from the dark web, but I would say they're so well done, it points to the Russian government—in my humble opinion."

"I remember him showing me all the ID, plus the photo he stole from the condo. He also had photos of love letters between my mother and father. I wonder if he had the letters or just took photos of them?"

"We found no actual love letters."

I choke back hot tears. The love letters. Where were they? Gone forever? But at least I have a few photos of them on my computer when Ian first sent them to me in Oregon. That seemed like decades ago. Before any of this happened with him in Florida.

"The condo hasn't been thoroughly searched yet. They might be there. Maybe he put them back."

I can't see Ian as a romantic or even caring.

"Detective Biboux thinks Ian might be Russian."

"What?"

"There's a Russian cartel that set up bases in Florida. The Russian government trains members to infiltrate both legal and criminal U.S. organizations. They're groomed in speech, idiomatic expressions, cultural ... you get my drift, right?" He goes on without me answering. "It's a fuzzy line between the Russian government and the cartels, but with this cartel, the members have a specific tattoo above their right clavicle so they can recognize each other." He smiles like he's going bust. "The tattoo is a flower. The chamomile."

"Oh, come on. That's ridiculous."

"I thought so too until Detective Biboux, who is a master gardener, said the state flower of Russia is the common chamomile."

I shake my head. Sometimes real life is weirder than fiction. "I guess it's less obvious than a tattoo of the Russian bear or two-headed eagle." Actually, I don't care. I'm so done with mobs, cartels, illegal operations. "What about the condo? It was my father's place, right?"

"Yes. Detective Biboux has been in touch with him, but he doesn't know about you yet."

"Is he coming to Naples?"

"No. He's had heart surgery and is recuperating. A couple of stents."

"Oh, no."

"He's doing well. His son is coming back from China. So don't worry."

His son. My real brother. What a way to get introduced to them. I certainly don't want to add more stress by announcing my existence.

Prosper says, "Detective Biboux will have to tell your

father the details of the case soon. Right now, it's a crime scene, and your father wouldn't be allowed back into the condo anyway. Give it some thought about contacting him. He will be surprised, but I doubt if it will give him another heart attack."

"Yeah, but we don't know that because we don't know him." I know I sound exasperated, so I try to tone it down. "In this case, I don't have much choice. Biboux will have to tell him how the fake Ian lured me into this mess." I want to change the subject. "Do they think they can ID the fake Ian?"

"No idea. The blood samples and evidence are being turned over to the Feds."

"How about the doctor?"

"The doctor doesn't exist. Surprise, surprise."

"Has Bibi been checked out?" I ask. "She was given drugs, and the fake doctor gave her an antidote that seemed to work. I've never seen anything like it."

"Yes, Bibi was checked out, somewhat."

"What do you mean?"

"They wanted to do some blood tests, especially after having an unknown drug in her system, but she said no. The more they wanted to do, the more resistant she became, and she left the hospital."

A woman walks by with a bouquet of lilies. I sneeze. I hate lilies. They remind me of death.

Prosper, who is still in his casual clothes, picks a leaf off his tennie. "Remember the blood on Bibi's coffee table?"

I turn in his direction. "Of course."

"We think that blood sample will match fake Ian. Also, he had a large dog bite on his leg. We think Otto bit him when he went into your sister's condo after Shawn took her away."

"Good ol' Otto." I laugh, thinking of the digital print that is now in Prosper's hands. He was able to get it from my room and have it examined.

Prosper gives me a sideways glance and then grins. Finally, he asks, "Have you talked with Bibi?"

"No. I think she's done with me." I barely choke out the words. "I represent way too much horrid family history." I wipe my nose on the back of my hand and then search my satchel for a tissue. "We don't have a lot in common other than my mother. Right after Bibi was born, my father took her away from my mom and her twin sister and left her at a fire station in Massachusetts." I suck back a sob. Thankfully, Prosper just listens. "The family history ... is ..." I snort. "I was going to say dysfunctional, but that's an understatement."

After a long silence, Prosper says, "She might come around. Maybe she needs time to process. She—both of you —have been through a hellish scenario."

I blow my nose and sigh. "What else did you find out? Has anyone had time to examine the digital art?"

"Your sister is a clever one. It was easy once we knew what we were looking for. Our IT department knew right away that a link was embedded in the painting. Didn't surprise them at all. The link led to an online site that led to another site, yadda yadda."

I chuckle. "Did you just say, 'Yadda yadda?'"

He ignores me.

"There's enough there to arrest Shawn and her gang—if the Feds ever find them. They're gone."

It's unbelievable how little I care. I feel nothing—except hunger.

Outside, the wind and rain torment those fighting to walk from cars to the hospital. Another tropical storm builds right on the heels of the last one. Or are they the same? I have no idea. No, they can't be the same. The first one was on the East Coast. This is the West Coast of Florida. I can't wait to get out of this state.

"What will you do now?" Prosper asks. "Want to get some dinner?"

I think about this. I guess it won't hurt. I remember the lobster roll Gerard bought me in New Hampshire. "Any place we can get a lobster roll?"

He calls Detective Biboux for a recommendation. On the call, he talks, laughs, looks a little shy, then smiles as he disconnects. I recognize a starry-eyed man when I see one, and Prosper is a good catch. I think of that lying sack of croissants now fighting for his life. Was he ever a good catch for anyone?

In the parking lot, Prosper stops and looks around.

The hair on the back of my neck prickles. "What?"

"I can never remember where I park my damn car."

We both laugh.

Then my cell rings, and I answer. The head nurse tells me Gerard is stable, awake, and wants to see me. I apologize to Prosper and head back into the hospital.

Maybe Gerard wanted to see me, but his handlers need to talk with him first, so it's almost midnight before I'm allowed in. The nurse warns me that he's tired, and I only have two minutes. The men in black have a confab in the hall, making it difficult for the staff to navigate. Detective Biboux has come and gone. I don't know what will happen to Gerard regarding his job in the FBI. He's broken so many rules. But if he's undercover, that's to be expected. I'm not privy to any of this, of course, and it no longer matters to me. Fake Ian was right. The mob will morph and keep going. There's no way to shut down a successfully embedded crime organization that, for all appearances, looks legal.

Unfortunately, Gerard was shot under the right clavicle, a nasty place for a wound. He'll be a long time recuperating, and who knows how it will impact holding a gun, never mind a myriad of other actions. I Googled it after the nurse told me the extent of his injuries. Because of the angle of the shot, it went into his chest and up through his shoulder.

When I worked as an attorney, my first case was defending a woman who had deliberately shot her abusive husband in the shoulder. When asked why she chose to shoot him there, she said she wanted to put that arm and hand out of commission for the rest of his life so he couldn't hurt another woman as he had her.

When the nurse told me about Gerard's injury, I was able to follow her medical jargon with words like *irrigation* and *debridement* when talking about the debris a gunshot left in the body, including shattered bone and destroyed tissue, along with foreign objects like bullets. Gerard will have a long rehab.

I open the door to his room. It's what you'd expect. A private room, a special agent sitting in a chair reading a magazine, and Gerard in a hospital bed hooked up to the usual equipment. Someone has combed his thick brown hair, but his skin looks thin and papery, his tan sallow. He's asleep, and I don't want to wake him. I'm about to leave when I hear him say, "Ang?"

I turn, smile, and say, "Hey, Gerard." I pull up a chair next to his bed.

He can hardly speak as his lips and mouth are dry. "Are you OK?" he croaks.

"Cracked ribs."

"Painful," he says.

"Want some water?" He nods, so I hold the plastic cup and help direct the straw to his lips. He drinks. "I should leave and let you sleep. I know you've been through the LE drill."

He takes my hand. "No, stay."

I do.

I've had plenty of time out in the lounge area to think

about everything we've been through and what doesn't make sense. "Hey, Gerard, remember when we were in New Hampshire? Two Feds came to Bibi's door while I was there. They wouldn't leave, so I mentioned your name and said I was going to call you. They took off like I was shooting at them. Why?"

He tries to smile, but he can't. I can barely hear him when he says, "They were supposed to nab me and take me back to Boston."

I chuckle. "And here I thought they were scared shitless of your very name."

He closes his eyes, a half-smile on his lips. We stay like that for a few minutes, and then the nurse comes in.

"I'm sorry, but your time is up. He needs to rest now."

Gerard won't let go of my hand. He says, "Ang, *je suis navré.*" He coughs. "So very sorry. I had your back. Always."

"You had a crazy way of showing it."

He coughs again. In a whisper, he says, "What did you expect? I'm FBI."

The nurse tells me again that it's time to leave.

I stand, push back a lock of his hair, and say, "You get better, OK? Do what you're told."

He smiles. "Yes, dear."

I want to smack him. Instead, I say, "Smartass." Then I bend over to give him a peck on the cheek, but he turns, and our lips meet.

"You are so bad, Duvernet," I whisper in his ear.

I leave quickly before I lose it. In the hall, I wait for the nurse. When she comes out, I ask how he's doing. She tells me he's doing surprisingly well, but he's not out of the woods yet. Lots of debris from shattered bone floating around in his body. They intend to keep him for a while for observation.

I'm tired, depressed, lonely, and need a shower. That night, I stay at a nearby hotel and fall asleep watching an old "Cagney and Lacey."

43

In the morning, I head back to the hospital. Gerard sleeps most of the day, and the duty nurse insists on no visitors because last night was too much for him.

I can't decide whether to head back to Hollywood or stay. I take a break in the cafe with coffee and the New York Times. I'm almost done when an older woman sits down across from me with her tea. I don't know why she's chosen to share my table, but maybe she's lonely. Naples Community Hospital is known for its cardiac department, so maybe she's waiting to visit her husband or a friend. The woman is stooped with gray hair and dressed in a matching coral top and capris.

I feel sorry for her. I ask, "Are you here for your husband or a loved one?"

Instead of answering, she looks up and says, "Like the wig?"

I gasp. It's Shawn. My paper crumples, my heart races, and I attempt to stand. She grabs my wrist.

"Sit."

Her fingers are cold, her grip strong. "I just dropped by

to tell you that Isaac, or Ian as you knew him, was my lover, my partner. But all is fair in love and war, right?"

I don't like the expression on her face. Is she going to kill me right here?

Then I realize I'm more pissed than scared. I fling off her hand. "You know what, Shawn—if that is your name—I don't give a rat's ass. He was going to kill Bibi and me. We defended ourselves."

"Isaac went against my orders. He wasn't supposed to take you two. He thought he could get all the information I needed playing his stupid game of being your brother."

I wait for her to continue, but she doesn't. "Why are you here?"

"Just checking in to see how our FBI special agent is."

My blood goes cold.

"You see, he bugged our place with your sister's help." She smiles. "But he found nothing. I know he lied to Bibi, told her that I killed Betty, and that's how he got her to cooperate."

I knew it.

She stops, pushes her tea aside, and says, "But we know that's not true."

I shiver. "What are you up to, Shawn, if that's really your name?"

"This agent? He means a lot to you, doesn't he?"

All my alarms go off. This time I stand and step away from her, then pull out my cell.

Shawn laughs. "I like you, Angeline. You're smart. You should come work for me."

I'm shaking head to toe and want to bash the bitch to a pulp. "Get. Out. Of. Here."

She unfurls herself and stands tall, no longer bent over,

and says next to my ear, "You know why the locals call this hospital NCH? It's for Never. Coming. Home."

I can't hold back. "Oh, by the way, did you know your lover was a Russian plant who cozied up to you to infiltrate your 'mob?'" I put mob in air quotes.

Bingo! She looks as if I've slapped her across the face. "You don't know that," she says, but with no conviction. Then she brightens. "I wonder what your dear sister will think when I tell her you were the one who killed Betty." She smirks.

"You're wrong. You don't know how she died. No one does."

Emergency buzzers go off. Shawn smiles and says, "Goodbye, Angeline." She hurries away.

I find the duty nurse's number on my cell and call. When no one answers, I rush back to Gerard's floor. FBI agents prevent me from entering his ward. I tell one of them about Shawn and give him a description. He makes a call. Hospital personnel rush past me. Gerard's doctor shoves past the men in black, and too many voices shout to make out their meaning.

I hug myself and stand there, immobile.

I smell my sweat.

I remember what Shawn called the hospital. Never Coming Home.

44

I pace the area in front of the door where two men guard Gerard's section. The two guards step aside as Gerard's doctor and a nurse push through the door. Someone comes out and speaks to one of the guards. I can't seem to follow. Who works for the hospital and who works with the Feds? Then one of the guards turns his back to me and speaks into a walkie-talkie.

When he's done, I ask, "Can you please tell me what's happened?"

He politely and firmly says he can't.

I walk over to a window and look down at the parking lot. A few media have arrived and are setting up outside the main entrance.

Someone behind me clears their throat. It's the nurse who's been keeping me apprised of Gerard's condition. We are on a first-name basis, and she's treated me with respect and has kept me from raging at others.

"I'm so sorry, Angeline. Special Agent Duvernet died about ten minutes ago."

Lights overhead buzz. Disinfectant hits my nose—the

cold sterility of this place. My first thought is *It's an awful place to die.*

"Angeline?"

I hug myself. "Do you know what happened?" I stupidly ask, knowing they won't know this so soon.

"We suspect a bone shard broke loose and pierced his heart because he died quickly. Unfortunately, that's not uncommon in these cases," she says. "Not with that amount of destruction of bone and tissue."

A chill runs up my arms. "Could anyone else have entered his room?"

She looks puzzled. "What do you mean?"

I clear my throat, searching for words. "Could someone have had access to him? Someone who isn't with the hospital or law enforcement?"

"No. He was closely guarded."

I'm numb and don't know what else to say.

"I'm sorry, Angeline, but I have to go."

I think of Shawn. My mind clicks in, and I reach for the nurse's wrist. "What about his food? Could someone have poisoned his food?"

She gently removes my hand. "What is this all about?"

I clasp my hands together and sigh. "Someone approached me in the cafe. She made a direct threat to Agent Duvernet."

She whispers, "Have you told anyone about this?"

"Just one. A man at the door. I called to tell you just as the emergency alarms went off."

"And?"

"This woman heads an extortion racket here in Florida. She could have been here to kill Agent Duvernet. Is Detective Biboux here?"

The nurse looks around nervously and shoves her hands into her pockets. "I don't kno—"

Someone calls her name.

I reach out to her, but she steps back. I don't believe he's dead. I need to see him. "Do you think I can see him?"

She looks at me, this time sympathetically, and I don't want to hear her answer.

"The FBI has taken control of his body and has already ordered an autopsy."

I swallow hard so I can talk. "You have to tell someone to talk to me, OK?"

"Of course." Her name is called again, and she hurries away.

I cover my face, forcing back nausea and tears. I don't know what to do.

When I look down the hall, a group of law enforcement has gathered. I recognize Detective Biboux. I rush over to her. When I tell her it's urgent, she pulls me aside and motions for me to talk. After I tell her about Shawn, she immediately puts officers on all the doors to the hospital. I'm sure, however, that Shawn is long gone.

I'm left alone in the hall. Even the two FBI men have gone.

Reluctantly, I head to the lobby where I call Prosper. He doesn't know about Gerard. I also tell him about Shawn. He says, "I'm very sorry about Agent Duvernet. As for Shawn, Biboux will handle it. How are you doing?"

I tell him I'm frustrated, angry, sad, and like a little kid, I say, "I just want to go home." But I know I can't, not until after there's an investigation or maybe even an inquest.

"Has Detective Biboux told you to remain in Florida?"

"No one has said anything to me yet."

"I doubt if you need to stay as long as you are available."

I'm confused. What is he talking about?

"Look, Angeline, you're in shock right now. Come back to Hollywood and when you get back, call me, OK?"

"What if Biboux wants to speak with me?"

"She can do that any time. How's your sister?"

"I don't know. She won't return my calls or messages."

"She's probably in shock too, so give her time."

Time? I don't even know the time. I look around. Inside the hospital, all seems normal except law enforcement at the front door. Why is it normal?

Detective Biboux steps out of an elevator, heads toward me, and tells me they did not find Shawn. Then she leaves.

So Shawn is MIA. She'll continue to outwit the cops. And that puts her out in the wild again and makes her dangerous—unless she doesn't care that I killed Ian ... Isaac ... whatever his name is. Maybe I did her a favor. But if he *was* a Russian player, Bibi and I are in even worse danger. It's well known in law enforcement that Russians don't like to leave unfinished business.

I need to get out of here. I'm so tired that my focus keeps drifting. But when I look out the window at the entrance, I groan. News crews have intensified. Vans and vehicles with logos from all the major networks have arrived with their satellite disks. News crews set up cameras and lighting. A hospital spokesperson tries to keep them out of the entrance. Official cars have also arrived, dislodging more men in suits. The word is out that this story is bigger than simply a shooting.

Someone behind me says, "And the circus begins." I've heard that one before. But I've never been part of the circus. Even at the law firm, I was not the spokesperson for what happened. I feel sick again. And dizzy. How will I ever get out of here?

I head to the ladies' room and close myself off in a stall. I finally recognize this numb feeling, this brain-dead sense that I have to do something, but in a way, I don't care. That feeling lets me know I'm in shock, just as Prosper said. I also need to eat, but I'm not hungry.

On my phone, I make a list in the Notes app.

- What do I have to take care of here in Naples?
- Call the hotel and check out.
- No, better keep the room.
- Talk to Biboux to see if I need to stay? How long?
- Need clothes & toiletries if I stay.
- Rent a car. What for?
- No, I have a rental in Hollywood.
- What else?
- Gerard is dead. He's gone.

I STARE at the last line. After a few minutes, I struggle with the lock on the stall door and wash my hands. Then my face. I call Detective Biboux. Yes, I can go back to Hollywood for the time being, but I need to be available. I call for a taxi.

Detective Biboux meets me outside the ladies' room. One of her officers takes me to an exit the hospital has made available. Still, a few media are there, ready to snap photos. Later they'll figure out who I am. The taxi driver finds me.

In the backseat, I'm afraid to lie down even though I desperately want to fall asleep and forget everything. I try to get comfortable with my satchel as a pillow but can't. I keep seeing Gerard smile as he sees Bibi and I are alive. I smile back. Then the shot.

I shut off my cell because the media has somehow found my number. The taxi is so quiet that it's like the whole world has stopped. I remember little about the ride back to Hollywood. When I'm dropped off at the hotel, I barely make it to my room. The room is freshly cleaned, and a large vase of flowers sits on the table. I flop onto the bed and cry myself to sleep.

45

I wake and sit bolt upright, my heart pounding. Light slits through the curtains across the bed like a knife cut. I'm still in my clothes from yesterday. It takes a few seconds to realize I'm back at the hotel. My chest fills with pain, remembering.

Outside, there's a cacophony of noise. I pull back the curtain an inch. It's the media. In the bathroom, I lean over the sink. My eyes are swollen, and my mouth tastes foul. Probably from the drugs Ian gave me. I brush my teeth then comb my hair. Everything takes effort. I don't want this day to begin, but I have no choice.

In the kitchen, I make coffee then call the front desk. The hotel is keeping the media from entering and bothering the guests. I wish I could call Gerard. I pinch my nose and squeeze my eyes shut, so I don't cry.

I turn on the TV and sip coffee. The story is all over the news.

"Two women, one from Boston and one from Oregon, were kidnapped by a suspected Russian mobster who was shot and killed. The alleged assailant is Angeline Porter, a former Oregon lawyer. An FBI special agent was also shot trying to save the two women. He later died of his injury."

THE PICTURE they show is from my law days. Now I'm more ragged and a lot less idealistic. I turn on my cell and scroll through all the numbers and voicemails to find one I recognize. Nothing from Bibi, but one from Prosper. He wants to know if I'm all right. I don't call back. I call Bibi instead. Again, she doesn't answer. I leave her a message.

"Please meet me at the beach. I'll be on a bench somewhere near the taco place. I'll leave you alone after that if that's what you want. But please give me some time before I head back to Oregon."

I slip out the delivery door wearing a baseball hat and sunglasses, and carrying a beach bag, all on loan from the hotel. I walk like a happy vacationer over to Publix, where I call an Uber to take me to the beach. I'm already exhausted. More emotionally than physically.

The beach is crowded and hot, and the people are unfriendly, almost prickly. On the horizon, a strange mercury-colored haze hangs there, poisonous looking. I have to push through a crowd that jostles me even though the walkway of multi-colored bricks is wide. I search for a quick fix, find the taco joint, and order a quesadilla.

After I find an empty spot on a bench, I stare out at the ocean and feel an emptiness I haven't felt ... since when?

I choke on a piece of the quesadilla and cough repeatedly, wanting to cry again, to bash something, to scream that I hate this place, all the while tanned and sunburned vacationers frolic in the waves, toss a beachball, lather each other with sunscreen. When was the last time I felt that happy and carefree?

Time passes with a slowness that fits my beleaguered body. Even though I'm on pain meds, I can't turn or twist without sharp pain reminding me of shooting Ian.

I keep checking my phone. Minutes crawl by. Maybe the drugs Ian gave me haven't completely left my body either. The drugs. I don't even know what they were. My fake brother is dead. Can't ask him. Wait, I have a real brother. No, I can't deal with that right now—as if he'd want a sister with this much baggage.

I repeatedly check my cell. I try to be patient. I'll wait for Bibi. But there's a good chance she wants nothing to do with me. Does she know I killed Betty? How would she know? How does Shawn know? She can't. Maybe she was guessing to see how I'd react. That doesn't mean that Shawn didn't tell Bibi. Shawn would do that to put a wedge of distrust between us.

I need a distraction, so I return calls from home. My lawyer says people have heard the news because it was a major story on local television and online. I FaceTime my dog sitters and ask about Tempest. The meddling media hasn't found them yet. They sit on the couch with Tempest between them to show me how great she looks. I'm trying to keep it together, but when I talk, Tempest woofs and barks and gets agitated. I can't even make my dog happy.

Now I'm agitated. Behind me, they sell lemonade, so I buy one. My hand shakes as I reach for the cup. When I return to the bench, an older couple now occupies it. I take off my sandals and walk back and forth along the beach not far from the bench so that I can look for Bibi. I sip my lemonade, but it upsets my stomach, so I throw it away. My skin is getting crisp, and I make a mental note to pick up aloe at Publix.

When a storm rolls in, turning the horizon black, there's a mass exodus of sun worshipers. Perfect. Even the weather has other plans for me. After returning to the hotel, I wait ten minutes and call Bibi again. No success.

I stop pacing. What if something has happened to her? Maybe that's why she hasn't answered my calls. I slip into my shoes, call an Uber, and rush to the street.

46

People shove mics at my face and try to cut me off from entering Bibi's residency part of the hotel. One news reporter chest bumps me, loudly saying, "Where's your sister? Was she part of a Boston mob?" I shove him to the ground. He calls me a bitch. Security at the door finally steps in and makes a path for me to enter. I hurry into the hotel.

At the front desk, I ask, "Is there any way I can check Bibi Brackston's apartment? She's my sister, and she hasn't returned any of my calls. We've both been in danger—"

"Yes, Ms. Porter, we are aware of your situation. But your sister left early this morning."

"What? To where?"

"I'm sorry, but we don't know. She had a flight. That's all we know."

I try to think. "Do you know if she went on her own?"

"I'm sorry. I don't. The police have been here looking for her also."

My face burns. "Do I have any messages?"

I'm handed a stack. "All news and media people," the desk clerk says.

I go through them on the way to my room. After I'm inside, I throw them away. What to do now?

Otto. Damn! Does Bibi know about Otto and where he is? I call the veterinary hospital. Bibi picked him up yesterday. I'm relieved at least about that. Did she pay the hospital? Of course. How did she know where he was? I call the front desk. Yes, they told her. How did they know? Did I tell them? I can't remember. But at least they've been reunited.

I'm sweating and feel listless, as if life has been squeezed out of me. I take the last of my energy and call Prosper.

"Hey, Prosper," I say.

"Porter, do you know where your sister went?" No friendly hellos this time.

"I can ask you the same."

"So you don't know?"

I don't like his accusatory tone. "I told you before. I've called and left dozens of messages. She hasn't responded."

"Darn." He still doesn't swear.

"Yes, *darn*. What did you want with her?"

"We need to talk to her, but I'm not at liberty to say why."

"Oh, give me a break, Prosper. It's my sister. We've just been through hell." I'm shaking. When I sit down too fast, I stifle a yelp as pain shoots through my back and ribs. "I need to know what's going on, Prosper. Please." My breath is ragged.

His voice lowers and slows. "First of all, she shouldn't have left town without letting us know. Secondly, we need to know what happened while she was at the mob's headquarters. We're working with the FBI. We need to know where she obtained the evidence on the mob's operations that she hid on the digital painting."

I sigh. "I've got nothing. Sorry." Then I say, "Maybe she's gone into hiding? Shawn might still be after her."

"Quite possible."

Goosebumps run up my arms. "Prosper, I can't blame her for leaving. If the Boston gang has joined hands with the Russians, I wouldn't want to be anywhere they could find me."

"The FBI is tracking money withdrawals and anything else that can lead them to her."

I groan. "You're kidding? What the fuck? Why aren't they putting all their energy into finding Shawn and her associates?"

"Don't worry. I'm sure they are. But your sister has more vital info than she left in that painting. The Feds need everything they can get their hands on to make arrests that will stick."

"Fuck them. They're going to get her killed."

"She doesn't need much help in that department."

"Thanks for the doom and gloom. It's my *sister* we're talking about."

"Look, I didn't push her into joining the mob. I didn't listen to an ostracized FBI agent who wanted me to go undercover with no protection. Duvernet screwed up. He did things that put you and her in danger."

It's too complicated to explain to Prosper. And too late.

I don't want to know, but I do want to know. Did Shawn poison Gerard? I can't seem to find my voice but managed to croak out, "Has the autopsy been done on Gerard?"

"Yes, but the results aren't back."

I swallow hard and ask, "Will you tell me what they find?"

"Of course. *If* the FBI let me know."

That's right. The FBI has Gerard's body.

Gerard's body.

I feel sick.

Prosper says, "Would you like to go to dinner tonight? Take a break. I'm sure you haven't eaten much. It would be better than sitting in your hotel room."

I'm taken aback. What do I say? To lighten the conversation, I jokingly say, "Do I have a choice?"

He chuckles. "Of course."

I don't feel like going to dinner. Eating is the last thing I have on my mind. But he's right. I don't want to spend the entire night in my hotel room. I blurt out, "OK, but it depends on where."

"Fine. You choose."

"Then I choose Runas." I don't know why I pick Runas. Maybe it's the place I met up with Gerard. Maybe it's where I was abducted. I have no idea. Call it intuition.

"OK," Prosper says. He's not happy about it.

But I don't care.

47

After dinner as we finish our drinks, Prosper gets a call. I watch his face intently, hoping it has something to do with the autopsy. He slugs back the remainder of his rum drink. "I need to get back. Biboux and her team think they have Shawn."

My jaw drops. I need to consciously close my mouth.

"They'd like you to ID her."

"What do you mean?"

"She's dead. Shot in the head, execution-style."

I think I'm going to be sick. I hold my head in my hands. "I don't want to go back to Naples."

"You don't have to. Just come with me to the precinct. You can officially ID her there by photo."

"Why do I have to ID her? I'm not related or even know who she really is."

"We need you to ID her as the person you met for the exchange outside Runas. That's all. We're still trying to find out her real identity."

"Excuse me." I hurry to the ladies' room. I wait there until my shakes subside and I don't feel like throwing up.

Then I head to the precinct with Prosper to identify the photo. It's Shawn, what's left of her. They will do a proper identification after the autopsy using other means to identify who she is—if they can.

Prosper drives me back to the hotel. My mind is in list mode, thinking of all the possibilities, trying to keep sane.

"Listen, at the hospital, Shawn told me Ian went against *her* orders when he took Bibi and me. What if it was the other way around? What if she went against the Russians when she met us in front of the restaurant and tried to nab us and the incriminating evidence before the Russians got to us?"

"Either way, she got in bed with the wrong guys," Prosper says with a finality I don't feel. "She also got in way over her head."

I lean my head against the window. "I think she stupidly went against the Russians, aka Ian. That got her killed." As much as I detested Shawn, I don't want to think about what it must have been like for her at the end.

When we draw up to the hotel, Prosper escorts me inside. Uniformed police officers now stand with the security guards as the media seem to have grown in size and strength. The same guy I shoved on his ass argues with a police officer at the door. Prosper pushes himself between the guy and the cop and says, "If you don't leave immediately, I'll have this officer arrest you for trespassing."

Instead, the guy sees me, rushes over, grabs my arm, shoves the mic at my face, and shouts, "Angeline Porter! Is it true that you're the one who killed the Russian mobster who then killed your friend the FBI age—"

Before he can finish, two cops are on him, and he's headed to the station. I rush into the hotel and take the elevator to my room. My arm hurts where the guy grabbed me. I rub it to help prevent bruising. The pain meds are wearing off, and I take two more, then call the airlines and make a flight for early morning. As I pack, I move slowly. Then I arrange with the front desk to have a town car take me to the airport. I can't get out of here fast enough.

I don't sleep. I've given up on Bibi. I don't blame her. Whether she knows about me killing Betty or not, we haven't connected on any level. She's right to run, to hide if that is what she's doing. I should too, but I'm done with that. If someone is still out to get me, so be it. But I'm such a small fish in their big pond. Without Gerard at the center showing me a way to swim in these polluted waters, I'll need to find my own way out.

I sit out on the balcony and smoke a cigarette that I bummed from one of the hotel staff. I know I'm rewriting what happened with Gerard. He wasn't always there to protect me. In fact, he put me in danger to bring down the Boston mob. But there were no innocents in this whole story. I wish the last time I saw Gerard wasn't when he smiled at me then took a bullet. It's not how I want to remember him. It will haunt me more than me shooting Ian because Ian deserved more than a bullet. Plus, I will always wonder if Gerard was actually chasing a rogue agent or if Gerard *was* the rogue agent. Does it matter? Not really. I'd like to know, but it's a moot point now.

"I'm going home," I say to Marilyn's portrait hanging on the wall.

The following day, Prosper calls while I'm sitting in the airport waiting for my flight.

"The autopsy results came back for Special Agent Duvernet."

I wait.

"The FBI say it's inconclusive."

I laugh. I can't help it. That's so Gerard.

"What's so funny?" Prosper asks.

"Oh, nothing. Now that Shawn's dead, it doesn't matter if she poisoned him or not."

"I see your point, but I don't think the FBI is telling me the truth."

"Why?"

"Let's just say years of experience."

There's an awkward pause.

"Are you going to be all right, Porter?" he asks.

I still like how he calls me Porter. "I guess. I just need to be home with my dog."

Another awkward pause.

"Look," he says. "Don't let this episode in your life color how you feel about Florida. I would enjoy taking you around to some of the nice spots, show you the good side of our state, you know, the ones without mobsters."

"You mean the ones with alligators?"

He runs down a bunch of places where he'd like to take me. He sounds like an advertisement. I don't want to tell him I won't be back. Ever.

"Thanks, Prosper. I appreciate that. But I'm going to hunker down in Oregon. Find a job where I can put my law background to work, do something good."

He doesn't say anything at first, then he says, "Well, good for you. I hope you find something that ... won't break your heart."

For a moment, I feel gutted. That hits hard. I cover my mouth with my hand to squelch a tiny squeal. Tears escape.

"Hey, Porter, I'm sorry. I didn't mean to upset you. It's just that it's hard to find something good to work for without it causing heartache. You're tough on the outside, but you're a creampuff inside."

I snort back a laugh. "Gee, thanks. I think."

"Well, good luck. Thanks for all your help on this case."

I nod as if he can see me. I'm so choked up I can't talk.

"Bye, Porter. Stay in touch." The call ends.

I whisper, "Bye, Prosper."

As the airplane ascends, I look out over the ocean. The storm worked its way up the eastern coast, and the sky above the southern Florida coastline is clear and sunny. I lean my head against the window. I refuse to say goodbye to Bibi. Maybe sometime in the future, we will have a reunion, maybe even find common ground for some kind of a relationship.

But I do need to let go of one person. Gerard. I know I haven't. As if he's still out there. Politics may make for strange bedfellows, but so does tragedy. Tragedy brought us together. Tragedy ended it. I didn't love him, but he loved my sister. He was an enigma, and I still don't know what he was up to. Again, it doesn't matter. He's gone.

Looking out the window as we pass through, and then over, a cloud bank, my lip trembles, and I suck back a tear, as I whisper, "Goodbye, Gerard."

EPILOGUE

I've been home one week and have barely touched the long list of everything I want and need to do. I've already installed a high-end security system on the house and near the street. I've gone to the range to practice. My goal is to become an expert marksperson. Tempest and I go on morning walks in any one of the many beautiful parks here in town. Sometime soon, I will reach out to a few women I like and try to deepen our friendships.

Naples, Florida law enforcement had me on two Zoom interviews, and then I was done. No one with the FBI will talk to me about Gerard. I get it, but it still pisses me off.

I ask Prosper to make sure Bibi's art piece of Otto P. Snowden gets back to her. I would have loved to have kept it just so I could have something of hers. Maybe in the future I'll buy a piece of her art. I'm giving her time before I reach out again.

My father called. He sounds sweet and kind, but I could tell he was trying to hold back tears. He was honest with me, saying his son, the real Ian, is worried about what has already happened around me as far as the mob is concerned. I understand. I told him there's no rush, that I will leave it up to him and his family as to how he'd like to handle a possible meeting and our relationship. But he said he wants to meet with me, he really does. I'm sure it's difficult that this brings up the past with my mother. He knows about the accident that killed my parents. He does not know, however, any of the details and that it was no accident. That my so-called dad drove them into a ravine. That will be a tough conversation if and when we reach that point. I'm having a difficult time processing that I have a father. Plus, I can't imagine what this is like for his wife, although he said, "Miriam is deliriously happy to now have a daughter in the fold." I think I'm going to like her.

One Sunday, I'm in my backyard, drinking coffee, tossing a stick for Tempest, when my cell rings. It's Prosper. He's called a few times and keeps me up to date on anything that has happened with the case. Not much is left. I think he calls about the case as an excuse to talk. I find we're talking more about our lives. He's told me about his wife dying of cancer, and I've told him about Hank falling down the stairs and ending up in a wheelchair, but not that we were fighting when it happened. I will never tell him that I killed two people or what I did in Portland to try to save my husband. I'll go to my grave with those secrets.

Prosper wants to know if I'll ever come back to Florida. I don't say what I'm thinking: *Not on your life.*

"What are you going to do now with all your time? Any ideas?" he asks today. He knows I'm puzzling over where to put my energy.

"No, haven't got that far yet."

"Didn't you tell me that you worked for an environmental group in Kauai?"

He remembers. He also knows that I had to do it secretly because the mob was after me.

Prosper says, "Why not put your brilliant legal mind to work with something like that?"

I smile. *Brilliant legal mind?* I know he's flattering me, but it feels good.

We talk about possibilities, then he asks, "Have you seen the black SUV hanging around?"

A few days ago, I saw a black SUV go up and down my street several times. I've walked with Tempest around the neighborhood to see if anyone has a black SUV that looks like this one. But there's a look to these vehicles when they're government or something else. Maybe I'm paranoid, but I've every right to be.

Prosper says, "Were you able to get the license plate number?" He'll check it out if I can. But if it's the Feds, they won't tell him.

Prosper knows I called the Feds about it right away, mentioning Gerard Duvernet, and how I was there when he was killed. But I heard nothing but apologies and bullshit excuses as to why they can't tell me if the vehicle is theirs. They ignored my mention of Gerard but asked me for my name and number. I thanked them and hung up. If they don't want to give me any information, then they don't get any. Not that they can't find out, but I'm not making it easy for them.

"Look," Prosper says. "I have a week's vacation coming up. What do you think?"

I'm speechless. Is he really asking if we can get together? I bite my lip.

"OK, too soon. Sorry," he says. "But is the door at all open? You know, even a crack?"

I laugh again, a nervous one. "Let's keep talking."

For now, Tempest is the only one I want around me day and night. I should talk to someone, a therapist of some kind, but that can wait. I need my own time, space to be by myself, to figure out what I feel and think about what's happened, and to get closure of some kind, whatever that means. "There really is no such thing as closure," as I wrote in my notebook the other day. "Why kid myself? No matter how closed a door is, it can always be opened."

On Thursday night, I'm getting ready for bed when I hear a buzzing. Walking around my bedroom, I recognize the vibration of a cell phone. My cell is on the nightstand, so it's not that. As I get closer to the open closet, I distinctly hear the buzzing, grab the satchel I took to Florida, and fling it on my bed where I rummage through everything I left in it, untouched, and find the burner I forgot about. As soon as I pick it up, the buzzing stops. The battery is almost dead. My throat goes dry, my brain numbs, my heart races. I don't recognize the number. I sit on the bed. Maybe Snoop has called me from a different number. We've spoken once since I've been home, mainly to catch up and for me to make sure she's OK. Gerard did a good job at keeping her safe and out of jail.

Then a voicemail pops up. I stare at the cell. If I listen to the call, my life may change again. Do I think it's worth it?

I slip on my sandals and take the phone to the garage.

I'll never know who's called if I destroy the burner. I could call the number back, but I think it's better that I don't open any more doors to the past. I pick up my hammer and place the phone on the concrete floor.

My hand trembles. I need to do it before I give in to curiosity.

I hold the hammer to my chest, agonizing over who it could be.

How long I stand there, I'm not sure. I'm literally frozen, both body and mind.

My head says I must answer. If I don't, it will also haunt me. Or will it?

Then the cell rings again. I grab it from the floor. It's the same number. I answer.

"Hello?"

I hear breathing on the other end.

"Who is this?"

I hear a heavy sigh. Male? Female? In the background, I hear a muffled conversation. If it were someone who wants something from me, they'd talk. If someone has found this number and wants to know who I am, they already know. But this is bullshit.

Crazy as it is, however, I almost say, "Gerard?" I don't. I don't believe in miracles, and besides, Prosper told me that he's definitely dead. God knows I've asked him enough times. Of course, Prosper doesn't know for sure. He only has the FBI's word. He never saw any evidence of his death, and neither did I.

Now I'm pissed. I'm done being manipulated. I feel a new Angeline kick in. I've had enough. I don't care who it is. I don't care who is outside driving the black SUV.

The battery goes on low power mode, a red line. Maybe it's a pocket or butt call. The line is still open, and I hear a sigh.

"Tell me who this is. Now." They don't. I disconnect.

A few seconds later a text pops up.

I'm safe. Don't look.

I SHAKE MY HEAD. A stillness washes over me. Even if it is Gerard, let someone else take over his games. Then, for some reason, I remember. When I left Portland for Florida, I promised I'd get a tattoo. Now I know what it will be. A woman's black lace glove in a fist holding a bleeding rose. Small, of course, because I'm not ready to do a major rebel yell. Yet.

I glance up. Tempest sits in the open doorway.

"How about it, Tempest? Are you ready to put this shit behind us?"

Tempest lies down, her chin on her paws.

"Good girl," I say. Then I place the phone on the concrete and bring the hammer down with all the force I have in my body.

THANK YOU

Thank you so much for reading *1 Last Betrayal* and being fans of my books. Because you're the best, I wrote a short story prequel to the Angeline Porter Trilogy. Find out how scary it was to be Angeline as a teen in her dysfunctional, but loving family. To sign up for my newsletter and download the prequel, click here:

LAKE WINNISQUAM 1982

If you are reading this in print, go to:
https://BookHip.com/GMHCTFN

And guess what? *The prequel is a contest*!
In the story, I've hidden three Easter Eggs. An Easter egg can be a character, a place, an object, or a bit of dialogue. The Easter Eggs in the prequel can be identified after reading *1 Last Betrayal.*

The *first reader* to identify the three Easter Eggs in "Lake Winnisquam 1982" will win not just one of my **Famous Mystery Packages** but will also have a character named after them in my next thriller.

Are you ready? Any questions?
Contact me with the answers.
valerie@valeriejbrooks.com

Good luck! And careful reading!

ACKNOWLEDGMENTS

Love, gratitude, and thanks go to:

My bestie, Jan Eliot, creator of "Stone Soup" cartoon, and my stellar LitChix writing group Chris Scofield, author of *The Shark Curtain*, and Patsy Hand author of *Lost Dogs of Rome*.

My inimitable Noirista Team: Alice Ahlstedt, Becci Crane, Caren Tracy, Grace Elting Castle, Jan Eliot, Kassy Daggett, Kay Porter, Kent Brooks, Kirsten Steen, Lory Britain, David Marks, Karla Droste, Mary Jo Comins, Mendy Sobol, Quinton Hallett, Rae Richen, Susan Glassow, Ted Lay, Jill Pearson, Christine Caldwell, Eve Miller, and Rev. Andrea Stoeckel.

My phenomenal friend and editor Lois Jean Bousquet.

Friend and green chemical engineer Terry Brix for his expertise and continued support of my work.

The people in my life who keep me going: Tom Titus, Susan Clayton-Goldner, Wendy Kendall, Kirsten Steen, Sofia Dumitru, Judith Watt, Marlene and Spud Howard, Jeff Fearnside, Carol Craig, Ruby Ratz Collette, Samantha Ducloux Waltz, and Jessica Maxwell for support in so many ways.

My sisters of the Professional Womens Network of Oregon who are always there for me and each other.

The bloggers and reviewers who keep authors and writers alive.

Kent and Debby Brooks, and Wendy Brooks for helping me research my settings in Hollywood and Naples, Florida, and answering the many questions I asked about where they live.

Helene and Thomas Lauer for letting me use their beautiful Naples condo for the setting in the last act.

My support group in New Hampshire: the fabulous Michelle Saia at the Book Warehouse, Tilton; my life-long friends Christie Abbott Fitzgerald, Kevin Walsh, Jane Lamanuzzi, Nancy Rand, Bob Read, Gus O'Connor, Linda Walsh, and Vicky Chase.

All the wonderful authors and fans I met at this year's Malice Domestic Conference and Bouchercon.

Scott Landfield and Tsunami Books, and Jeremy at J. Michaels Books for keeping the faith and continuing to give writers and authors indie bookstores we are so proud of.

Cindy Casey & the fabulous crew at Vero Espresso House.

Oregon Writers Colony for providing a second home and writing retreat at Colonyhouse in Rockaway Beach, Oregon; Wordcrafters; Willamette Writers; Pacific Northwest Writers Association; and Sisters in Crime along with the Columbia River and NorCal chapters.

Elizabeth George Foundation for a grant that led me to writing noir.

The residencies that gave me time and immersion to explore my writing: Hedgebrook for Women, Playa, Villa Montalvo for the Arts, Soapstone, and Vermont Studio Center.

My sweet family: Jason, Alexx, Maddi, Iree, Promise, Roy, Zylan, Holdynn, P.J., Mia, Gia, Zailah, and Mama Joy. You lift me up and carry me, always.

My pooch, Stevie Nicks who took over one of my writing desks. She's a great watchdog but a lousy editor. Plus, she can't sing. But I love her anyway.

My one and only, my heart and soulmate, Dan Connors, the best traveling companion and scout ever.

FANS INTERROGATE VALERIE

∽

If you have questions for me about my books or author's life, please send them via my website or message me on social media. I'll collect them and answer them in a newsletter. Thank you to Lois Jean Bousquet, Caren Tracy, Lory Britain, and others who forced me to think and answer these questions.

Also, readers beware! If you haven't read the novel yet, there are spoilers ahead.

Angeline is a unique character. How did she come about? (A composite? An emerging surprise? A niggling tap-tap on your writer's brain?)

I always start with setting. I was in Paris in 2015 with my husband for Christmas and New Year's. I knew I wanted to set a femmes-noir thriller there. We arrived a month after the November bombings of the Bataclan, a historic theatre and concert hall where 89 people were shot and killed at the Eagles of Death Metal concert.

I've been to Paris half a dozen times, but this time was different. People were amiable but cautious. The city, overall, was low-key. Soldiers who looked fifteen years old walked the streets loaded with firearms. The details in *Revenge in 3 Parts* came from my experience walking the city, including the homeless Santa and a photo exhibit of Marilyn Monroe. When I went home, Paris haunted me, and in imagining a character there, Angeline popped up. She walked down Boulevard de Grenelle, wearing a disguise, her anger thick on her sweaty skin, ready to seek revenge for her sister's death. The story took off from there.

(If you're interested in seeing the photos of that trip and the details, visit my Pinterest page.)

How do you immerse yourself in dark plots (as an author) and still maintain happy "normal" thoughts in your personal "real" life?

I think of my thoughts as being about stories of human nature. I'm a happy person most of the time, and my stories don't affect that. I've never been a reader who escapes in happy-ending stories. In childhood, I read Nancy Drew, but as a teen graduated to *The Moonstone* by Wilkie Collins and *Rebecca* by Daphne du Maurier, both dark and resonant novels. Growing up in New England gave me a love of the dark side with its gothic and secretive atmosphere. I was never scared of anything except one nasty-looking guy who tried to push his way into our house on the pretext of selling encyclopedias. I slammed the door on his foot and called the neighbors.

Where did your love of noir first grab you?

I was working at a college as a strategic planning specialist. Employees could take free classes. I'd already earned my degrees, so this was an opportunity to indulge in classes for fun. Little did I know that a one-year course would lead me to a writing career. Up to that point, I'd been a visual artist, graphic designer, and strategic planner.

The course, "Film as Literature," was conceived and taught by Susan Glassow, now a very dear friend. I blame her for my career change. That year, she concentrated on film noir. For me, handing in assignments wasn't necessary as I wasn't taking the class for credit, but I loved writing about these films and the symbolism, the stark reality, the history, anything!

I did the end-of-year assignment, writing a paper about film noir and its aspects, using the films we'd watched as examples to show the noir tropes, symbolism, camerawork, story arc, characters, etc. Naturally, as an artist, I illustrated it too. I found out later that Susan used my paper when she made presentations to other universities and colleges about her course. At the end of the year, on my paper, she wrote, "You should be a writer."

How did your creation of the genre "femme-noir" come about?

I knew what I was writing when I started the trilogy. Unfortunately, no subgenre of crime represented it. Yes, the books could be called psychological thrillers—but they're not by definition. Noirs usually end badly, or at least the good guy doesn't get his objective. For those of you who remember the film *Chinatown* (one of my all-time favorite neo-noirs), Jake the detective (Jack Nicholson) cannot save his client (Faye Dunaway) from her father, who owns the L.A. water rights. Power wins. In most psychological thrillers, the good guy wins and brings about closure for those involved. Not in noir.

I searched for subgenres written by women. I could name novels that I would label femme noir, but they were thrown into other subgenres. Then I stumbled across a British writer, Julia Crouch, who applied the term "domestic noir" to her books. She defined it this way:

> In a nutshell, Domestic Noir takes place primarily in homes and workplaces, concerns itself largely (but not exclusively) with the female experience, is based around relationships, and takes as its base a broadly feminist view that the domestic sphere is a challenging and sometimes dangerous prospect for its inhabitants.

This definition fits her books and many others. In fact, I was overjoyed she had broken out a subgenre that represented women writing noir.

However, my novels don't take place in the domestic sphere. Mine are concerned with the female experience in a larger world. I figured if Julia could create her own genre, so could I. As a call-back to the classic noirs, I took the femmes from "femmes fatales" and used it in an inclusive sense to cover all noir focused on women as the protagonists.

Why the heck does Gerard seem to love Angeline so much when he professes this great love for her half-sister Sophie whom he royally f#@%*d over by dragging her into this criminal scheme? That is such a bad cop/FBI move.

I don't think he loves Angeline. I think he sees Sophie in Angeline and is driven by guilt. He was following orders at first when going undercover in the mob. But love has no boundaries. I don't know how FBI special agents keep their emotions out of their work. With Gerard, I wanted him to be an enigma, fully human, a guy who has been undone by his involvement with Sophie. I also think he has a secret that hasn't come out yet. My characters often confound me. I loved writing him as he had me conflicted.

Why is Gerard so singularly focused on exposing the double agent? It clouds his judgment and exposes those he loves to great risk. Yet he continues to pursue this path of self-destruction to the detriment of his career and all whom he loves. This has to come from more than just losing Sophie.

As I wrote above, he's human and an enigma. I don't think he knows—unless he's fooled me and is darker than I thought. Maybe he's a hero, and this rogue agent has caused the death of many people. Maybe he's at the mercy of his emotions. Perhaps he found love with Sophie and never thought he'd ever love or feel deep emotions. So many human conditions can affect him.

Gerard has survived multiple attempts on his life and

what seem to be actual deaths. Is he really dead, or will he once again resurrect to cause more chaos in the life of Angeline as she continues to find some order in her life as she pieces together a family of half-siblings she never knew existed?

Who knows? If I do continue writing about Ang, we'll find out if he's dead or not. But right now, I'm not sure if I will turn the trilogy into a series. I'd love to explore the half-siblings and how they could fit into a noir. Then again, poor Angeline if I do!

Art Prosper, the Florida detective, is he really a good guy? There is just something too perfect about him, especially since there seems to be a mole in his division that he is not actively pursuing. Does he perhaps play a bit on the dark side?

No, I don't think so. I'm sure he's looking into the mole behind the scenes. I like him. I'm sure he's not perfect, but I think he represents the good cop who tries to do his duty and keep a moral high ground. Sometimes when someone tries to do that, they are blind to the dark forces near them and want to think the best of people. I think he tries not to bring the dark into the job as much as possible. For example, he's even changed the interrogation room into something more comfortable, but he has a good reason for that.

Then again, I could be all wrong about him. I hope not.

I love the way you highlight rescue dogs in your books. Where did the name Tempest come from? It seems to be a perfect name for Angeline's dog.

I'm glad you asked. Back in the day, a few other women in Vida, Oregon, and I were left alone as young, single moms when our men or husbands went off to "greener pastures." Our neighbor, Kendra, was a beautiful weaver, older, and had moved to the river from Haight Ashbury. We'd go to her house on Saturday nights. She'd have the fireplace going and coffee brewing. We'd work on crafts to sell while watching *Rockford Files*. Dan, the guy who would later become my husband, nicknamed Kendra "Tempest" because she was a fiery Leo with long dark hair and a penchant for the dramatic. I couldn't resist using her nickname. Plus, I think the name fits what the poor dog has to deal with.

Why does Ang still love Sophie so much after all she's done to her. It's Sophie's fault that Ang has been chased by the mob and has to deal with Gerard.

Yes, she does seem forgiving. But their younger years together and the suicide of their parents formed a bond that can't be broken. I hope the prequel (free short story) I've offered to readers who sign up for my newsletter will give a better understanding of what Ang and Sophie had to endure early on in their lives.

I hope you make the trilogy into a series. There's so much more to Angeline's story that I'd like to follow. You could write one more novel and have a zero in the title! LOL.

Gosh, you've really thought this through. Does that mean I'd have to go into negative numbers? I'd like to get away from the numbers. I could do that if I gave Ang something else to pursue now that she's home with Tempest. I would love to set a novel in my area. It's perfect for noir. Then again, I think every place is perfect for noir.

What made you want to write a story about the mob and the FBI? Was it something you saw in a movie or on a streaming show or tv?

I stay away from getting my ideas from films or streaming series. I do love to watch them, but I have enough in my life to draw on.

You asked about the mob and the FBI. That's an easy one. In high school in New Hampshire, I worked as a switchboard operator for New England Tel and Tel. (Yes, I'm giving away my age.)

One day, I had a call come in from a local phone booth to a Boston number. At the time, all calls from phone booths had to be paid in coins before I connected the call. The customer was given three minutes to talk before I had to ask for more money. After three minutes, I pulled back the switch to listen for a break in the conversation so I could ask for an additional deposit.

I heard the man in the phone booth setting up a hit! He was talking about someone in Gunstock Acres, an exclusive housing development with a gate and a guard on duty. I didn't know what to do, so I wrote down the names and the numbers of where the call was from and to whom. I was shaking. Naturally, I didn't interrupt the call. After the parties hung up, I went to my manager and told her. She said I couldn't say anything because we weren't allowed to listen in on conversations.

After work, I went home, told my parents, and asked if we could call the FBI. I don't know how I knew this, but Dad made the call. Half an hour later, two men in casual clothing arrived and showed us their FBI credentials. They took my story, thanked me, and the one who had asked me questions said, "You won't hear from us again or about this unless it becomes a big story in the news. But we've had our eyes on Gunstock, so thank you so much for the information." Mom and Dad showed them out, and that was all that happened. I never saw a news story, and my parents never read anything about it in the paper. But it intrigued me and has stuck with me ever since.

Where would you like to set your next novel?

I'd like to set it close to home. I'd also love to set a femmes noir in Thailand, England, and Majorca. I need to smell the place, discover unique details, and immerse myself in the culture. I also need to track down who's hiding in the alley and has a story to tell.

ABOUT THE AUTHOR

Multi-award-winning author **Valerie J. Brooks** writes femmes-noir psychological thrillers where the women are badass and take center stage. The first in the Angeline Porter Trilogy *Revenge in 3 Parts* was a finalist for the Nancy Pearl Book Award and a winner in the International Readers' Favorites Thriller Awards. Her second novel in the trilogy *Tainted Times 2* won the Book Excellence Award for thrillers and was a finalist for the CIBA CLUE Award. NY Times bestselling author Kevin O'Brien called *Tainted Times 2* "... a real nail-biter from first page to last."

A lifelong writer and reader, she reads everything from Daphne du Maurier to the latest Scandinavian crime writers. Her English war-bride mom and artistic army officer dad raised her with my two siblings in ultra-conservative New Hampshire during the 1950-60s. Growing up in puritanical New England, she was drawn to the gothic, to secrets, mystery, and the dark side of human nature. As her English mum once said, "You're a good girl who wants to be bad." Now she has the perfect conduit for her "bad girl" side —writing noir.

After studying film noir in college, she found her noir voice for fiction. She received an Elizabeth George Foundation grant and was the recipient of five writing residencies. She teaches classes and workshops in writing noir and creating plot twists, plus reviews mystery, suspense, and thriller novels, podcasts, and streaming shows on her blog.

She's a member of Sisters in Crime (Columbia River Chapter), Pacific Northwest Writers Association, Oregon Writers Colony (past board member), Willamette Writers (co-founder WW Speakers Series) and Professional Women's Network of Oregon.

Brooks lives in Oregon's McKenzie River Valley with her husband, Dan, and their Havanese pooch Stevie Nicks.

Please visit me on any of my social media sites. I'd love to connect with you!

Also, check out my articles and reviews in "Mystery and Suspense Magazine."

facebook.com/NoirTravelStories

twitter.com/ValinParis

instagram.com/valeriejbrooksauthor

linkedin.com/in/valeriejbrooks

pinterest.com/valinparis

tiktok.com/@valeriebrooksauthor

bookbub.com/profile/valerie-j-brooks